WHAT BECOMES OF US

Henrietta McKERVEY

HACHETTE
BOOKS
IRELAND

First published in 2015 by Hachette Books Ireland
First published in paperback in 2016

A CIP catalogue record for this title is available from the British Library

ISBN 978 1444 794 113

Typeset in Cambria by redrattledesign.com
Printed and bound by CPI Group (UK) Ltd, Croydon, CR0 4YY

Hachette Books Ireland policy is to use papers that are natural, renewable and recyclable products and made from wood grown in sustainable forests. The logging and manufacturing processes are expected to conform to the environmental regulations of the country of origin.

Hachette Books Ireland
8 Castlecourt Centre
Castleknock
Dublin 15, Ireland

A division of Hachette UK Ltd.
Carmelite House
50 Victoria Embankment
London EC4Y 0DZ

www.hachette.ie

For my mother,
and for hers.

Pra **McKervey**

'A fascinating read that deals with big questions about female

KY

CHAPTER ONE

She was sure they wouldn't make it. Maybe they haven't. *Yet*. Her fingers drum on the table. She has bitten her nails so low that the sound is muffled, and with every tap against the Formica the raw, ragged edges of her fingertips sting. It's already ten past – why haven't they left? Sailed, undocked. Whatever it's called. Their table is in the furthest corner of the smoking lounge, beside a window that will soon look out over the galloping white horses of the Irish Sea, but Maria's not interested in the view. She licks the torn skin around her thumbnail, and when her tongue finds the pink rips, the pain is reassuring. It is a sensation she knows well. Calm, found in the familiar.

'These aren't taken, sure they're not?' An accusing finger is pointing at their two spare seats. Coats, cardigans, Maria's suitcase and their exhausted-looking ham sandwiches wrapped in greaseproof are piled on one. Anna's teddy, Jocky, has the other to himself, his furry little body making no impression on the padded vinyl.

The woman is in her sixties, seventies maybe, and pinchy-looking with it. Maria opens her mouth to put her off, but the woman is already shouting, 'Molly! Here!' And again, louder this time, over the clatter of people and engines, 'MOLLY HALPIN! I've two here!' A large leather handbag plonks down on the table, followed by a bag of knitting, a pillar-box-red Thermos and, last, *Weldon's Home Journal*.

'Will I get a man to move your suitcase?' Hers is an old-fashioned accent, the buttermilk sort that reminds Maria of her own Wicklow childhood. The front-row-at-Mass-every-Sunday and daily-Rosary-at-home type. Maria shakes her head and, with a rough shove, pushes the case under Anna's seat. As she scoops up their coats and cardigans two curious blue eyes peer over the ramparts of *The Topper Summer Annual* and briefly meet her own.

A solid heft of a woman in a red and green checked coat with a rabbit collar winds her way over, precise directions for her passage – 'Not that way! Lord in Heaven, woman, go round him. AROUND! Look at the size of him!' – bellowed across the crowded lounge.

'Ada Rogers! You'd find a dropped stitch in the dark, so you would!' Younger-looking than her friend, she has a head of tight silverish curls and eyes like currants. Maria's slip is glued to her back with sweat, but this second woman doesn't appear to notice the heat of the lounge or the sun ping-ponging off the water and in the windows. Maria glances from the new arrival to the clutter dumped on the table. Between the pattern of the woman's coat and the steel of her hair, she has a look of her pal's Thermos.

'Quick!' Maria nudges Anna, who whips Jocky to safety just in time. Another vast handbag, another flask, a small net of oranges and a paper twist of toffees with *Sweet Sights of London* in jaunty red script across the wrapper are laboriously offloaded onto the table. Anna's face lights up and Maria lays a warning hand on her arm.

'Oh, help yourself, pet. A little of what you fancy and all that,' says Mrs Thermos. She takes a long, admiring look around the lounge and coos in delight, 'Ada, you're great altogether! I'd say these are the last two seats on the boat!'

She's probably right. Even the seats on the deck outside are occupied. Uncomfortable sea-sprayed benches, they face hard into the breeze and the glare of the sun, and are at the mercy of the incontinent seagulls and their banshee cries. She turns to Anna, 'It was that other boat on the way over. The old one. We were up to our ankles in the-Lord-himself-only-knows-what.' Anna, her little face puzzled, shyly waves Jocky's paw in response.

Once seated, the two women embark on a voyage of their own that calls at every fixture and fitting of this, the aft smoking lounge. And when they have assessed its every detail ('Oh, Ada, real curtains!'; 'Nothing but dust-catchers, Molly'), they move on to the greater merits of the ship. The captain himself, Maria reckons, can't possibly know more about the *Holyhead Ferry 1* than these two pensioners. Anna watches them intently, her head turning as she follows their conversation, serious as a spectator at a tennis final.

Did Molly know that the walls on the stairs are lined with real wood veneer? What about the seats with the padded headrests on the upper deck? Ada has it on the best authority that they are *exactly* the same as you'd be in on a plane. The two grey heads shake in disbelief at the cut of it. You'd know she was new to the water, they conclude. Isn't she just the last word in style?

Getting stuck with such talkative companions is the last thing Maria wants, but there's nothing she can do about it. She's not prepared to give up their seats as she won't be able to find any others. She's too jittery for one thing, frayed at her seams. The rattling train journey from London to Holyhead had been long and stifling, and their suitcases bumped relentlessly against her knees. Anna cried for an hour, then slept the rest of the way, her head hot and uncomfortable in Maria's lap, her cheeks stained with dust and tears. The carriage was full of returning Irish, louder and dowdier than their London counterparts. Plumper, too; a pale starchy look to the lot of them. Every clunk and swish as the carriage door opened had her twisting in her seat, desperate to see what was going on but reluctant to disturb Anna.

She won't believe they're really leaving until the water swells beneath them. Sssh now, she silently tells herself, as if she were the child. Stop your fretting. What with getting those cancellation tickets, haven't they been lucky enough so far? And the train got in early so they'd had a chance to board before the worst of the car crowds showed up. Sssh now. It's going to be all right.

The klaxon sounds and the engine's busy throb is softened by the roll of the sea. For the first time, Maria leans back in her seat and exhales so deeply she realises she's been holding her breath.

The two women get busy with their flasks. Mrs Rogers and Mrs Halpin have been on a visit to Mrs Halpin's daughter, Norma, and her husband, George.

('He's a policeman,' Mrs Halpin sounds very proud of her

son-in-law, 'and doing very well for himself, he is too. Rising up the ranks, as they say!'

'It's a waste of such a big house, if you ask me,' Mrs Rogers adds and, with a click of her tongue, continues, 'To have no sign of a child and them married, what is it? A decade?'

'Twelve,' Mrs Halpin corrects quietly, without looking at her friend. 'It was twelve years in May.')

And after that, didn't they head to Mrs Rogers's sister, settled in Ealing these last thirty years. Lovely trip it was too. Lovely. And you are? Maria and Anna Mills. And would Maria like a cup of tea? No, she wouldn't, but thank you. The teacups rise and fall in harmony. Does Maria know Ealing at all? No? Pity. Lovely spot. Very respectable. Maria forces a smile. God, how is she to stand this pull and push all the way to Ireland?

The incessant bang of the door has stopped. Wales is behind them, Holyhead getting chewed up by the ever-widening coastline. People are settled at tables or queuing at the snack bar down the other end of the lounge. There is a rising *clack-clack* of cutlery and delph. It's safe to look away from the door and out of the window now. The whiny diesel stink has disappeared, overwhelmed by the smell of frying. Her mouth waters as a man carrying a tray of vinegar-soaked chips walks past ('Yum,' Anna whispers, staring at his plate). Maria is very tired and very hungry. Has been for ages, she's just realised.

'We had to bring our own tea,' Mrs Rogers says, 'after that fiasco the last time!'

Mrs Halpin nods furiously, 'Pure dishwater, on the old boat.' She turns to Anna. 'Take yourself a sweetie, pet.' Before Maria can object, Anna has one winkled out of the bag. Jocky's paw waves thank you before his owner quickly stuffs the toffee into her mouth, as if concerned the offer might disappear. With her palm, she presses the wrapper flat and traces her finger over the illustration.

'Big Ben,' she whispers stickily to her mother, and slips the paper between two pages of her annual.

And what is the new world Maria and Anna are moving towards at a top speed of – Mrs Rogers is dying to tell her – 19.5 knots? As if they can read her mind, the two women launch into a complicated cross-referenced discussion about what may and may not have changed back home while they've been away. From time to time they pause and nod at Maria, as if waiting for her to claim her rightful third of the conversation, though it concerns people she has never heard of and topics she knows next to nothing about. The holiday must have stretched their friendship too thin, she thinks. They need an audience to unite them once more.

They begin with the traffic in Dublin, fierce, these days. Mrs Rogers wonders if their local greengrocer – a man with hands heavy on the scales and eyes heavy on the good-looking customers – will have been up to his usual tricks. Only a matter of time, they concur, before he gets his just deserts. They agree, too, what a shame it is they've missed that lovely Robert Ryan's variety programme *Town Hall Tonight,* by far the best show on Radio Éireann. Mrs Halpin holds the view that Taoiseach Seán Lemass is no good at all, but what else would you expect from a boyo who took hold of a gun in 1916 and was up to all sorts of who-knows-what? Now, now, go easier on him, Mrs Rogers tells her. Wasn't all that business over and done with nigh on fifty years ago now? Lemass may be no de Valera, it's true, but didn't the late Mr Rogers meet him that one time and declare him as proud an Irishman as ever walked? She *had* forgotten that, Mrs Halpin nods at Maria. How right Ada is to remind her.

Mrs Halpin is more hesitant with her next comment that, what with the graphical printing strike, there's not been a newspaper in weeks. 'And with all respect, Ada, that's down to your Mr Lemass. He has the unions as mithered as children.' She takes a long swallow of her tea before concluding that even the pictures must be suffering by now, because how can anyone know the times of the films?

'What's a fillum?' Anna stretches over and whispers in her mother's ear.

Too tired to attempt to follow such tangled threads, even if she had a mind to, Maria lets their conversation slosh around her. The pensioners remind her of an Ireland she had forgotten: a country where road directions are given as if every pub is tied to the next by invisible string, and where strangers are dogged in their determination to connect you to someone they already know. The London she took Anna from just this morning – was it really this morning? How can that even be possible? – is more than a different city: it is a different world. A jingle-jangle of ever-shifting faces and colours and sounds and lives. A city where you can be as lost to yourself as to others.

The two women pause and drain their flasks. Mrs Halpin screws the lid tight back onto her Thermos. 'That was a good cup.' Her accent is a winding path, all dips and twists.

Maria's fretting again. She's been gone from Ireland for too long. What was once familiar has become unfamiliar. The thought frightens her, like a dream in which every movement is nothing more than panting, hard-won steps on marshy ground and nowhere is safe.

Mrs Halpin bends her head low over a dog-eared copy of *Stitchcraft* and peels an orange. Her clipped nails move quickly through the creamy white pith. Fresh zest rises through the thin minty smoke of Mrs Rogers's menthol cigarette, now abandoned in the ashtray inset in the table. Its owner has nodded off, her hat squashed to one side and glasses low on her nose. The hum of the engines below them gives a slight blur to every movement as the ferry butts its way across the Irish Sea. The jagged coast of Wales now long left behind, they are in open water. Ireland, a country where questions answer questions, lies ahead. Dublin, a city she hasn't been in since she got the boat to England a decade before, is getting closer. No, more than that: life is getting closer.

Mrs Halpin has kept Anna steadily supplied with toffees and they have begun to chat quietly about the landmarks on the wrappers. 'Look, another Tower of London!' Anna says, her initial shyness dissipating as the silver papers mount up. 'Did you know that in Dublin there's a tower you can climb up to see the whole city all around? It's my birthday in three weeks and that's where we're going for my present.'

'Maybe,' Maria interjects, her voice a warning.

'Maybe,' Anna repeats, in such a way as to exorcise her mother's meaning. 'Did you ever go up it?'

'The Pillar on O'Connell Street, do you mean?' Mrs Halpin laughs. 'Ah, sure Dubliners never go up Nelson's Pillar. What age will you be, Anna?'

'Six. My mum is twenty-nine.'

'I don't think anyone was looking to know my age, Anna.' Yet Anna's tone was so determinedly grown up that Maria can't help but smile. For ten years Maria's own voice announced her as Irish, and now this is about to be reversed.

Every time Anna opens her mouth she will draw attention to them. For Maria is no holidaying emigrant, desperate to compare the old with the new and determined to find the old wanting. No, what she wants is for them to slide seamlessly into a different, fresh life, to slip it on as easily as one might a new coat. Or a disguise.

'Six! Aren't you great altogether? Try this one next, pet.'

'Ooh, liquorice! Fank you!'

The new school will help, Maria reassures herself. It will smooth over the sharp blades of her London accent. Anna will be sure to make friends and learn to talk like them. *Fank you.* Jagged straw-like wisps stick out in all directions from Anna's hair. Maria licks her fingertips and traces the arc of her daughter's head. The hair is fine enough still to feel baby-like. Her jaws clamped shut, Anna grins up at her mother as widely as Callard & Bowser allow. The corners of her lips are stained a shiny black, as though her mouth was packed full of wet earth.

'That hurts.' Anna's voice is sticky. 'Ouch! Stop rubbing, Mummy!' She wriggles her head away from Maria's hankie. 'Can I go outside now?'

Before Maria can reply, Mrs Halpin looks over Anna's head and says, 'Isn't it a lovely start to her holidays, a trip on the new ferry?'

'But we're not going on holidays,' Anna says, her teeth now unstuck. 'We're going to live because my dad—'

Her next words go unheard as a loud *bang* is followed by a scream, a 'Jesus, Mary and Joseph!' from Mrs Halpin, and a 'Holy Mother of Divine!' from Mrs Rogers, jolted awake by the noise. A seagull has thudded against the long window next to their table. Its huge body doesn't move at first: some horrible failure of gravity keeps it glued to the glass. Its neck is twisted at a grotesque angle, one vast greyish wing outstretched. The pinprick black pupil in its yellow eye stares straight at Maria.

The wing twitches and the bird thumps to the deck. Two men approach and nudge it softly but it doesn't stir. They begin to kick the corpse from foot to foot as far as the edge of the deck, getting quicker and more confident as they approach the rail.

'There's some weight in those birds.' Mrs Rogers pushes her glasses up her nose.

'Flying turkeys.' Mrs Halpin nods, and Anna's eyes widen.

They watch as a man on the deck lands the seagull a solid whack. 'Goal,' someone shouts, and the crowd inside the lounge applaud and laugh as the dead bird disappears over the side of the boat. Maria alone is still standing, her hands clutching the table. Mrs Halpin and Mrs Rogers are looking at her, one quizzical, the other frowning. Jocky and Anna huddle together, paw-in-hand. Even his little glass eyes appear startled. Maria looks around the table and understands, from the faces staring at her, that the loudest cry had been the one that came from her.

The door leading out of the lounge is inset with a frosted-glass panel. Dark unreadable shapes pass by on the other side. Shadow after shadow flickers. Who are these people? Beyond the door is the deck. Beyond the deck lie the deep, dark waters of the Irish Sea. And beyond them, the low, dun-coloured curves of Ireland.

An eggy-looking smear matted with feathers trickles thick and disgusting down the window. And despite the hot day and the sun falling yellow and panting onto their table, Maria stares at the glass and shivers. Sssh now. It's going to be all right, she repeats silently and her torn nails sting afresh as she pushes the blunt tips of her fingers into her palms.

CHAPTER TWO

'Look, Mummy!'

That insistent tug at her sleeve again. She leans as far forward as the metal cage allows and the cold metal presses hard against her warm cheek. It smells of stale cigarettes. Far down below, small dark bodies scurry to and fro in formless patterns. They do look like ants. Anna's right.

'They're not really ants, though, are they, Mummy?'

'Don't put your hands through the gaps like that, sweetheart. No, course they're not, they're people, the same as us.' Men and women, together in the dance of their days. Up here they are soaring high. On the ground below the parade of Dublin turns, marches and performs just for them.

'But small.'

'That's only because we're up so high. We're over a hundred feet from the ground.'

On street level, the city had teemed with buildings, shops, cars, strangers. Mid-height is all windows and words. Anna, a good reader for more than a year now, spells out the advertising billboards: *Guinness Is Good For You* and *Fly Pan Am!* She reminds Maria not to forget the Sweepstakes, that she's never alone when she smokes a Strand.

A grey giant, his uniform streaked white with guano, stands sentinel overhead. Maria follows Admiral Horatio Nelson's gaze over the river-sparkling city. His sightless stone eyes stare across the Liffey at the Dublin Mountains in the distance: the hills the purple of heather, the lonely blue of turf-smoke. If he could only turn to the side, his sea-faring eye would have a view of the seal-grey horizon, that caress of water and sky. She turns and looks across at the roof of the General Post Office. Considering its famously troubled past, the GPO – which also houses Radio Éireann, the national radio station – is ordinary, the street doors small and unimpressive. It wears its scarred history modestly.

'That's a famous building.' Maria points across O'Connell Street. 'It's where the Easter Rising started.'

'The what?'

Maria smiles. It's been only three weeks; Anna is a London girl still. 'It was a battle. You'll hear about it in school, I'm sure.' She hopes Ireland will quietly take root inside her London-born daughter. Because life has to work here, it has to. If it doesn't, there is no trail of breadcrumbs to lead them back over the water. She made sure of that.

'And that big shop on your left – no, that's your right. Left is the one that makes the L shape, remember? That's Clerys Department Store.' Striped awnings stretch tight as skin and the sun glints off Clerys' flagpole. O'Connell Street's intricate carved façades run torso-straight until, after the site of the old air-raid shelter, the road spreads its two legs: Westmoreland Street and D'Olier Street. Cars hang back behind a slow-moving dray horse. A fuzz of trees parts the middle of the road. She remembers that the view north is neater, more manicured. In all directions, church towers point into the sky.

'No, not needles. They're called spires,' Maria explains. 'They point towards Heaven. People believe the spires bring their prayers closer to God.'

'God must look like a pin cushion.'

Maria is still laughing as Anna leans into her and says, 'I wish Daddy was with us.'

'I know,' Maria says, and she remembers another view, another time: Hampstead Heath with John. The two of them had been wrapped up in coats and scarves and each other, the dense closeness of his body as real as though he were still as naked in her hands as he had been an hour before. It must have been only weeks after they'd first met. They stood there for ages that day. He laughed at her when she marvelled at how London seemed to go on and on for ever. It fascinated her, the dark, greenish blanket that stretched from the vast worker-bee sprawl far into the hazy shingle of the horizon. Unlike home, it had no edges. Ireland was all edges.

'Just think, Maria,' he said, 'there's millions of women scratching about out there, and I found you.' He pulled her even closer to him. 'You're all mine,' he said, his breath misting her ear and cheek and his arm so tight around her shoulders that, even through their coats, she could feel the sharp mark of his hip rubbing hers. 'For ever and ever.' And she had smiled giddily, delighted with a view as wide and generous and certain as the future that was surely rolling out before her under a blanket of careless winter sun.

She leans in again to the metal barrier, so close now that she could lick its rough surface. Dublin is different. It is solid and dumpy, butted up between the mountains and the sea. Today they are at the heart of the capital; even their bus from Ranelagh listed 'The Pillar' as its terminus. Street level will be dull by comparison. The viewing platform is busy and people squeeze around each other to get closer to the front. City-smart pigeons on the ledges beyond peck at cigarette butts. Nelson has his back to them and when they walk into his shadow Maria shivers in the sudden gloom.

Jocky's paw points through the railings, and Anna says, 'You never told me Dublin was bigger than London.'

'It looks that way from up here, but it's not. London is much bigger.'

Anna tucks Jocky under her arm and clasps her hands. 'Well, this is an excellent spending of a birthday shilling.' Turning six is a serious business.

'Ninepence, love. Children are half price. Well said, though. It *is* an excellent spending.'

'Will I ever be grown up enough to pay full price?'

'Course you will! And to prove it, we'll come back when you're a grown up and pay our sixpences.' Maria bends down to hug her. 'But there's no rush. You'll be your whole life grown up.'

'I wish we could climb down the outside instead of those twisty steps in the middle.'

'I don't! Come on, love. It's time we were off.' The black limestone steps were steep and narrow on their way up, the handrail as tight a twist as the writing in a stick of rock. The stairs curled about themselves, a promise offered and withdrawn at every turn. 'This way, it's quicker on the way down.'

A few feet further on she pauses. She looks back over her shoulder, as though she might catch her ten-year-old self there: that small girl, quiet and tired, standing in silence at the Pillar railings, waiting for her father and wishing she knew which direction home was.

'Anna?' She'd been there – right there! – just a second ago. Maria pushes her way back to the edge of the platform. It's getting busier, people everywhere, blocking her path. 'Anna?' She runs back to the doorway and shouts down the spiral stairs, but only her own voice comes back to her, the words spiked by footsteps coming up. She pushes her way around the platform. It's hard to see past the clusters of people. Backs obscure her view; a man's hat is in front of her face; a handbag jabs her ribs. Christ, where has she gone? God, no, Maria thinks. *No, no, no.*

'Anna!' She sees her crouching, her little hands through the wire cage tugging at something. '*Anna!* Get over here. Now!' The world slows down until it is no more than a single breath as she drops to her knees. She wraps the child in her arms. Should scold but can't. Her voice catches. 'What on earth were you doing?'

A whisper against her shoulder: 'I had dropped Jocky. He got stuck. I called but you didn't hear me.'

'You'd keep a better eye on your childer, missus.' His voice is low and too close, the accent a Dublin one. The sun is behind him and his hat is tipped forward – it's hard to make out his face. 'All manner of things can happen up here. It's easy done,' he says, and is gone, disappearing through the doorway.

Anna breaks away from her mother's grip and her eyes fill. 'Why is that man cross with you?'

'Don't mind him, love. It's all right.' Maria looks at her bewildered face, the fresh gleam of her tears. 'I got a fright because I couldn't find you. That's all.'

Her heart thumps as they make their way down the steps.

There is no sign of him. A man alone on the Pillar like that? Who was he? Didn't that woman on the ferry say something about locals not being bothered with the Pillar? Anna trots just ahead, round and round the dark stairs. Bony shoulder-blades flutter like closed wings against the summer cotton of her dress. It's hard to believe they're not tunnelling far underground into the labyrinthine passages of Hell.

'I'm dizzy,' Anna says, her feet trip-trapping down the steps.

'Me too.' One hand is a beak on the child's shoulder. She would pick her up and fly away with her if she could.

'Oh, no!' Anna stops so abruptly that Maria's knees bump her back and she has to grab the handrail to steady herself. 'We didn't go back to look properly from the far side, where all those people were in our way.'

'Doesn't matter. There isn't as good a view from that side.'

Anna frowns up at her mother. 'But you've not been here before. How do you know what the views are?'

'I must have overheard someone say it,' Maria says quickly. She takes a deep breath to steady herself. 'Now, we've still got that threepence to spend. What do you think about a birthday bun?'

'Ooh, yes, please!' Anna cries, her upset forgotten. 'And a postcard?'

Fruit-sellers trade at the entrance by the postcard stand and the porch is full of the fleshy stink of plums and peaches. Already overripe, they will have gone off by tomorrow. Anna's small hand clasped in her own, Maria hears her child whisper, 'Just think, Jocky, if people look like ants, how small must the ants be!'

CHAPTER THREE

Another warm August day, two days since their trip to the Pillar. They have idled the afternoon away in the park, then done a few bits of shopping in Ranelagh village.

'"We're for tummies, we're for yummies, we're the biscuits with the big grin . . ."' The way home has taken them through a series of red-brick terraces that lie quiet and drowsy in the sun. Maria hears only the soft sound of Anna singing her favourite jingle and the distant *thwock-thwock* of a ball in an unseen back garden. The sloping pavement on this side of Redoubt Terrace is shaded by trees planted into the concrete. Veins of weeds run the length of the street where roots have broken through.

'". . . we've icing nosies and toesies, and our home is your biscuit tin—"' The singing ends abruptly as she bumps over a crack and the toy pram takes flight down the street. 'Mummy, help!'

'Anna! I told you, never let go of the handle!'

Through an unseen gate in a hedge a woman has appeared and Anna's wriggling fingers freeze in mid-air ('Uh-oh') as the pram collides with the back of her knees. A Red Indian doll catapults out from under the pram apron and hits the pavement head first. Maria runs to the aid of the tartan overcoat protruding from the boxwood hedge. 'Are you hurt?' she calls. 'I'm so sorry.'

'Fine, I think . . .' The woman rights herself. 'Well! If it isn't yourselves!'

It's one of the pair from the boat. The smaller one with all the toffees, Maria doesn't remember her name.

'Anna? Apologise at once, please!'

Anna's mouth trembles and tears spill. Her wet eyes make Maria's heart twist. They are the colour of January.

'Don't worry yourself, pet,' the woman says. 'Sure I'm grand, and isn't it lovely to see you again?' She plucks stray leaves from her coat and a tiny plastic tomahawk falls to the ground. Maria struggles to remember her name. Halfin?

'Are you visiting the terrace?' Mrs Halfin straightens her flowery headscarf. Petals yellow as egg yolk stretch tight and smooth over the dome of her head.

'That's our house down there.' Anna stands up from the pavement and points with the tomahawk. 'The upstairs of the one with the red door.'

They turn as one at a croak of 'Good afternoon,' and see an elderly man in a long overcoat on the far pavement. He is wearing one cracked boot and one slipper. The boot lifts high from the ground, but the slipper shuffles along. 'Rain's held off again, Mrs Halpin,' he says, without breaking his uncomfortable, loping stride.

Halpin. That was it.

'Thanks be to God, Mr Owens,' Mrs Halpin shouts back. She turns to Maria and, in a carrying whisper, says, 'Number thirty-nine, top flat. Tess McDermott has the ground. I'd say the stairs have him crippled. Poor man's a martyr to his health.

'Well now,' she turns to Anna, her tone brighter, 'seeing as how you're new to the terrace, why don't you and your mam come in with me and have a cup of tea by way of a welcome? I can get my few messages any time.'

Maria's swift 'No thanks,' isn't quick enough to beat Anna's 'Ooh, yes, please!'

'We have to, um . . . we should be going,' Maria adds limply, knowing even as she speaks that her refusal was too weak to form any serious opposition. Anna trots past her mother and, eyes glowing, hopscotches her way up the red and black tiles to the door. Mrs Halpin gives Maria a broad smile. Clearly delighted with such a doughty accomplice, she says, 'Sure let's get inside so. I don't trust that sky.'

Maria hoists her basket of shopping onto her arm and grabs the handle of the pram. She looks at what must surely be a perfect sky and wonders if this dog-end of a late August afternoon is hanging heavy on Mrs Halpin's hands. Is that deep story-book blue, dotted with tiny cotton balls of cloud, not to be trusted? Already this week she has learnt to doubt the veracity of the bus timetable from Donnybrook and the prices in the butcher's on Ranelagh Road. Even small doubts add up. They fuse together, form a vast and unstable universe.

Mrs Halpin's hallway smells of boiled cabbage and an unidentifiable meat. The parlour she ushers them into feels stale, as if its very air has been kept-for-good for too long. The velourette pile of the seat is cold to Maria's touch and she wonders when their hostess last sat in here. Anna picks up a plastic effigy of the Virgin Mary and shakes it. Holy water sloshes up and down inside.

'Don't twist her halo or you'll end up spilling it,' Maria warns. 'Her halo is the lid.'

Anna fiddles with the brown tassels that drop neatly from the cushion corners before making a beeline for a row of china animals standing guard on the windowsill. 'This is nice, Mummy.' They are ranged in order of height and her hand hovers over a perky Scottie before settling on a larger dog. 'Wolfhound?'

'Alsatian.'

'Here, kitty kitty.' She crouches and clicks her fingers.

'No touching, Anna.'

'The cat?' she asks, her hands buried in its fur.

'The cat. The dogs. Everything. Please, no touching.'

'Ah, you touch away, love.' An expertly steered tray rounds the door. 'I see you've met my Chuzzlewit. Now, you have the look of a girl who loves cake. Would I be right?'

Anna looks dizzy with pleasure at this fairy-tale turn their afternoon is taking. 'Are there any children here?' she asks hopefully.

'No. My Thomas and Norma are long grown up.' In a series of studio photographs from black-and-white children to Kodak-colour adults, Thomas and Norma ladder side by side down the chimneybreast. They meet in the middle on the mantelpiece in their respective wedding photographs.

'Do they have any children I can play with?'

'No. Thomas has two sons, but he's in Boston these last eighteen years so I've not seen them in a long time. My Norma's in London. We'd been visiting her when I met you on the boat.' Mrs Halpin's back tenses as she bends over and straightens the gleaming white tray cloth before pouring tea. 'I don't light a fire in here any more – the one in the kitchen is enough for myself. But let me know if you get cold. I could put a bar of the heater on.'

'It's fine, thank you,' Maria replies.

The pause that follows settles like a weight on the sofa next to her. Maria says nothing, content to let it take up the space between them, but Mrs Halpin shoos it away: 'And tell me this: when will Mr Mills be following you over?' Anna looks up from the cat on her lap. She holds him so that he is standing on his back legs, and she is dancing with his front paws.

'My daddy is dead,' she says. Mrs Halpin blesses herself in a single motion – forehead, chest, left shoulder, right shoulder – and Maria remembers the distractions and deck walks and toffees it took to ensure Anna didn't return to the subject of her father that day on the ferry.

'Lord rest him, is that so? I'm very sorry for your loss.'

'It's all right,' Anna answers. 'Dip, kitty, dip. You don't have to say sorry. It wasn't you who killed him.'

Molly Halpin's tea is as good as spat back into the cup. Maria imagines the phone call Mrs Whoever-the-other-one-was will get as soon as they leave: *Pure shocked I was, at the cut of it. Heathen child! That's London ways for you.*

'He was away for his job on a rig.' Anna twirls the cat. 'That's a sort of factory for finding oil under the sea,' she adds helpfully. 'The boat taking him there had an accident and he drowned.'

'God have mercy on the poor man.' She turns to Maria and says, in a loud whisper, 'Was the body recovered?' Maria shakes her head and Mrs Halpin looks down in respect for a few seconds before leaning across the cushion between them. 'I wouldn't talk about that sort of thing in front of the child,' she says, her lips pursed. Maria nods faintly, wishing that were the case. Since they arrived in Dublin, the subject of John has been kept alive by everyone *but* her.

'Please can I have another fairy cake, Mrs Helping?'

'One is enough,' Maria answers automatically, though she is so relieved at the change of subject she would happily have fed Anna every cake on the plate.

'Halpin. Of course you can, my dear. Tell me, do you go to school?'

'I'm starting next week.' Anna peels back the greaseproof paper. 'It's called St Columba's.'

'Isn't that where my own pair went! You must tell the headmaster that Norma and Thomas Onions's mother sends her very best wishes.'

'Onions!' Moist crumbs splutter onto the cat's fur.

'Anna!'

'Scally, the boys used to call Thomas.' She sighs. 'For scallion. He was always small for his age. The late Mr Halpin was my second husband. Will you be in the Holy Communion class, Anna?'

Anna looks to her mother, confused. 'No,' Maria says.

'So you're going into High Babies?'

'First Class.' Anna frowns, her mouth full.

'We'll be sure to pass on your regards to the head.' Maria rises. 'And now we mustn't delay you any longer. Anna? Finish up.' Anna shoves the last of the cake into her mouth and her cheeks swell as she hurriedly tries to chew some moisture into it.

'You must visit some morning, while Anna's at school.' Mrs Halpin sweeps away Anna's crumbs with the side of her hand. 'Ada Rogers and a few other pals call by every Wednesday after eleven Mass. We're like clockwork. Why don't you join us next week?'

'Mum will be at her new work.' Anna extracts a waxy plug of chewed paper from the back of her mouth.

'Will you? Where?'

'RTÉ,' Maria replies, grabbing the paper from Anna's fingers.

'Really? Radio Éireann in the GPO?'

'No, Donnybrook, where the television studios are.'

'Will you be on the television? I don't have a set myself but I must tell Ada—'

'No, no, nothing like that.' A little information might be the price of escape. 'I'm a copytaker.'

'A whatty-whatter?'

'Copytaker. Reporters phone in their stories and copytakers transcribe them for the news department. It's typing mainly.'

'And that's while Anna's at school?'

'It's all day.' Maria had asked to move her start date already and the lady in Personnel had made her feel like a beggar. 'You do remember,' the woman had said, her red lipstick radiating away from her mouth in dry, spidery cracks, 'that this is a full-time position and essentially secretarial?'

'Don't mind her,' Eve had said afterwards. 'That old weapon, what does she know? I'll see the job is held for you.' A head secretary in Telifís Éireann, Eve has always had the knack of getting her own way. The smartest thing Maria has done, she realises, has been to get in touch with Eve again. She'd be lost in Dublin without her help. Between finding the flat and putting her up for the job, Eve has been great, no two ways about it. She organised everything, just as she always did.

Even at boarding school she was the only one who seemed able to get around the miserly nuns. Secretarial college, too: Eve could always put anyone in the ha'penny place without it ever being clear exactly how she'd done it.

('Eve Cawley!' the head nun Sister Magdalene had once shouted across the classroom in exasperation. 'Are you the matador or the bull?'

'Both, Sister,' Eve replied politely, knowing only too well how much the nuns hated it when they weren't addressed by their full name. 'I'm both.')

After secretarial college Eve moved to Dublin and Maria, with nothing left to stay for in Ireland, had got the boat to London. She had met John within weeks and, almost without her noticing, had let Eve slip out of her life. Yet Eve hasn't looked for explanations or audits of the missing years. She seems happy simply to have picked up where they left off a decade before. Maria has wondered if Eve is discreet – which honestly seems unlike her – or disinterested. Probably better not to know, she's decided.

Eve's intercession with Personnel gained Maria an extra week, which has just begun, but the problem of what to do with Anna during working hours is keeping her awake at night. A newspaper ad would have done the trick but, what with the printers' strike, she hasn't seen an Irish newspaper since they arrived. There wasn't a single response to the *Mother's Help Wanted* notices she pinned up in the shops. She has the perfect person in mind too, if only she'd make herself known. Maria pictures a local woman, one with children of her own for Anna to play with. She bakes and knits and tells stories. Keeps hair free of nits and her brasses polished. And if this ideal of womanhood doesn't materialise in the next few days, Maria will have to get the bus in from Donnybrook every lunch hour and bring Anna back to work with her. It's a couple of miles each way but she reckons it may be just about manageable, if they hurry. Eve swears there is a woman in the drama department with a son squirrelled away in her office every afternoon. Maria can't imagine how that would work, and pictures Anna tucked into the bottom drawer of a filing cabinet (under T for Trouble) or hidden in the ladies' loo. She hates the very thought of it: of displaying and denying her daughter all at once.

Hell. If Mrs Halpin's face and sudden silence are anything to go by, she's missed a question. She keeps doing that, getting derailed by her own thoughts.

'What I was asking, dear, is what will Anna be doing while you're at work?'

'I'm making arrangements for a local woman to look after her in the afternoons.'

'And who would that be, now?'

'I'm not entirely sure.'

'You don't know her *name*?'

'No, I haven't quite . . .' She feels exposed, as if confessing to a crime. 'I mean I've nearly . . . I've not found someone yet.'

Mrs Halpin tut-tuts. 'And school about to start any day now? That's no good. Anna, why don't you come to me?'

Ill-adjusted clocks chime: 'Yes, please!' and 'No, thank you,' into the room.

'Just to be going on with,' Mrs Halpin adds, her curranty eyes bright, 'while you get yourselves sorted.'

'Please, Mummy?' Anna's feet strike up an excited jig.

'It's very kind, but I couldn't possibly impose.'

'Of course you could. Aren't I a neighbour now and all?

And a few bob on top of the pension would do me no harm. Being a widow, well, it's a hard station.'

Three eager faces (including that of the cat, now curled tight in Anna's arms and purring like a motor) stare at Maria. Her money is almost gone: she has to start work. Life is a dead end otherwise. Would it be so bad? London, Dublin: adding the ends of her life together is impossible – it doesn't matter where she is. Perhaps some strange quirk of Fate has arranged this. And she can't ignore the fact that Anna and Mrs Halpin appear to have taken a real if inexplicable shine to each other, just as they had done that day on the ferry.

A hard station. She wonders which of them Mrs Halpin is referring to. 'I suppose, maybe . . . just for a week or two. Until I arrange something . . .' she pulls herself back from the brink of the word *proper* '. . . something permanent. Thank you.'

Maria imagines her carefully written *Mother's Help Wanted* advertisement crumbling to ashes. That perfect, warm-hearted woman, clustered around her warm-hearted hearth with her nit-free, clean-nosed children, fades slowly until all that remains is a gleaming pinpoint of light, a tiny reflection in her immaculately polished brasses.

Anna hugs the cat and wiggles his paw at the box of gingerbread men in the basket by Maria's feet. She couldn't look happier had the biscuits waved back, clicked their gingerbread fingers, whistled their happy tune.

That evening Anna falls asleep quickly. Maria envies the ease with which her daughter gives herself to the night, to the vast dreaming world of her own imagination. Alone, she stands at the window and parts the curtains. They smell of dust. The blue sky is tired, darkening at the seams. The street is empty. Summer is nearly over; the winding path through autumn and into winter will soon be waiting for them. As a child she lived her life as though she were on an escalator. The route was fixed, determined by the incomprehensible, never-explained rules of others: her father, Aunt Josephine, the nuns at school. Especially the nuns. Her role was to stand quietly on her step until the escalator dropped her off at adulthood. When she had first met John she had assumed London would be different, but it turned out to be much the same. Within a year or two her steps followed a route that wasn't her own choice.

It's different here, in Redoubt Terrace. Her movements feel small and wobbling, but at least they are hers. Every day spent quietly living this new life is successful simply for its being complete. She takes a final look up and down the empty street, then turns her back on the window. Anna's souvenir postcard of the Pillar is tacked on the wall to the side of the mantelpiece. It tilts awkwardly on its drawing pin and Maria reaches over to tweak it. From nowhere she can see the same hand clutched tight to the handrail of the Pillar on the day her father had driven the two of them the forty miles up to Dublin from Rathdrum.

Her tenth birthday. *A proper treat*. He had kept saying it. *A special girl deserves a special treat*. The Pillar, a new doll from Switzers, an ice in the Shelbourne Hotel. He'd repeated their itinerary over and over during the drive till it had begun to sound as thunderous as Aunt Josephine when she muttered her devotions. Maria's fingers had been crossed for the zoo, but he had looked so disappointed – no, more than that, so *upset*, as though she was deliberately hurting him when she asked could they maybe, just maybe, go and see the animals instead – that she had smiled and said, 'No, Daddy, the Pillar's fine, thank you.' When she walked up the steps she wished it didn't feel as though she was clambering up the hollowed-out spine of a giant.

'Mr Desmond Power,' he'd say, his hand out, ever quick to introduce himself to people. 'At your service, sir.' Nearly twenty years later she can hear the echoes of his bluff voice. She was well used to the compliment he'd produce for every woman, the hearty back-slap for every man. Yet on her birthday she had found herself blushing at his relentless best-friendliness with every Tom, Dick and Harry who crossed their path. The two hours spent in the bar of the Shelbourne Hotel felt so long she'd thought she'd be yet another year older again by the time they got home. She had sat alone with a bowl of ice-cream, the new doll sitting next to her, while he leant one elbow on the bar and talked to men like himself. He only ever drank small glasses of red lemonade, quickly, one after another.

By her eleventh birthday he was gone. Their house had come with the job, but the bank gave her and Aunt Josephine a few weeks to make other arrangements. 'Leopards and their spots,' Aunt Josephine said, when no card arrived. She'd made a fruit cake and cut them both a birthday slice at teatime. They sat in the kitchen and chewed. Maria silently told herself her favourite story (about a warm-skinned, kind-voiced mother and the blessed, golden-haired infant she adored more than life itself) and stared at her plate when Aunt Josephine turned up the wireless in time for the bongs of the Angelus.

Bank agents were moved around the country regularly to prevent them getting in too thick with the locals. They'd been in Rathdrum for six years by then, which was too long for a man like him. He'd lent bank money he shouldn't to people who couldn't repay it, and got himself involved in buying up plots of land he'd no business with. ('If there was a rat-trap in an empty room, my younger brother would get his foot stuck in it,' said Aunt Josephine.)

But on her tenth birthday did he realise he was already in over his head? Could he feel the tremble in the walls that, brick by brick, he was to pull down upon their heads? The adult Maria hopes not, she really does. Because if he knew that day in Dublin was to be their last outing, would he not have wanted to give her the day she'd asked for and taken her to the zoo?

Maria picks up Anna's discarded cardigan from the floor. Let the past be, she reminds herself. There's nothing more to be done with it. This is their life now. Why can't she have a new past as well as a new future? It is intoxicating, the idea that she can remake herself. But is it possible to be so unanchored to the world? She rubs her tired face. The night shadows have begun to creep out from the corners, eager to begin their ghostly céilí. There is nothing left to do but go to bed herself. Anna's postcard sits soldier-straight on the wall. The brass drawing pin rises high in the black and white sky, high as a noon sun over a blind empire.

CHAPTER FOUR

Thursday evening on Dame Street. Civil servants got their cheques today. Girls are lipstick-fresh and laundered, out together in clutches. Lads jingle the few bob in their pockets, enjoying the freedom of payday, forgetting it will be gone by morning. Maria recalls the happiness of that feeling. A tiny joy, like having an ice-cream in winter just because you can, because you have the blaze of a fire to warm you up afterwards. Thoughts of rent and food and coal, of money for Mrs Halpin, new school clothes for Anna and a decent winter coat for herself jump out at her. *Boo. Gotcha.*

The autumn air is chilly. She pulls her scarf tighter around her neck and tucks it under the collar of her coat. Eve's bus is late. Why did she ever agree to this? She can't afford an evening out. But that's the thing about Eve. Before you realise the best thing is just to say no, you've already, stupidly, said yes.

'Have you the time?' He is stopped right in front of her, blocking her path. Maria raises her hand so the handle of her bag bumps down to the tight crook of her elbow. 'If you don't mind, missus,' the man adds, a fur of beer warming his breath.

'Quarter past seven,' she says sharply, his *missus* sitting heavy on her. He looks her up and down and smiles with wet lips. The spark of his match is a twin for the glint in his eye.

'And would you want one yourself?' He extends the box till it's just shy of the green paste brooch pinned to the swell of her coat.

'No, she would not!' Eve's voice is loud as she grasps Maria's arm. 'Now get lost, you chancer.' Through the thin boiled wool Maria feels the sinewy strength of Eve's gloved hand. Eve links arms and gives hers a squeeze. 'I'm so glad you showed up!'

'I didn't know I had a choice!'

'You didn't, really.' Eve grins. She is petite, with regular features, but there is an energy to her that translates into a wiry, fizzing prettiness, and when she talks – which, according to the nuns in school, was far too much of the time – she is a Roman candle. 'It'll do you good to have a night out, Maria. You keep too much to yourself at work.'

'Where are we going?' Maria asks, and Eve nods in the direction of a tatty pub across the road. The Percy French seems to Maria to be an odd choice. Dublin is full of Victorian pubs like this. London was as bad. She's been in plenty of them, sometimes with John, in more recent years looking for him. The bitter smell of stout, the dark stools worn smooth by lazy backsides. The drink, the backsides, the bars. All the same. Even the accents.

'Really? I assumed we'd be going to a milk bar.'

Eve says nothing. As they cross the road she tugs off her headscarf and bright red hair bounces down her back. It's like watching turf blaze. Maria adds, 'I told Mrs Halpin I'd be back before nine.'

'Still delighted with the understudy granddaughter, is she?'

'They seem completely charmed by each other.'

'Aren't you lucky her own children haven't provided her with any?'

'There are two in the States that she never seems to hear from. I got the impression that the daughter and her constable husband would oblige if they could. I really don't want Anna to get too used to her, though. It's only temporary.' It's been just three weeks, yet Anna and Mrs Halpin seem to have found a genuine attachment to each other. Maria's search for a replacement has been half-hearted at best, and when she raised the subject again earlier, Anna's face had darkened.

'So why not just leave it as it is?' Eve says. 'Sleeping dogs and all that.'

'The woman's a pensioner. Looking after a child all afternoon is too much for her,' Maria replies, though in fact she's thinking of some fresh phrases in Anna's vocabulary, and a *well-Holy-Mother-of-Divine* tucking of arms under a non-existent bosom.

'If I were you, I'd be worried about her being too much for Anna,' Eve replies. 'Girls!' she calls. 'We're here!'

Maria is introduced to Bernie, a clerical assistant Eve knows from her first job in Dublin. They seem unlikely friends, and Maria summons up a memory of a long-ago letter of Eve's in which she crossly described a conversation with Bernie as 'trying to do a jigsaw with no picture on the box'. Eve's cousin Mary-Anne is there, too, a pretty, shy girl. Maria hasn't seen Mary-Anne since they were in school. Mary-Anne is a primary teacher now, and the children have her driven half demented.

Maria can't help but notice the nervous glances Mary-Anne and Bernie are giving each other. They're waiting, she's sure of it. She's seen it enough by now to know the signs. The two of them must be wondering who should go first with the sorry-for-your-loss, the and-how-are-you-in-yourself? Eve interrupts the start of whatever halting sentence Bernie is putting together: 'And this is Alicia. You won't have met her before.' Alicia leans forward and shakes Maria's hand. Tall as a man and nearly as broad, she smiles but doesn't speak.

Of course they want to know. Well, possibly not Alicia, whose disinterested expression suits her slacks and sharp bobbed hairdo. The others want to say something, it's obvious. News of a sudden death does that. The questions are hard to ask but they burn in your heart until you get an answer.

'Me and Maria together, then Bernie, then Mary-Anne. Alicia is . . .' Eve is saying as she pushes the worn brass handle of the street door. Her voice is low and busy, and Maria misses the last few words as they crowd into a small lobby. Scratched gold lettering on brown and red glass panels reads *Public Bar* to their left, *Saloon* to the right. Alicia runs a finger over two words painted in black on the brown: *Men Only*. 'One at a time, eh?' she says softly, and touches Eve's arm. Eve doesn't appear to notice Alicia's thumb resting on her thin, bare wrist.

Curls of blue and brown smoke greet them and the carpet sticks to Maria's shoes. Two men review them before returning to the gaze of their pints. The walls are panelled to waist height, their chipped plaster mouldings stained brown by tobacco. Over the counter a pearly glass lightshade is suspended from the ceiling on brass chains. Small dead shadows scatter its opaque base. The printing strike finally over, *Evening Press* carcasses litter the counter. Today's headlines – *ESB To Demolish Georgian Houses* and *Fire Destroys Ice Cream Factory* – are history already, sprinkled with beer and ash.

Their reflections stare back from the fly-spotted mirror on the wall behind the bar. *Guinness Stout* is a swirling bower over their reflected heads, *Take the Time It Takes* written beneath. The barman puts down the four drinks Eve asked for. There is an odd quickening in the way the others look from Eve to each other that Maria doesn't understand. He extends a hand for Eve's money just as Alicia appears at the counter. 'Be ready.' Eve pushes Maria's drink closer to her.

'What was that?' Must have misheard, Maria thinks. But Eve ignores her and Maria is distracted from asking again by the low rumble of Alicia's voice.

'Pint of Guinness.'

'Go way out o' that!' The barman rolls his eyes as if to say, *That's women for you*. 'Quick now, love, what'll it be?'

'Pint of Harp.'

Didn't Alicia hear him? Maria doesn't understand. 'What's going on? Eve?' she says, but Eve ignores her.

'Ah, stop your messing,' he goes. 'I've not got all night.'

'Pint of Smithwick's.'

'There's no pints served to women, you know that. Have a port'n'lem like your pals here.'

'Pint of Beamish.' Her expression hasn't changed.

'Listen to me, will yeh? No pints, same rules here as everywhere.'

Alicia doesn't reply and, without moving her eyes from his, takes a deep drag of her cigarette. She holds it with the lit tip pointing inward, like a man.

'So that's it, is it?' He stands taller, hands on the edge of the counter, as if finally smelling trouble in her woody cigarette smoke. 'Right. The rest of yis, pay up double-quick. You.' He leans over the bar, his face close to hers. 'Out.'

'And whatever you're having yourself.' Alicia exhales a smoke ring and doesn't move. 'Go on.' She looks him up and down and her lip curls. 'Have a half.'

'You little bitch!' He scuttles off down the bar, yet Maria can tell he's heading for a hatch built into the counter at the far end.

'Now! One – two – three – *now*!' Eve's head flashes from side to side. Bernie gulps and splutters her snowball. An opaque, milky trail runs down her chin. 'Quick!' Eve's voice is firm and unarguable-with as she shoves the drink into Maria's hand. 'You've to drink it, so he can't put it back!' Maria raises her head and pours the port and lemon down her throat. A sugary taste, like Veno's cough syrup, mixed with a burning sharpness flows directly into her, a sensation that registers immediately in her stomach.

'Thieving wretches!' He's on their side of the counter now. Eve plucks the glass from Maria's hand and slams it on the counter. There is a rough shove on her back as Eve hisses, 'Bloody hell, run!'

The barman half-heartedly gives chase for a few yards down Lord Edward Street then stops and, with one arm raised, shouts, 'Yis aren't fit to be let out!' Eve laughs and calls something back to him. She grabs Maria's arm and, ignoring her splutters, tugs her down the road. His shouting has faded

by the time they reach City Hall and, though they slow down,
Eve doesn't let her stop until they have crossed the road and
reached the shelter of a doorway at the cobbled corner of
Temple Lane.

Eve pokes her head out. Her face is glowing. 'All clear.'
She unbuttons her coat. 'That went well. Good work, Maria –
you're light on your feet.'

Maria is bent over, her hands on her knees. 'Went *well*?'
she pants, furious and dizzy. She never drinks, and can feel
the alcohol on her as much as the unexpected sprint. 'Eve,
what in God's name were you doing?' Mary-Anne and Bernie
have piled into the doorway with them. Alicia alone is on the
pavement outside, her cigarette still in her hand.

'Best to leave it at the one for tonight,' Eve says to the
others. 'Next Thursday meet me under Clerys' clock at seven.
Leave a message at my digs if you can't come, but I'll be
expecting to see you all.'

'I'm not pint next time.' Alicia throws her cigarette on the
street and jams her hands into the pockets of her slacks.
'Didn't even get a drink out of it.' She strides away and is
almost immediately swallowed by the ancient shadows of
Temple Lane. The other two troop towards the bus stop at
College Green. When Bernie lifts her hand to wave goodbye
she stumbles and bumps into Mary-Anne, setting her bag
swinging from her arm like a pendulum.

A door opens and fills the doorway with the smell of frying
meat.

'Can I help you, ladies?'

Maria hadn't realised it was a restaurant. 'Good idea! Let's
have a bite to eat,' Eve says. 'Don't look at me like that, Maria.
I'll explain everything.' Maria's still furious. They've stolen

drinks from that pub! Eve has made thieves of them! Seeing how calm Eve is makes her even angrier. 'No chance, Eve,' she hisses. 'Not if you're going to run off without paying!'

'Don't snap at me. Of course I'm not!' Eve has the gall to look shocked. 'It's not about money, Maria,' she whispers, as the waiter leads them inside. The restaurant is dimly lit and empty, apart from two leathery priests steadily and silently chewing.

He seats them in a flourish of menus and declares, 'Welcome to the Chopstick, ladies.'

'Lord above!' Eve looks around the room. 'This is a Chinese restaurant!' One of the priests frowns over and she holds his gaze until he looks away. 'Missions, do you think?' she says, with a sideways nod, her voice thankfully lower this time. 'They've nothing to do back home but eat and get filled full of tea.' Eve cranes her head around the room. 'Have you ever been before?'

'The Missions?'

'A Chinese restaurant, you eejit.'

'There was one near our first flat in London.'

'What did you eat?'

'Sweet and sour chicken.' She was nervous, she remembers. Asked for a dish she thought she understood.

'Sweet and sour *together*? Sounds disgusting.'

'It wasn't too bad,' Maria says, but Eve is right: it *was* disgusting. And yet how silly to be wary of a meal. And her living in a new place with a new husband and a baby in her belly. Swirls of black and red had curled around the edge of the plate. She remembers the twisting tail and open mouth of a gilt dragon. The food was dense with knots of tinned pineapple, which irritated John: who in their right mind would put fruit in their dinner? How was he expected to eat it? You'd never think he was from a big city himself. He was scrappy with the young Chinese lad serving them. They never went back after that.

The waiter appears and Eve beams up at him. 'So, what should we have, seeing as how we've never been here before?'

'A nice chop suey.' He smiles back. 'And,' he leans over, closer to Eve's ear, 'if you don't like it, I'll make Chef do you an omelette instead.' Eve closes her menu, hands it to him and they grin at each other, the happiest waiter and customer in all of Ireland.

The door to the kitchen swings behind him and still silence hangs over the table. Eve sips her water, apparently oblivious. Maria has no idea where this conversation will go. Worse, she doesn't know where it should start. Eve has been so kind to Anna and her that she hates feeling angry with her. Hasn't she got enough to deal with without getting dragged into whatever thievery and lies Eve is up to, these days? But there's no avoiding it. She takes a deep breath. 'Go on, then, Eve. What was that about? Stealing those drinks – you've done it before, haven't you?'

Eve puts her glass down. 'It's not about getting a drink for free. Who could care about that? Doesn't it annoy you that we can't go into a public house and ask for a pint? That it's not,' she sneers, '*ladylike*.'

'But I don't want a pint. I don't even like drinking.'

'It's not the pint, it's the right.'

The words trip off her tongue and Maria is sure this was no spur-of-the-moment idea. 'But, Eve, what happened back there . . . . that wasn't fair. You should have told me what you were going to do.'

'Would you have come if I had?'

'No!'

'That's why, then.'

They are still glowering at each other when the waiter reappears. He puts their plates down and gives Eve a wink. Maria rages wordlessly, furious at Eve's presumption in involving her in her stupid, reckless nonsense. It swells between them until Eve cries in exasperation, 'Oh, for pity's sake, Maria, don't you want Anna to be treated the same as everyone else?' Her knife scrapes against the side of her plate and the *ding* causes the priests' heads to shoot up from their silver ice-cream bowls like greyhounds after a lure. 'Well? Where it's the very *fact* of her, not her personality or her face or what she's good at, that means she will be treated the same?'

'*What?* What are you going on about?'

'All those women who fought for our rights, died, some of them, to get us – that's you and me both, Maria, not to mention Anna – a vote, and we can't have something as ordinary, as pointless, as the same drink as a man?' Eve eats and talks all at once. A splash of sauce, dark as oxblood, smears the white tablecloth.

How sure of herself she sounds. Maria can hear the conviction that pumps through her friend's blood, though she is too annoyed still to admit it.

'It's not stealing,' Eve is saying. 'It's righting a wrong.'

'How can a drink change anything?'

'I told you, it's not about drinking, it's about rights. And I want the right to choose my own battles.'

Maria looks at her friend's flushed cheeks. What is she talking about? 'Battles? Eve, there's no war.'

Eve frowns. 'How long were you gone? Eight years?'

'Ten,' Maria says.

'So much should have changed while you were gone and yet –' Eve gestures around the restaurant with her knife '– nothing has, really. The road we're all meant to be dancing on is a hiding to nothing.'

'You make it sound like we're all . . .' She pauses, confused. She's never considered any of this before '. . . stagnating.'

'Because we are! That's exactly it. Maria, think of the fight women had just to get the vote.'

'And what of it? They won.'

'*They?* You should hear yourself. And, no, *they* didn't, because it wasn't the end of something, it was the beginning of a war. No single win will ever be enough. This is our inheritance, yours and mine. Anna's too. And before you shake your head at me again, Maria, it's true, whether you like it or not.'

The priests have carefully counted out their coins and departed. The Chopstick falls quiet. It is half past eight and they are the only customers. Maria pushes her plate aside. Her appetite is gone. Inheritance? What inheritance? A life of lies for ever and ever until death us do part. A trousseau that might as well have been cut from old newspapers.

'I just want a quiet life,' Maria says. 'To have a job and save some money and make Anna happy.'

'Stick with the first and I don't think you'll get the last.'

Maria wonders does she look as worn down as these words make her feel because Eve suddenly changes the subject. She describes Bernie's job in the office of the Swastika Laundry in Ballsbridge: 'She's got an eye on one of the van drivers, good luck to her.' And Mary-Anne, teaching with the Sisters of Mercy in Drimnagh: 'The kids sound like animals, the way she tells it. Fifty to a class, and whatever bits of her carcass they leave behind the nuns go for.'

Maria smiles at this. 'And Alicia?'

'Alicia is just Alicia.' The words are muffled as Eve wipes her lips. 'How're you getting on at work? Hilda's a pain, isn't she? You'd think she invented bloody radio the way she goes on. The others are all right, though.'

'It's fine.' Maria answers the phone, transcribes what the caller tells her in shorthand, types it up, and either she or a messenger takes it to another room. She never sees the page after that, because it's on to the next call, the next report, the next human she will never meet. GAA matches in faraway townlands, political meetings in half-full parish halls, wars abroad and daily tragedies at home . . . These worlds fill her ears and guide her hand. She can do a full day's work and not be able to recall a moment of it by the time she gets to the bus stop. She brings sandwiches and spends her breaks alone on a bench outside, where there are no phones, no voices.

'You'd be surprised the pig's ear some of the girls make of it.' Eve piles the last of her chop suey onto her fork. 'And then they whine that it's dull, and it's this, that and the other, and why can't they be over in the Drama department instead? The 1916 Programmes Committee secretary got moved down to archiving last week, she'd made such a hames of her job. And it's one of the easier ones!'

Maria has heard the other copytakers talk about the 1916 Programmes Committee, newly charged with organising the station's schedule for the jubilee year of the Easter Rising, now just months away. According to Hilda, bitter words have been spoken across the canteen because funding for other shows has been withdrawn to finance the commemorative programmes.

Eve puts her fork down and stares across the table. 'Maria?' She hesitates. 'Is it too difficult, being here? I mean –' her voice falters '– what with losing John so suddenly? What I mean is . . . it was such a tragedy, you must be still in shock.'

Maria has dreaded this for weeks, but now that Eve has finally asked, she feels something close to relief. 'Eve, I haven't been . . .' she begins. 'John, he used to . . . the thing about us . . .' She pauses, the words stuck tight in her chest. They're not ready to come out. She knows the words, feels the weight of them hard against her, yet can't force breath into them.

'I was – am – so sorry,' Eve says. 'You know I am, don't you?' Maria nods dumbly, afraid that the lump in her throat, sudden and thick, will choke her. 'But,' Eve continues, 'I was so glad to hear from you again after all those years, I really was.'

Maria gulps her water, desperately forcing the pain back inside, back where it belongs. Safe and contained. Familiar. 'I know,' she says, with a splutter. She forces a smile at Eve's concerned face and the words remain unborn. 'Don't mind me, Eve, I'm fine.'

'Are you sure? You're all right in yourself?'

'Eve, please don't look at me like Bernie and Mary-Anne did earlier. I can't bear it. I don't want your sympathy, honest. I told you that our first day here.' Don't deserve it, she thinks.

'But don't you hate being here, after London? Doesn't Anna miss her friends?'

'This is nothing like London and that's just what I want.' Eve, she realises, doesn't understand at all. How could she?

She doesn't live life like that. London was hard. Mean. London *was* John. 'Anna misses her pal, Cheryl. She lived on the same street and we used to see her and her mum quite a bit. But it's the best thing for us both, that we came here.'

Eve seems relieved to be back on surer ground. 'In case I forget,' she says, 'I've got the doll Anna wanted for her birthday. It took me ages to find it – I had to go to that new toyshop in Terenure in the end.'

'You shouldn't have put yourself to so much trouble.'

'It wasn't trouble.' She grins. 'I support her right to be choosy about her toys.'

To prove a point, Eve insists on paying for them both. 'This thing with the pints is just the start,' she says. 'If we get them in the pubs, we get their attention.'

'You got the barman's attention tonight, that's for sure.'

'You've got to join us, Maria. It's Blackrock next week. I've made a list of pubs from the phone book. We'll go straight from town, get three, four maybe, done in an hour.' Her eyes shine. 'Will you come?'

Maria pictures her daughter, three achingly long miles away. 'No. I've Anna to think of.'

'But Anna is exactly why you should come with us!' Eve says.

Maria picks up her gloves and bag, and before Eve can jump back on her soapbox, she asks quickly, 'What was it you shouted back to that barman earlier?'

'*Sláinte.*' Eve giggles. 'Cheers from the Campaign for Pints.'

Back outside on Dame Street the Thursday giddiness is nearly done. The shillings have been given over, the flirting will soon end. Maria stands at her bus stop with only the click of her own heels on the pavement for company. It's impossible to stay cross with Eve for long; she should have remembered that. Eve is impervious to anyone else's opinion and disapproval runs off her feathers. The bus is almost at Ranelagh Bridge when a different thought strikes her, one that makes her sit up straight in her seat and frown at her reflection in the window. What if Eve has got it all wrong?

What if they are the heiresses of nothing?

Friday is hair-wash night. Anna has fed the ever-hungry gas meter in the bathroom and Vosene-scented steam now rises from her head. She is kneeling sideways to the fire and one half of her face flickers red and orange. Single hairs wave, pushed up by the heat.

'It's dripping down the back of your dressing gown.' Maria lifts the wet rope of Anna's hair. Water sizzles on the grate and fallen hairs singe. 'I should have towelled it more.' She nudges her closer to the hearth.

'But that makes my ear go on fire.' She cups one hand over the side of her head while the other pulls at the green pile of her dressing gown. This constant picking has given the candlewick the scrappy look of a playing field in winter. Wet bed-sheets and blouses are draped over chairs and splodge slowly onto the newspapers that Maria has overlapped on the lino. *Splat, splat* onto the paper. She hears it as the sound of quiet poverty, of her inability to succeed at the business of living.

'Keep turning around, Anna. You'll never get dry otherwise.'

Anna looks at the cardboard box the grocer in Ranelagh gave her. 'Can we make the window now?' Two of the larger panels of the box have been removed and two exposed sides trimmed into an angle. The floor is lined with a piece of green and yellow lino, the walls papered in newspaper coated with pink poster paint. She inspects the outside. 'And I'd like rose trees on these parts, here.'

'Roses grow on bushes, not trees.'

'Big pink ones up the walls. Like Mrs Helping has in the summer. She told me about them this afternoon.'

Who else? Anna's conversations are peppered with encyclopaedic references to Mrs Helping (the name seems to have stuck) and both of her dead husbands. 'Her roses grow high as the window, she says. Guess how she makes them stand up so high?'

'How?'

'Stockings!' Anna chortles. 'Her old ones that have ladders in. I said, do the roses climb the ladders, but she said no. The stockings are the ropes that hold the roses to nails that the Late Mr Helping put in the wall.' She pats the box. 'I want roses for my house.'

'All right. But no nails. Or stockings, for that matter. Fetch your colouring pencils and we'll draw them on.'

'Can we cover the outside first?'

'People don't wallpaper the outside of houses.'

'But houses don't have *Kellogg's Corn Flakes* written on them.'

'When the box is on the shelf in your room you won't see the outside of it.'

'The sides of it.' Her voice rises a notch. 'I'll still see the sides of it, there, where it says *Sunshine in a Bowl*.'

Maria sniffs defeat through the Vosene, through the wet-dog steam of damp wool and flannelette. 'How about,' she sighs, 'if we paint the sides white, and draw some roses on when it's dry?'

'Perfect. Now.' Anna holds out a paper frame the size of a small envelope. 'Let's stick a picture on the inside first!'

Maria fetches the Red Cross 1965 Year of Older People calendar. It was on the wall when they moved into the flat, but they took it down in favour of Anna's Pillar postcard.

'But I don't want to cut it up when the year's not over. It might be bad luck.'

'There's no such thing, sweetheart,' she replies, yet puts the calendar to one side without argument.

Anna points at a sheet of newspaper on the floor. 'How about that one there, where the people are having a picnic?'

Maria picks up the scissors.

'But . . .'

Maria puts down the scissors.

'. . . I don't think having a picnic at night is a good idea, and it's a bedroom as well as all the other rooms.'

'So?'

'That one there! No, the one that's half under the chair.'

'Wouldn't you prefer a picture of Ireland?'

Anna shakes her head. Maria cuts out the photograph and together they paste it to the cardboard wall, then stick the paper window frame around it. Anna gathers up the tiny furniture, the product of two weeks' make-and-do. The bed and table are cigarette boxes wrapped in newspaper and painted brown. One box for the bed, two for the table. Two old spools of thread with scraps of fabric stuck to the top are the seats. Anna saves the three-matchbox chest of drawers for last. It's her favourite piece because she thought it up herself. Stacked, wrapped and painted green, the drawers have drawing-pin handles. She makes up the cigarette-box bed with a coverlet cut from an old hankie and a cotton-wool-ball pillow.

'It's perfect, Mummy.' She sits back on her heels. Newsprint shows faintly through the uneven poster paint on the walls, random words – *statute, agricultural, nation* – shining eerily through the pink. Through the window frame the Eiffel Tower stands majestic in grainy black-and-white newsprint.

'It's the most beautiful room I've ever—' Suddenly she drops the box. 'Phone! Can I answer it? *Please?*'

'It'll be for the lads.' The telephone is in the hall downstairs, shared between the three flats of the house. Two trainee accountants have the ground floor. From Sunday night to Friday morning the hall is filled with the odours of cheap cigarettes, sausages brought up from the home place in Louth and burnt, and oil from the bicycles that appear and disappear at random.

'Not on a Friday. And it never rings for upstairs.' Larry and Alfie go back to Castlebellingham every weekend. A nurse who works night shifts lives alone in the top-floor flat. She is a shadow to them: a creaking ceiling, a hum from behind the door of the shared bathroom, a smudge of navy uniform. 'You promised I could, the next time.'

'Go on, then.' Anna is already pulling at the door as Maria continues, 'But don't make noise on the stairs, just in case.' The pad of Anna's slippers on the carpet soon gives way to the slap of lino. Maria trails her out onto the landing and feels the heat of the fire sluice out of her body in seconds. She leans over the banister and watches the top of Anna's head as the child picks up the receiver. The light coming through the opaque glass of the front door is a dead grey and Anna's dressing gowned body blurs in the gloom. Only the parting in her damp hair shines. The white line bisecting her skull looks strangely cruel, a path highlighting the fragile bone underneath. Anna has the receiver clutched in both hands and is nodding seriously at the wall in front of her where the phone instructions are pinned.

'Ranelagh seven three nine four. May-I-please-help-you?' She must have been practising her telephone voice. 'Yes, this is Anna Mills speaking.'

Maria's palms prickle.

'*Really?* You have? And you're definitely coming to see me? For sure?' There is a pause. 'Mu-MMEEEE!' Anna shouts. She takes a step back to look up the stairs and screams. Maria is right next to her, a silent apparition in the dark. 'Mummy, you gave me a fright!'

'Who is it?' Maria grabs the receiver from Anna's hand before she's had a chance to answer and snaps, 'Go upstairs and shut the door behind you.' Her blouse sticks to her back, despite the cold gusts whistling around the hallway.

A fly-spotted mirror hangs on the wall next to the instructions. She stares at the woman reflected in it. Dark hair falls onto thin shoulders. A pale face with full lips, hollow cheeks and a frown etched into her forehead. She watches the lips open, hears them speak.

Eve is hard to derail once she gets going and Maria's ankles are numb by the time she gets back upstairs. This morning she was still puzzling over what had happened the night before in the Percy French. No matter how you dressed it up, calling it rights or a campaign or whatever other rubbish Eve had come out with, stealing was what they did. What stupidity. Dangerous, even. Eve has the energy and enthusiasm of a dozen – she always did – but in deciding that winning is more important than honesty, she's gone too far.

Maria is determined that under no circumstances will she go on one of those ridiculous outings again.

Anna is back beside the fire, the box in front of her. Her hair is nearly dry and back to its usual dark blonde. She has switched on the lamp and Maria is grateful for the spill of light on the dull colours of the room. Kitchen, bedroom, sitting room, shared bathroom on the return in the stairs: it's not much, their flat. The opposite side of Redoubt Terrace is identical and the view from the sitting room is of other, gently bowing bay windows. Red bricks dulled to the colour of old tea, grubby white net curtains, small gardens growing bicycles and dustbins. She often expects to pull back the curtain only to see another Maria and another Anna wearily staring sentinel across. Their bedroom is at the back and overlooks a lane. A repair shop in a long garage runs across what must once have been several back gardens. An overalled man there fixes sewing machines. The chain across his workshop door is too loose, and when the wind is up, it clangs like ropes hitting a ship's mast. On breezy nights Maria lies in bed and listens to the relentless *tack-tack* and pretends they're drifting through a peacock-blue sea with clear skies above and no horizon in sight.

She looks at Anna, now touring Jocky around the doll's house with the energy of an apprentice letting agent. Anna tugs open each drawer of the chest in turn and shows him the painted insides of the matchboxes. Maria looks down at the box, its out-of-scale furniture the colour of beef stew. We've made it as murky as this flat, she thinks. At least the box has a better view: the Eiffel Tower now looms, impossibly close and impossibly high, behind the paper window frame.

She picks up the torn newspaper. The Eiffel Tower photograph had been used to illustrate a film review. She skims through the article. *For any squeamish or nervous readers among you,* it concludes, *although* The Great Race *ends with the destruction of the Tower, it is considered virtually impossible for such an imposing edifice to be knocked down in this way.*

'Mum, Eve said she has my birthday doll for me! With yellow hair and a green mackintosh, just like the one I made up in my head!'

'I thought you asked her for a doll you'd seen in a shop.'

'No, I made her up. What is it? Why are you laughing at me?'

'It's nothing, sweetheart,' Maria says, enjoying the thought of Eve traipsing determinedly from shop to shop.

'Can we make a wardrobe to put the dolly's mac in?'

'We've no more boxes.'

'When we get more. Mrs Helping is saving hers for me too. Oh, I nearly forgot! She gave me these earlier to put on the walls.' Anna takes a piece of tissue paper from her school satchel and unwraps two pictures. 'They're spares. She cut him out.' A man faces the camera square-on, a black-and-white body in a suit that can't have graced the fashion pages since before the war. The white border of the photograph cuts him off at the ribs and gives him the look of a hand puppet.

'Who is it?'

'The Late Mr Onions, of course!' Anna gums the man to the wall over the bed and laboriously draws a thick black line in pencil around the picture. At each corner of the frame she loops the line around on itself then colours in the tiny oval. 'Mrs Helping has heaps of them.'

'Of what?'

'Little cards with a picture on. When somebody dies you give one to people so they don't forget what the person looked like. She has lots of people, not just him. She keeps them between the pages of her Bible, a different person in each page.'

The photo cut from Mr Onions's In Memoriam card is stuck to the wall over the brown bed. With the thick sheen of Macassar oil on dark hair and the broad, untroubled forehead, he looks the spivvy type. She can't picture Mrs Halpin as anything other than a fussy pensioner in a housecoat, while the man with those hard eyes could be her ne'er-do-well son, the sort of boy who breaks a mother's heart and is devoted only to her purse.

'I wanted a lady picture, too, but she doesn't have any spare in her collection,' Anna says. 'I tried drawing plaits on one of the Mr Onionses, but it didn't work out.'

'I can see why it wouldn't have,' Maria says, with a glance at the second Mr Onions, now regarding himself with satisfaction from his perch above the chest of drawers. The top of a packet of cigarettes protrudes like a sly tongue from his breast pocket.

'Yes.' Anna nods sagely. 'The moustache.'

CHAPTER FIVE

The window through which the Eiffel Tower is visible is draped in baby-blue curtains, trimmed from the thin skin of aerogram paper. 'Remember not to pull them, won't you?' Maria says, when Anna reaches out to touch the *Par Avion* just legible down one side. 'They'll rip if you try to close them.'

'I want them open. This way we can look at Paris all day and all night.'

With the glint in all four of the Late Mr Onions's eyes on her, Maria pats the tiny coverlet smooth. A small hand touches her own, warm and soft on her arm, fingertips on her wrist. 'Mum? Why do we not have any in-memory card for my daddy?'

Why? It had begun softly. So much so that Maria was never quite sure when it turned bad, could never figure out which bite of the apple had been the poisoned one. Wasn't it his job to keep her safe, to protect her from the world? She'd heard that often from him in their first few years. Whispered at first, and even when said with breath that was hot and beer-scented against her cheek, she had welcomed it as a caress. What else could that be, only love? What else could she want from him? It was what every woman wanted: a man to look after her, a man who had chosen to keep her safe. Find a man with a future and you'd find a future for yourself: at school that's what they all believed. And yet, without her noticing, his meaning had shifted from a question to a statement and, finally, an order.

It was as though one day she had looked up from the baby dandled on her lap only to see her world had shrunk until it was no more than an arm's stretch in any direction. Invisible walls were cemented around her and she had let him build them, had whispered loving words of encouragement while he did so. She had tried to explain as much once, quietly, carefully, on a day when he was just started in a new job and in a good mood because of it. He was always at his best then, when he was not long after getting a position with a new firm. When it was all fresh and all the successes he was certain of were out there just waiting for him to claim them, and whatever misunderstandings had occurred in the last place had been sluiced down the plughole in his shaving water. Without mentioning fear or anger, she tried to make him understand that they – she – couldn't go on in that manner. She could see now, she said, that it was her fault and she wanted to make it good, for them to sort everything out and start afresh and— 'And that bairn's after turning you softer than you already was,' he cut across her, then took a long pull on his cigarette. He smoked like a movie star. John wasn't a tall man but he had long, thin hands and smoking suited him.

'You can do whatever you like, Maria, anytime you like,' he said. And she had lifted Anna's pudgy hands and clapped those soft fingers together in patty-cake. Of course she could – he was right! A chink of light cracked the grey fog she lived in. She was being silly, had been so for ages and just hadn't realised. Wasn't she in a cage that she had built herself?

'That said,' he called, over his shoulder, as he opened the front door of the flat, 'I'd like to see you try.'

The door clicked shut behind him. The slap of his boots on the tiled stairs, the bounce and slap of his hand on the rail, called back to them. His whistle. The greyness settled around her once more. She knew that somewhere beyond it was a world that was bright and warm and knowable, but she couldn't figure out how to get there. He had taken understanding from her, shaken it out of her. And wasn't everything that had happened her own fault anyway? He had told her that often enough. She had told herself, too. John's hand was her punishment and her penance.

When Anna was born Maria had hoped the baby would prove to be the lamp that would lead them both out of the fog, yet Anna had become as trapped as Maria was, walled up by the uncertainty of his occasional indifference to her. One day he'd come home, pick her up and whirl her round, tickling her until she was nearly sick with hysterical laughter; the next it would be like she wasn't in the room. She would run to greet him only to be waved away and Maria would drop to her knees and try to distract her, to smooth out the child's crumpled, confused face.

By Anna's fifth birthday, the work had got more erratic. He'd long since given up the building business entirely – wasting his time, he said, herding a bunch of navvies and thieves – and, after a few weeks' work in a pub, had got a position as a sales rep with Antony Wise Car Dealership. That had suited him well. John had grown up in Leeds where his father had worked as a mechanic and he grew up knowing more about cars than any boy on his terrace. Life had been easier then: he was happy in his job. Antony Wise valued him, understood what John was made of. John made more sales than anyone else, got himself promoted. He had to travel to different garages in order to teach the other sales reps his techniques. He'd go out early, get back late, if he came back at all. It suited.

When the trouble did come calling, Maria realised she'd been holding her breath, waiting for it. Police at the door. Some misunderstanding, he told her afterwards, him and another fellow in what John was calling a *racket*, though the police had used the word *fraud*. Cars getting bought cheap, done up and sold on the side under the famous *Wise Buy Guarantee*, but Antony Wise not seeing so much as a farthing of the commission. John had been given his cards that morning. Wise had got the police in but, to Maria's relief, decided afterwards that he wouldn't take it any further in case a scandal might damage the business.

'Please tell me what's been going on.' Maria had tried to keep her voice even, though to her own ears she was squeaking like a child. She felt like one. 'Why are you in trouble with the police?'

He looked frightened. It was the first time she'd ever seen him so. He lit his cigarette. 'It's all finished with now. A caution,' he said, yet there was a shake to his hand. 'Wise could have made a packet if he'd only listened to me. He needs his head examined. Every pound a prisoner, that's his problem. Doesn't matter, there's plenty more opportunities out there. I was talking to a man only last week who said the big money's to be made on that new rig.'

She said nothing, bewildered in equal measure by his carelessness and his fear.

'Come on, Maria, even you must have heard of it. Oil rig? The Sea Gem, it's called. Do a stint there and you leave the place made of money. Dripping with it.'

She went to put dinner on. Why wasn't it ready? he asked. What had he done to get himself landed with her? He could have any woman he wanted. And maybe it was time he did. Anna was making too much noise: could she not shut her up for once? Maria stayed silent. Two policemen had been at their door! The entire street must have seen them. No good could find them from this point on, she knew it: John had taken them away from its touch, had chosen his path. She stayed inside her grey walls and said nothing.

The kitchenette was so small she could put a pan of water on the stove to boil and, without moving, lean into the sink to wash the potatoes. She tugged at the stiff cold tap and took down the potato peeler. From the other room she could hear him begin to tease Anna by pulling at her plaits. Could she not say her numbers any quicker? Why wasn't she better at spelling? She didn't want to grow up thick like her mother, did she? Maria dropped the peeler and went through to the sitting room to send Anna to her room until dinner was ready. But he moved so that he was in front of her, blocking her path just as Anna skipped past her into the kitchen. Maria sidestepped to walk around him and he grabbed her hands. She pushed against him but he had his hands flat against hers and wouldn't let go. He started on at her again, hissing in his anger this time.

Maria looked over his shoulder and realised Anna was tugging a chair to the sink to get a drink of water.

'Anna!' Maria called, but Anna ignored her. Couldn't she see that her arm was inches – less! – from the handle of the pot of water on the hob? Maria pushed him but John wouldn't drop her hands. 'Let me go! Look at her!' she pleaded, and he glanced behind him, into the kitchen. Anna was standing on the chair now. Steam had begun to billow up next to her but she was concentrating so hard on twisting the tap that she didn't seem to notice. And he understood. She knew he understood because he looked at their daughter, then carefully gathered both Maria's wrists in his one hand while he leant past her to the radio on the sideboard. He turned the volume up. One twist, then another.

She struggled but he wouldn't let go. She was afraid to scream over the music again in case it startled Anna into turning – or, worse, falling – and knocking the handle. He watched her watching Anna and he sang softly, matching Elvis word for word. He stared into her eyes, his own glittering, the entire time. And then he opened his hands wide and let her wrists drop to her sides.

Maria ran forward and grabbed Anna, pulled her off the chair and onto the floor. She pushed the pot back. She was never sure how it happened, but the pot slipped in her grasp and water splashed out and down her hands. For a split second it registered as very cold before a burning sensation around her bitten nails told her it wasn't. Quickly she turned and sank her hands into the sink. The grey scummy water rose up to meet the red marks on her wrists. She pushed her hands in further until the weals were submerged.

When she turned back to face him her hands felt strangely heavy. Her fingers were swollen and pounding, the skin the blotched pink of raw sausages. A grey potato peeling slid from her wedding ring and landed on the linoleum at her feet.

This is what will happen to me, she thought. To us. And as she stood there Elvis wept with her, crying his tears of joy in the chapel.

That day in the kitchen she had understood what would become of her – of them both – if she didn't act. Anna's question about the memorial card echoes in the room long after she is asleep and Maria sits alone in the near-dark. The fire has nearly gone out; the last few bits of coal she threw on, to be sure the washing dried fully, are damp and sputtering. She'd promised herself that she wouldn't let herself pull at all that again, that it was over and done with. It has to be, for how could she wish her life any different? To do so would be to deny Anna her existence, to disown every single scrap of her, every smile and scraped knee, every hair, whistle and giggle. How clever of Anna to ask about the card. Maria is annoyed with herself that it never occurred to her before. Of course John Mills has no In Memoriam card. He has no grave. How could he?

Graves are for the dead.

CHAPTER SIX

The rule is that the copytakers have their tea break in turns, no more than two out at a time, but Hilda, Deirdre and Mags invariably go together. They've been gone ten minutes and by now are sure to be two biscuits deep in a conversation as familiar and dependable as the blue lines of their stenographer's notebooks.

'Please? Take this one, it's only some old football match.' Michael is sprawled across his desk, his phone resting in the crook of his arm. Like an overgrown schoolboy, bony wrists extend from his cuffs. The only man among the five inhabitants of the copytaking office, Maria soon realised that Hilda, Deirdre and Mags regard him as their lovable yet unreliably housetrained pet. In the two months since she started in the copy office, Maria's become fond of his lazy giddiness, the good humour he turns equally on them all. It's easy to see how the others have come to treat him as their puppy and turn a blind eye when he snoozes on the beds or pilfers scraps from the table. 'Go on, Maria, I can never make out a word. The man has a mouthful of marrowfats. He's not drunk this time. At least, I don't think so.' Michael raises his head and says, 'Well? Are you stewed?' to the caller.

'Sorry,' Maria looks up from her typewriter, 'but the Rolling Stones are waiting on me.'

'Get you, Maria Mills! What about them?'

'A promoter wants them for more shows here but the Conference of Irish Catholic Bishops has demanded that...' she checks her pad '... "they and their heathen ways be banned from entering Ireland again."' She glances up. 'It's probably our own fault for entering the Eurovision Song Contest. Now everyone knows where we are.'

His guffaw is more than her joke deserved and she realises that her frivolity surprised him. He must think her the quiet sort.

'When are the shows?' he says.

'Never, if the bishops get their way. But the report's due in a few minutes.'

'Oh, all right . . . Yes, yes,' he says to his caller, 'with you in a moment.' She hears a squeak of response, tinny and irate.

'Honestly!' Michael puts the receiver on his desk. 'Will you read it over for me at least?'

'When you've typed it up,' she says, but he pouts and puts his head to one side. 'No, Michael!' Maria has yet to see him complete a full day's work. 'Typed only! Those squiggles of yours aren't even shorthand.' A clatter of coins thuds into his caller's payphone. 'I learned Pitman's, not Michael Brennan's, shorthand. Go on, before that poor man runs out of change.'

Michael sighs and rolls a biro up from the desk. He has neatly trimmed nails and never seems to get the ink stains and callouses that she does. He takes up the receiver and mutters, 'You'd better not be stewed.'

Maria's electric typewriter is being repaired and she is using the office spare, an old manual one. The wands are stained black and red with ribbon ink, the *t* is sticky and crosses over the *y* on its journey home. She teases them apart and they click back into their wide metal smile.

The bishop concluded that it was incumbent upon every priest to warn their own parishioners about the immorality threatening the very fabric of decent Irish society.

There are days when these turns in the lives of strangers, phoned through by faceless voices, sit heavy and indigestible on her. But on other, brighter, days – when she has woken up feeling stronger, convinced that she has done right by them both – her work is nothing more than coding and decoding her own scribbles. These are the days, she suspects, when she's closest to being the woman Eve thinks she ought to be.

With a final *ding* from the carriage return, Maria rolls the page out and puts it into a satisfyingly full brown folder. At the desk opposite, Michael is making heavy weather of his call. 'He passed the ball to *who*?' he's saying. 'Repeat that . . . Are you making these names up?'

She runs a finger gently along the dip and arc of the metal type inside the casing. The shapes are ciphers for what appears on the page. She types four letters directly onto the roller, watches how they suddenly appear the right way round when they hit the surface. It puts her in mind of a baby turning in the womb.

Today is pleasantly quiet, though there's no predicting when such days will occur. Mondays and Fridays tend to be busier, but a serious accident or a bad storm will have her phone glued to her head and her fingers typing rapid fire for hours. A plane crash that killed forty-one in England not long before she started had Michael run ragged for days. 'My fingers were worn down to the bone,' he told her, adding with relish, '*and* it was the same week as Cheltenham!'

She picks up a fresh sheet of paper. The letters she typed onto the roller shine, the faint gloss of black ink on black. J-O-H-N. If only the past could be rolled out of sight as easily.

Is he out there somewhere? Waiting in the dark night, in the bright morning, in the rain, in the sunlight? Maria allows herself breathe her fear in and out, to let that which she usually keeps packed down inside consume her for a moment. Sooner or later is he going to come looking for her? For them? No, she thinks, angry with herself. *No.* Every day that passes makes them safer. If he's not found them by now, he's not likely to. She doubts he'd want to try, even if he had any idea where to look. Remember, she consoles herself, how well covered their tracks are.

J-O-H-N. *Click-click-click* and the letters disappear.

'Michael!' Brian O'Toole appears around the door. A drama producer, he pops up in the copy office at regular intervals. The world-weary air he affects is undermined by the unyielding sheen of his new paisley scarf. 'Oh,' he looks at Maria, 'he's on the phone.' He is twirling one fringed end in his hand. Presumably he's affecting a burlesque-style tassel, but it gives him the appearance of a pantomime villain.

'That's how it looks to me,' she replies drily. He doesn't register her tone. Brian wouldn't have acknowledged her presence at all had Michael been free to talk. Maria doodles a plump face in her stenographer's book. A speech bubble floats above flushed cheeks like a hot-air balloon. She grins to herself.

Michael points to the phone clamped to his ear and mimes shooting himself in the temple. 'Lunch?' Brian stage-whispers and turns to leave. 'Call me!' He twirls his goodbyes, his scarf the colour of bruises.

'Ta-daa!' Maria mutters under her breath. The scarf is a foolish choice, she decides, for a man working in drama.

Michael's 'Cheerio!' is snapped in two by the closing door. 'No, not you, caller,' he sighs. 'You're to keep going. Impressive lead by when?'

Brian O'Fool, says the speech bubble in her doodle. Maria scribbles over it, then decides to rip out the page altogether. Better to be careful. Hilda is a graduate with distinction from Miss Galway's Secretarial College and carries the weight of her profession heavy on her shoulders. She lifts their notebooks at random to examine them. It would be awful to lose this job now. On the days when she gets home and Anna is full of school, and what fun Mrs Halpin and Chuzzlewit are ('The Late Mr Helping,' Anna said seriously, when Maria questioned the cat's strange name, 'was a Great Devotee of Charles Dickens'), this job feels like the only thing she has that is purely her own.

'I've got another waiting. Must ring off. Scores, yes, yes. Got you.' Michael's head is on top of his desk, his nose almost in his ashtray. 'Lord,' he says, his receiver finally put to bed, 'but that was a hellish one. What else did Brian say?'

'Nothing to me.'

'I'll see if I can catch him up for tea break. I'm parched. Did you hear the cut of that one? Half stewed. Most of them are, I'm sure of it.' His phone is exchanged for a cigarette in a single motion. He holds it the same way she recalls Alicia did. Foolhardy Alicia that night in the Percy French! Facing the barman square in the eye and asking for pint after pint. Maria can't imagine what it must feel like to live inside her skin.

'Get Mags or Deirdre to run an eye over this, will you?' He drops his notebook on her desk and rushes out of the door. 'You're a pet, Maria Mills,' he calls back. She looks down and smiles. The page is a mass of squiggles, his writing as bad as she's ever seen on a doctor's pad. Even Michael often can't make out what he's written and types up a fair approximation from memory and guesswork. When he's really stuck he asks one of the others to phone the reporter back 'for verification purposes'.

It's unusual to be alone in the office, free of the stream of reporters and messengers, the occasional impatient producer or editor harrying them to type faster. The room isn't really big enough for the five of them and it gets stuffy when they're all there together. On rainy mornings their coats steam over the backs of their chairs until lunchtime.

Michael's fading cigarette smoke has a distant, melancholy tinge, the blue of faraway hills. The morning sun illuminates the dust motes whipped up by the thud of his pad. Tiny separate existences mixing with her own. She flips her own notebook through her fingers. Her pages rustle with stories in a never-ending refrain of changed lives and fresh days.

Handbags over their arms, Hilda, Deirdre and Mags reappear in a formation as solid as a filing cabinet. Hilda, a large woman who lists forward on small feet ('trotterish', Eve had described her), started as a radio copytaker in the old days, when the staff were employed by the Department of Posts and Telegraphs and were, she insists, '*proper* civil servants'. Back then, she claims, the entire office was permitted to take a break together if they chose to do so. A cloud of freshly applied Tweed around her, Hilda sits down and tucks her chair under the apron of her desk.

'Copytaking office?' She breathes the heavy sigh of the overworked. 'One moment, please, caller. We're very busy just now.' The whirl of the rollers, the clack of clean sheets waiting to be dirtied, begins again. Maria is free to go.

Outside in the corridor two men are leaning against the wall. 'Go on.' The taller of the two nudges the other. 'It'll be a laugh.'

'Are you . . . ?' She holds the door to the copy office open for them.

'No, no,' the tall one says. His dark hair is slicked back, his accent confident. 'Just waiting . . .' he nudges his friend and winks '. . . for a special someone.'

She walks past the canteen. As people in RTÉ are very fond of saying, RTÉ people have great style, and through the gap in the swinging doors she glimpses table after table of fashionable Dacron-wool suits and the latest shirt-waisters and twinsets. She spots Eve just inside the door, chatting intently to a lady she recognises as Edna Corrigan, the head of women's programming. Eve doesn't notice her but Maria hurries past, just in case. The odd thought strikes her that, a few hours earlier, all of these people had woken up alike and dishevelled, the crumpled truth of sleep still in their eyes. They dressed themselves into roles they will perform for each other until the end of the day.

The clatter of trays follows her as far as the Ladies. She remembers Hilda taking her aside on the Monday of her second week. 'You didn't go on your tea breaks last week, Maria. Tea break's a right. It's our entitlement as part of our working conditions.'

'Thanks, Hilda,' Maria replied, 'but I wasn't thirsty.' Hilda sighed in response, exhausted by Maria's stupidity. 'You don't have to drink the tea, but you're expected to take the break.'

Maria smiles. Despite Eve always referring to Hilda as dull and petty, they might just have more in common than she realises. As she soaps her hands she thinks of the woman Eve told her about, the one with the son hidden away. She's never seen or heard anything else about that unknown and invisible little boy yet often expects to find him skulking around the Ladies, haunting it like a ghost desperate to be released into the other world. She can't imagine how she ever considered she could hide Anna here even for a day. The idea of parking her daughter at her feet, like an umbrella or a parcel, now seems ridiculous. And the tales she'd overhear! Anna's ears would be out on stalks at the stories of falling in love in time for the last bus, the wriggling and wrestling in the back seats at the pictures.

Back in the office, Michael is still at tea break. The others are on their phones and scribbling furiously. The smaller of the two men she saw in the corridor is now bent over Michael's desk. Callers are so frequent that no one takes any notice.

'Can I help you?' she asks.

The man jumps. 'You're grand,' he says, his grin wide yet unsmiling. 'Just leaving a note.' He slips a piece of paper into Michael's typed copy folder. 'Don't say anything, will you? It's a surprise.'

Fifteen minutes later Michael returns and, only an hour behind schedule, laboriously types up his notes. 'Oh, bugger and damnation. He couldn't really have said *dexterity and skulls*, could he?'

'Skills?'

'Oh, yes, that must be it.' After a last flurry of typing, he pulls the page from the machine and shoves it into his folder. 'Right, the job's Oxo. Patrick Keady told me to get this lot to News by lunch or I'm for it.'

She turns back to her own copy, a short piece just phoned in from the High Court about a dispute over land between two farmers that has rumbled on for years. As the seasons passed, the reporter told her, the sly remarks and mean tempers grew. One sunny morning the previous February the younger brother drove his tractor into the other's yard. The court was not yet in full possession of the facts as to what tipped the man over the edge; it was hoped that the truth would emerge after lunch.

The prosecution claims, she typed, *Joseph Murray pulled John Murray to the ground before putting the blade of his shovel against John Murray's open hand. When he leant his shoulder to the handle, the shovel went through his brother's palm like a knife through butter.*

'Did you get that last bit?' The reporter had been insistent. 'A knife through butter?'

The prosecution claims, she typed, *that Joseph Murray acted in plain view for all to see and was laughing for the entire duration of the assault.*

She types the sentence slowly, something jarring in her mind. Something about the man leaning over Michael's desk. The grin that was more of a sneer; his wink.

The News Department is at the other end of a corridor that is nearly the length of the building, and Michael has just reached the office by the time she catches up with him. An executive is standing at the door, one hand outstretched.

'You're really pushing it, these days, Michael,' he is saying. His pinstriped navy suit and irritated expression suggest a man unused to waiting.

'It's just gone one now!' Michael hands over the folder, adding, 'Sorry,' as the man's eyebrows rise.

'No!' Maria leans past Michael and plucks the folder out of the older man's hand. 'I mean, there's been a mistake. This is mine.'

'Maria?' Michael says. 'What are you doing? Of course it's not.' He puts his hand out but she keeps the folder close to her chest. He looks from her face to the executive's. Christ, I don't know either, his shrug seems to say. Search me.

'Excuse me, but who are you?' The pinstriped suit is impatient. 'And can I have my report now?'

Holding the folder awkwardly close, Maria flicks through the pages. Her heart thumps. She singles out a report about newly observed patterns of behaviour in migrating bird pairs. She doesn't answer but instead turns to Michael and says, 'Yes, this one, here. Look.' She points at where the typed page ends with the handwritten line, *Newsflash: Michael Brennan enjoyed himself in Bartley's bar last night, didn't he?*

'You see?' she says. 'Mine.'

Michael pales. 'Em, this is Maria Mills, she works in the copy office. Maria, this is Patrick Keady.' His voice is sticky.

'Mr Keady, if you give me a minute I'll get Michael's report.' She turns away before he has a chance to reply. The page she returns with is still warm from a Xerox machine. Only a faint shadow indicates where the handwriting once was.

'Everybody happy now?' Patrick Keady asks. 'Is it possible for you two to share an office without getting your work mixed up, do you think?'

'Maria is an excellent copytaker,' Michael says, his face still pale.

'This little scenario would suggest otherwise,' he replies, but he's looking at her, staring straight at her, in fact, as though Michael wasn't even there. There is a tired handsomeness to him. Fancy suit aside, his careworn manner has the frayed dedication of a busy doctor in a market town.

Just before Maria rounds the bend in the corridor she takes a quick glance back. She knows her cheeks are flushed, and hopes he can't tell from that distance. Patrick Keady's eyes are on her still, his expression that of a man who won't turn away until her body has disappeared and she is no more than the *tap-tap* of heels receding into silence.

At ten minutes to five Hilda goes to the Ladies and fixes her make-up. At two minutes to five, she puts on her coat and headscarf. At one minute to five, she tucks all the brown folders into a neat pile on the shelf outside their door for a messenger to collect. This brings her to five exactly, the time at which she leaves the building. 'In the P and T,' she regularly tells the room, 'a day's work was always done by five.' This unbreakable obstinacy about her conditions is such that Michael has speculated to Maria that if Hilda needed the toilet at five o'clock she would wait in agony until she got home rather than 'wee in work on her own time'.

Folders collected, the typewriters are put to bed under their covers. Deirdre and Mags are freshening up for a visit to the Club. Mags has eyes like chocolate drops and needs only a wave of her lipstick, whereas Deirdre – Michael calls her Rudolph behind her back – has a more laborious Pan-Stik routine. Maria pushes her phone away and stretches. There is a grinding pain in her shoulders.

'Anyone want to come with us?' Mags asks. 'Maria? No? Looks like it's just us chickens, Dee.'

At the far end of the corridor Eve is waiting. 'Hurry up, Maria. It's Rathmines this evening. You're coming, aren't you?'

'Nice try, Eve! You've asked the last four weeks and I've said no each time.'

'Maria?' an unseen voice calls. She glances through an open door. Through a second door, Patrick Keady is looking out from behind a large and cluttered desk. 'Step in a minute, would you?' he says, his voice that of a man in charge.

'What's all this?' Eve whispers.

'I've no idea.' His formal-sounding tone is worrying.

'Go on.' Eve nudges her arm. 'I'll wait out here.'

'Shut the door, please.' He gestures towards the chair on the other side of the desk, then swivels around until his back is facing her. 'I know,' he says, the phone now against his ear, 'but it's not like we ask them to spend a week whitewashing the yard and pressing their Sunday suits, is it? They know that's not the image of farming we're looking for.'

When he turns back he looks surprised to see her still standing and raises his forefinger. *Wait!* the finger says. *You are next on my list.* His dark hair is greying at the temples and there is a tired droop to his blue eyes. His shirt collar looks properly starched, yet she can see from his unbuttoned suit jacket that the shirt itself is creased. He must look quite different when he laughs, she thinks, and wonders what age he is. He's bound to be younger than he seems. He rings off and rubs his eyes with the back of one hand. 'My mother was a poultry instructor many years ago and she takes a keen interest in the problems we come up against in making our agricultural programming.'

'I see.'

'It's not my area at all, but helpful to pass on comments, don't you think?'

'That rather depends, Mr Keady.' Maria imagines the response if she were to phone up whoever is in charge of *School Around the Corner* and pass on Anna's detailed and often scathing remarks.

'Patrick, please.' He gestures again at the chair and she sits this time, her bag standing to attention on her lap. The desk between them is cluttered with pages and clipboards. Densely typed pages scored with red pen spill from brown folders and there are enough half-full cups of cold tea and dirty ashtrays to give Mrs Halpin heart failure. Two framed photographs teeter at the edge of his desk. The one nearest to her is of three children on a stony beach, a dark sea just behind them. The two girls have jumpers pulled over their swimming costumes and are making faces at the camera. The youngest child, a boy, hugs himself against the cold. He looks pale and miserable and has one foot tucked behind his knee. The toes on his standing foot are splayed out and gripping the pebbles. A shadow from the photographer – Patrick? – falls in front of the boy and the water behind laps at his small heel.

Patrick's elbow nudges a folder, which shoves a box, which in turn falls on the photographs. This is the desk equivalent of the game Anna plays in which she stands dominoes up in a curved line and gently taps the first one to bring the lot down in sequence. 'Sorry,' he says, and carefully rights the picture of the children. The second photo – a woman in evening dress with a high bun and a crochet wrap as thin and fine as her expression – he doesn't touch. The woman's patent-shod feet are lying flat and pointing towards him. How could he not notice it?

'What was that about today, with Michael?' he asks. 'That wasn't really your copy in his folder, was it?'

'It was nothing, sorry. A mistake.' Stay quiet, Maria, she tells herself. It's none of your business and he's an executive and you're a secretary.

Michael has the tight dirty-blond curls of a fallen angel and underneath his chirpy manner a shadow shifts of something darker, more complicated. He had cried when they were alone that afternoon. 'It's a bar,' he said. 'What's so wrong with that?' One of the journalists regularly uses the payphone in Bartley Dunne's and Maria has noticed Hilda always passes on his calls to someone else to transcribe. Michael made her swear not to mention what happened to anyone. 'Especially Eve,' he said. 'She'd never let me alone.' Maria nodded, promised not to say a word. This is the Ireland she remembered from a decade before: a land built on telling one man a tale of another.

'It was nothing,' she repeats, looking straight at Patrick Keady.

'I know there may be some people here who take amiss Michael's, um, manner. But if there is . . .' he pauses, seems unsettled '. . . wrongdoing, then nobody should be protected.'

'I don't agree.' It is only as she hears the words leave her mouth that she realises this is the truth. 'Michael should be protected,' she continues, 'but how is up to him, not you or me.'

Patrick Keady's eyebrows arch but he doesn't respond. She stands up, her heart knocking in her chest. 'So, if there's nothing else, will you please excuse me?'

'No.' He leans back, his blue eyes unreadable. 'There's nothing else.' She has one hand on the doorknob when he says, 'I'd heard of you before today. Liam Mavin mentioned you.'

Her stomach contracts with nerves as she turns to face him again. So this is the real reason Patrick Keady called her in. That business about Michael was a decoy and now she let herself be put on the back foot over it. Has Mavin been giving out about her? She can't understand why. It's not as though she's rude to him, like the others sometimes are. Getting him off the phone is a job in itself. It's not that he's a bad reporter – in fact Maria thinks of his reports as perfectly aimed arrows even when the first few sentences sound as though he's misfiring blindly. What causes the entire copy office to sigh when he phones is the prospect of listening to the lengthy epilogues that follow. In these, Liam 'The Mavin' himself is the story. Who else was it stood shoulder to shoulder with Harry Boland in the 1916 Rising but The Mavin? Wasn't he so close to Cosgrave at Arthur Griffith's funeral that he might as well have picked the man's pocket? And – this one is Maria's favourite – wasn't it none other than The Mav himself who'd go to the circus with Jack B. Yeats? ('And the big bulging head on him,' he had added.)

'Has Mr Mavin made a complaint about me?'

He ignores her question. 'Liam Mavin has been guest of honour at four separate retirement parties yet turned up for work again within days each time. We'll never get rid of the old bugger. Or his stories.'

'His *derring-did* years, I think of them,' she says hesitantly, and Patrick's unexpectedly hearty guffaw suggests that, whatever is going on, she mustn't be in any trouble.

'Mavin said when he's finished dictating his copy you often ask him about where he's telephoning from.'

'Yes.'

'Why? Most people can't wait to get him off the phone.'

'I know.' Deirdre and Mags like to tease Michael about the time he panicked and said he had to ring off because the office was on fire. 'I'm curious, that's all.' She has wondered why she asks some of the reporters about where they are. It's hard to believe it's real.

'It would be interesting to see the places where all the different reports come from. Mr Mavin describes them so distinctly,' is the answer she gives. She can't tell Patrick Keady that it's because there are days when she needs to picture the real Ireland outside this building, days when a voice telling a story doesn't feel enough to keep her tethered to the desk, to stop her floating away, high over the Irish Sea, like a lost balloon.

'It'll go that way in time. There'll be fewer studio-based reports as the equipment gets more refined and we can do better outside broadcasts. If we had cameras trained on Mavin now we'd be showing one pub payphone after another.'

'I wasn't implying that—'

'It's all right, I know you weren't.' He grins, seeming to enjoy her confusion. 'Though some day I'm sure every blasted piece will be broadcast by the reporters themselves instead of newsreaders. God love us when that happens.'

'They already are broadcast, Patrick,' and she returns his smile for the first time when she adds, 'to me.'

Eve is waiting impatiently outside. The flurry of departures over, the corridor has that air of ruffled calm, as though it needs to settle back into itself again. 'Hark at you, chit-chatting with the top brass.'

'Were you listening at the door?'

'I'm a secretary, aren't I? It's what I do best. I wonder what else does Patrick Keady want with you.'

'Nothing. You already heard. A misunderstanding earlier, with Michael.'

'Hmm, I wonder. He'll be a big shot, mark my words. Did he tell you he's just taken over as head of the 1916 Programmes Committee?'

'No. It was nothing like that, honestly,' she says, her mind on the note and Michael's tears. You can smell the spill of tears on a person. All afternoon his face had been the dull, weathered grey of metal sheeting, his eyes two bolts beaten far back into it.

'Right, let's go.' Eve can be like a typewriter herself sometimes. It doesn't take much for her to click on to the next topic. 'We need to hurry.'

'I told you already, I'm not going. Not this week, not any week.'

The oily sheen of Eve's astrakhan cuffs gleams under the strip lighting as she buttons her coat. 'Your Mrs Halpin won't mind. She'll be delighted to have Anna for another few hours.'

This is hard to disagree with. Anna even has her own bedroom there now, though Maria won't hear of her staying overnight. 'It's for her to rest if she ever wants to,' Mrs Halpin said, 'and to keep her few bits and bobs, like you'd have at your nan's.'

Maria shakes her head, and with a final 'Oh, all right, but it's your loss,' thrown over her shoulder, Eve is gone.

It's nearly half past five. Talking to Patrick Keady has made her late and she'll have missed her bus. She pops back to the copy office to telephone Mrs Halpin. The room is quiet, the air overused. Ah, sure there's no rush, she's told. Aren't they baking scones for the tea, and they'll be twenty minutes or more yet in the oven. Maria pictures her daughter wrapped in Mrs Halpin's spare apron. Flour in her hair, her tongue stuck to her lip in concentration and those thin wrists bending to and fro as she kneads.

Mrs Halpin rings off because the serial is about to come on the radio, but before the receiver is in its cradle, Maria hears her say, 'If you're to be a good Irish girl, you'll have to pronounce your words right,' and Anna's reply, 'Sko-inns. Isn't that right? Sko-inns?'

Through the window she catches sight of Eve striding towards the main road. She didn't believe it was any of her business to ask Michael about the two guys earlier and the note, yet his tears were a secret door opening in a wall. Even though it quickly slid closed again, she knows it is there. As she watches her friend, something pinches inside her, a recognition that all of it – Michael, Eve's nonsense about the pints, the deceiving half-person she herself shows to the world, even Alicia's solid bull-headedness – is all connected in some strange, opaque way. As though a similar emptiness rests in all their hearts. As she turns away from the window there is a flash as Eve conjures her headscarf from her bag. A red ripple, of blood spilt in water.

CHAPTER SEVEN

The 1916 Programmes Committee played with their pipes and cigarettes like bored amateur actors fiddling with props. Eve did a silent head count around the large table in Patrick's office – six out of nine, not a bad hit rate as meetings go – and put an agenda in front of each person. She enjoyed the fact that the divisions among the group were such that when Eamon O'Mara brought the page up to his milk-bottle glasses, Hugh Clarke was obliged to read his without lifting it rather than appear to be following Eamon's lead.

'Shall we get started, then?' Patrick's hand bumped an ashtray, which sent a folder skittering to the floor. 'Buggeration,' he muttered.

Ham-fisted. Eve threw her eyes to Heaven. She picked up the folder, its pages fluttering obediently back into their homes at a wave of her hand.

Just as the meeting was beginning, Robert Ryan's secretary Dolores phoned through his apologies. Eve didn't care: the pride of the radio waves was no loss. In fact, with the possible exception of Patrick Keady himself, the 1916 Committee were a bag of eejits. Patrick had headed up Telifís Éireann's JFK Visit Committee three years before, but it had been small fry compared to this jubilee. As she watched him glance from one cranky face to another, she decided there could be no bigger curse for an executive than ambition. The previous head of the 1916 Programmes Committee had cited pressure of work as the reason for his resignation and Patrick's expression suggested he was finally twigging what his predecessor had really meant.

'Run us through this lot quick as you like, Patrick,' said Hugh Clarke, a senior drama producer. 'I've a lot on today.' Lured to Dublin from Granada Television at the launch of Telifís Éireann, it was widely assumed that he regretted his decision to leave *Coronation Street*.

'These are not insignificant matters!' Eamon O'Mara, an engineer promoted beyond his training and ability into an executive job, bristled inside his hairy tweed suit. A man in the habit of using the phrase *all things considered*, Eve had noticed that the more often he said it, the less consideration he applied. 'The jubilee of our nation's founding chapter is a serious undertaking. I will not sit here to be told otherwise.'

How much more enjoyable it would be to record the unspoken, Eve thought, as Hugh fired a glare across the table. The thick ice of Eamon's glasses whacked it back but Hugh was ready, and lashed it over the crossbar with the stem of his pipe.

Clink-clunk. The committee's eyes turned to the closed door. The station has an entire department devoted to the creation of sound, yet the jangle of crockery on the tea lady's trolley is the most recognised and most loved noise in the building. It grew closer then faded, taking the promise of tea with biscuits – one for Eve, two for each executive – with it. Only when it was so faint as to be no more than the jingle of sleigh bells over a distant frozen land did the heads turn from the blank screen of the door back to the table. Eve said nothing. She alone knew the tea break was arranged for ten thirty, the point at which they would be as cranky as small children and in need of a sugary biscuit.

The wall clock across from Patrick's head showed nine fifteen. He straightened in his chair and sighed, but so softly that only Eve, now sitting to his right, heard. 'Right,' Patrick said, 'Let's begin, shall we?'

Her pen feeling like an axe over her stenographer's notebook, Eve stifled a yawn.

PK opened the meeting with . . .

'It's just not analytical enough!' By nine forty-five EO'M's embers were thoroughly stoked. He frowned at HC, who ignored him in favour of the bowl of his pipe.

'We must stimulate . . .' EO'M stumbled over the word and Eve had to mask her snigger with a cough '. . . more debate, more rigour. We are talking about the founding chapters of our history.'

'Yes, Eamon,' PK agreed. 'Founding chapters, you have mentioned. But it has been agreed that the work of the station is to present a uniform approach to the Rising, and our perspective is to be one of nationalism, not socialism. Producing successful and interesting programming is what Upstairs has tasked us with.' Eve had heard him practise this nationalism-not-socialism response aloud in advance of the meeting but she suspected even he wasn't entirely convinced by it.

'Uniform?' The cheeks beneath EO'M's scrubby beard looked hot and itchy. Smoke rose through one of the chimneys created between his nose and his glasses. 'Prescriptive more like. Oppressive. The very thing that those men, who should be held aloft as the idols of our nation, were rebelling against.' It was like watching a greedy baby on its bottle, the way he sucked at his cigarette.

'Our task is to bring the events to life, to invigorate what happened for the listeners and viewers,' HC interrupted. 'The purpose of commemorative programming isn't to present events as one might a mere history lesson.'

'Commemorating history is exactly our purpose!' It is well known that EO'M believes television is where the theatre buckos come to earn a regular wage and, by doing so, inflict on the public the profane nonsense paraded across the stages of Ireland.

'Our purpose, *Eamon*,' HC lifted his name with invisible tongs, 'is to get ratings.'

'Dramatic tension is so important, Hugh, I agree,' PK spoke quickly, 'and we have no better man than you for understanding it, and how it can best be used to improve ratings.'

Eve put down her pen and flexed her fingers. She had spotted this argument as she would a faraway bus: there is nothing else to do but stare as it rumbles slowly towards the stop.

'Also important,' PK continued, as EO'M opened his mouth to protest, 'is maintaining faith with historical accuracy, as Eamon has so wisely noted. So, thank you both, for such . . . considered contributions. Have you got all that, Eve?' She nodded a not-entirely-truthful yes. She had already decided to reconstruct the conversation later, using the minutes of the last meeting and a fresh selection of PK's comments.

Eamon sat back and lit another cigarette, gratified. He's wise. It will be in the minutes. And if it's in the minutes, it's the truth. HC called his pipe to order by tapping it against the table. ('He does everything,' she told Maria later, 'except smoke the stupid thing.')

'Right. Next item: the newspaper advertisement looking for anyone with direct knowledge of the events or the leaders to contact us. It has now been placed, and there'll be a second this week asking people to post in relics for use in a photographic feature in the *RTV Guide*.'

By eleven thirty PK had coerced and cajoled the room down the dead end of the agenda until only two items stood between Eve and freedom. First up was *Easter Rebellion*, the eight-part television series directed by Keith Kirwin that was to re-enact the events of the Rising and present them night by night as if they were news reports broadcast fifty years before. Unusual, ambitious and expensive, the station is hoping to sell it internationally. Eve knew the words *Easter Rebellion* made Patrick more fearful than anything else on the agenda.

'The scripts have all been signed off by Upstairs,' PK said. 'So what stage is this at? Has the final shooting schedule been agreed?'

'Excuse me?' Eve spoke for the first time since the tea break. HC craned around his neighbour for a better view. 'Mr Kirwin is finalising his locations today in town. He asked me to let you know that the complete schedule will be circulated on Friday. The indoor filming starts next week. Outdoor starts in the first week of the New Year, scheduled to run until February.'

'I cannot support a decision to reconstruct such momentous events and depict them as merely the news of the day.' EO'M had fired himself up all over again. 'All things considered, we must not sacrifice the historical accuracy of our nation's revolutionary past. We cannot replace a national memory with a selection of – of staged fiddle-faddles!'

There's one for the minutes, Eve thought. *Fiddle-faddles.* Honestly. Can it really be so difficult to think before speaking?

'For Heaven's sake, what do you think history *is* except the news of its day?' HC snapped. 'Your so-called revolutionaries were flesh and blood. They walked the same ground as the rest of us.'

'No,' PK said. 'I mean, yes. We all take your point, Eamon, but *Easter Rebellion* is primarily a drama series. And its first priority is to do justice to the dramatic tension of the events. You've read the scripts? Yes? I think we're all agreed that they're excellent.'

'I would like my concerns to be recorded,' EO'M huffed.

Just as his predecessor used to do, PK nodded at the minute book. And not for the first time, Eve wondered how the instigators of the Rising would respond if they were to eavesdrop on these interminable meetings. What blunt advice would they have for the people who had less than six months to reanimate their lives and legacy?

'Who is liaising with the clerical unit for this committee?' a hitherto silent voice piped up from the far end of the table. 'I haven't heard mention of it yet.' *The clerical unit*? Christ, another minute of this and Eve would be throwing herself under a bus on the Stillorgan Road.

'I'll take care of that,' PK said, then continued, 'And our final item for today, gentlemen, is a new addition to the commemorative schedule: a radio documentary on women's participation in the events leading up to and during the Rising. Robert Ryan and Edna Corrigan are the producers, and Robert himself is going to present it. He will brief us fully at the next meeting.'

PK approached the close of the meeting with the determination of a jockey facing the last fence. Finally, the 1916 Programmes Committee stood, stretched and – thanks be to God – left the room. Another meeting over, successful if for no reason other than its completion. Radio Éireann and Telifís Éireann are the country's two barometers, national arbiters of taste and judgement. And posterity in the guise of Eve's notebook has recorded another day of their participation in its life. Even better again, with another morning nearly over, the downhill trot to lunchtime well under way.

'I appreciate you helping out, Eve,' Patrick said, as she tidied away loose pages and emptied the ashtrays, 'but I know you're busy enough already. The workload of the committee will increase so much over the next few months that we still need a dedicated secretary. Has someone been arranged yet?'

'Someone from the copytaking office, Personnel said. They can spare one person on a secondment from next week until the middle of April.'

'Good. Will you make sure she's up to date on everything before the next meeting?'

'She? I haven't heard who it is yet. It could be Michael.'

Patrick pushed his chair back from the table, taking two folders and his own ashtray with him. Cigarette ash rained down his trouser legs and onto his shoes. 'Dammit.' He plucked a butt from his trouser turn-up and lobbed it in the general direction of the wastepaper basket. 'Eve, do something for me, will you? Make sure it isn't.'

'And that brings me . . . here!' With a flourish Eve finishes her story of the meeting. 'You did see where all that was going, didn't you? I promised I'd sort you something more interesting!'

'Interesting?' Maria splutters. 'They sound like they've been let loose from a county home! And I don't want something *more interesting*. I told you that before! I'm fine where I am, thank you very much.'

'Oh, there's no need to thank me,' Eve says. 'Anyway, it's only for six months – you can go back to copytaking afterwards. Some meetings go quicker than today. It depends who's there. Here, I've made you copies of the minutes of all the previous meetings so you'll know the schedule and who's doing what. You'll be based in Robert Ryan's office. He's the only one on the committee with a spare desk in his secretary's office.'

'What's he like?'

Eve sniggers. 'If he was an ice-cream he'd lick himself.'

Robert Ryan, the popular presenter of *Double R's Rovings* and *Town Hall Tonight* had believed himself to be a shoe-in for the television programme *The Late Late Show*. Bragged all round the Club for weeks that the job was as good as his. Eve had overheard him say so. But it had bypassed him, and instead the wry, eager face tucked behind the desk every Saturday night is that of Gay Byrne. By a happy irony of scheduling, at the same time Gay is preparing to introduce his guests to the live studio audience, Robert is stuck in a cubicle on the third floor of the GPO presenting *At the Pictures*, a weekly radio programme about the latest movies. 'So, not only does he miss watching *The Late Late* himself, but he has to present his show knowing that no one who owns a television will be listening!'

Maria pulls a face. 'Sounds like I'll have a lovely time.'

'You'll be grand. You're not his sort.'

'What do you mean?' Although she has no interest in being Robert Ryan's sort, Maria has vanity enough to wonder why Eve thinks so.

Eve laughs. 'You'll see what I mean when you meet Dolores. Oh, before I forget, I bought this for that eejit who used to be the 1916 secretary. It might be a help to know what they're all talking about, and for spelling the names and that.'

The Cradle of a Nation has its paper seal on it still. Together they leaf through the pages, pausing at the illustrations and cartoons. Eve frowns at the photograph of Padraig Pearse's surrender. *General William Henry Muir Lowe*, the caption notes, *is holding Pearse's sword-stick and pistol, which Pearse handed over along with his ammunition and a canteen containing two onions.*

'Look.' Eve points at the two pairs of feet just visible beneath Pearse's coat, the frustration loud in her voice. 'That woman walked the length of the street carrying the white flag of surrender, and her feet are the only part of her not doctored out of the picture.'

She's right: there *are* two extra feet Maria hadn't noticed. The second pair, Eve tells her, belong to Nurse Elizabeth O'Farrell of Cumann na mBan, the Irish republican women's paramilitary organisation. 'And if you thought that was bad,'

Eve adds crossly, as she flicks on a few pages, 'in other books even her feet are gone.'

'Wait! Go back a page.' A photograph of an oddly shaped brooch has caught Maria's eye. 'Aunt Josephine,' she says softly. 'She had one of those. She kept it wrapped in a hankie in her wardrobe.' The brooch had felt light in her hand, she remembers. She can picture it now. It was long and light and shone like Rumpelstiltskin's gold. Aunt Josephine must have polished it in secret.

Summer holidays. Maria was nine and bored. She was always bored. Aunt Josephine Power had come over from Scotland to keep house for them after her mother had died, and didn't she harp on and on about it? How she'd been saving for years to go to the States, only hadn't she put her own life to one side to help her younger brother with his motherless bairn? The motherless bairn once overheard Aunt Josephine refer to her as 'the only one of five that took, and it was the fifth killed the poor woman. But Veronica was the soft sort.'

Maria was five when her mother died and she missed her without really remembering much about her. Her memories were similar to a pleasant dream that fades on waking and leaves behind a hazy sense of loss, as well as gratitude for having had the dream at all. What a terrible burden Maria must be on Aunt Josephine, she thought, if living in Rathdrum with her and her father was worse than staying in Glasgow during the Blitz.

Aunt Josephine did the church flowers on a Wednesday afternoon, and Maria sometimes had a little poke around her room while she was out. There wasn't much. Some dull letters, postcards. Tucked between copies of *Ireland's Own* there were a few cheap paperbacks. She was both unnerved and fascinated by their covers: women with big skirts and exposed bodices, their hair tumbling back over milky shoulders, and villains towering over them like highwaymen. Maria's best discoveries by a long chalk had been the photograph and the brooch. They were wrapped in hankies that were hidden in her heavy woollen underthings. A studio shot, Josephine wore a shirt and loosely knotted tie, and a heavy wool military-style coat with patch pockets, epaulettes and brass buttons. She held her left arm slightly away from her body, as if to highlight the first-aid armlet just above her elbow. It was unbelievable that the strong young woman with fire in her eyes in the photograph was the same creaking, complaining aunt Maria spent her days trying not to annoy. Unbelievable, too, that the brooch on her lapel in the photograph was the same as the one in the picture.

Maria takes the book from Eve's hand and touches the photograph, tracing it with her fingertip. The brooch is the shape of a rifle, gold, gleaming and beautiful, with the letters *CnamB* curling around the barrel.

'She must have been in Cumann na mBan!' Eve says. 'That sounds exactly like the uniform. The brooch was an active service award. It was given to the women who participated in the Easter Rising. Did you ever ask her about it?'

'How could I? She'd have killed me for snooping in her room.'

'You should be proud of her. I'd have joined them.'

Maria laughs. 'Eve, you'd have joined Joan of Arc as they were lighting the kindling.'

On the next page there is a picture of a Cumann na mBan meeting in Cork. Two lines of women wearing loose dresses and hats stand close together behind a trestle table littered with half-made sandwiches. One woman has her arm slung lightly around another's shoulders.

'Wouldn't you love to walk into the photo and hear what they're saying?' Maria runs her finger lightly across the picture. She imagines them stretching, stamping their feet, after the stiffness of the pose.

'They'd have some tales to tell, right enough. Good advice too, I'd say.' Eve nods. But Maria isn't imagining them discussing rebellions and battle tactics over the crumbs. The whispers she hears are those coloured by the scrimping of daily life: complaints about wailing children and money and distracted husbands. She finds it hard to believe that these women really believed the fight that was to come was more important than everything else; that to them it was worth the sacrifice of themselves and their men, their children's future. Were they honestly as united in real life as this picture would have her believe?

'We could do with another Irishwomen's Council now, if you ask me,' Eve says, her eyes alight.

'But it says here they believed in force and using arms.'

Eve's shrug is a *so-what*. 'That's war, Maria. You don't believe me, but that's the way it was. Should be again! Here, take these.' With a mock bow, Eve passes her a bundle of manila folders. 'You'd best get back to the copy office. Hilda will have kittens if you're gone any longer.'

In Eve's freshly typed minutes, the morning's meeting has become a model of collegiate democracy. Excoriated are the ums and ahs, the ifs and buts, the coughs and sneezes, the incessant snap of cigarette lighters. Two and a half hours are reduced to five pages of decisions, notes, action. Even the dissent is now agreed upon. Maria stops at the final item:

PK briefed the meeting as to a one-off radio programme about the role of women in the Easter Rising, scheduled for broadcast on Easter Monday 1966. Programme to feature interviews with Rising participants and contributions from historians of the period. He asked the meeting for suggestions for a title. EC suggested

'You included yourself?'

'Why not? I spoke, didn't I?'

Maria finishes the page in silence, then looks up at her friend and says, 'I'm sorry.'

Eve looks away. Everyone except Patrick had stared when she made her suggestion. To her own ears her voice had sounded so feeble, a fading echo called from the bottom of an abandoned well. She left the meeting believing herself a fool. It was only later, as she explains to Maria, that she realised she was foolish only for feeling that way.

CHAPTER EIGHT

The first patrons of the Club arrive promptly at opening time; the last to leave – they are often the same – are asked repeatedly at ten to go. A secretary to 'one of the big bosses', a man who shook the hand of none other than John F. Kennedy himself, regularly tells the switchboard to put his calls through to the bar phone first before trying their office.

'Swear to God!' Michael protests, as if Maria doesn't believe him. 'There's a book next to the cocktail cherries just for his messages.'

It is a Friday evening in early December and the Club is busier than usual because it's playing host to a party for *The Kennedys of Castleross*. Radio Éireann's most popular drama serial is a decade old this week, and, as Maria hears one producer say to another, 'Sounds mighty well on it.'

'It'll run for ever,' her companion replies. 'You mark my words, we've hit on something there. We really have.' And they clink glasses in a toast to the Kennedys, to their living happily for all eternity in Castleross.

The windows overlooking the car park are fitted with green-tinted plastic. Even during daylight it gives the room a curiously murky underwater atmosphere. It could be early afternoon in winter or just before daybreak on a dull summer's morning; it's hard to tell. The leatherette booths that mark the further outreaches of the room are darker, and popular for it, according to Michael.

Strings of tinsel and paper decorations hang in greasy fringes down the sides of the bar. It's hard to believe it will soon be Christmas. Anna has been busy assisting Mrs Halpin with her Christmas cards. When Maria collected her the previous evening they were on what Anna referred to as 'the overseas batch', the first card of which was addressed to Mrs Halpin's daughter, Norma, and her policeman husband. George had been promoted, Mrs Halpin said with pride. An *inspector*! Would you believe the cut of it! Maria congratulated her, privately convinced that such a title alone would be enough to earn Mrs Halpin's praise, irrespective of the profession George was paid to inspect.

Anna's tongue had stuck out of the side of her mouth as she laboriously copied Mrs Halpin's address onto the reverse of each envelope. As Maria gathered up Anna's scattered school things she could hear Mrs Halpin muttering on about what good etiquette it was to write the sender's address on the back. No wonder Anna was coming home with all sorts of nonsense.

'Can I send Cheryl a card?' Anna had asked, but Maria's quick 'We'll see' (which she and Anna both knew well as the not-while-we're-in-company equivalent of 'No') played second fiddle to the older woman's 'Ah, sure I'm bound to have a spare, pet.'

Michael takes a long draw from his beer. 'You will stay for a while, won't you? I never see you now, so you're to spill the beans about life on the second floor. I'm so glad they picked you, not me,' he says, and before she can answer continues, 'I mean, 1916? Honestly, who cares?'

She sips her lemonade. 'Lots of people do! It's only fifty years. That's within your parents' lifetime, isn't it?' Michael is more of a child than Anna sometimes.

'You can be sure it is, though my old pair are old as the hills. Though I'm not sure they had a Rising in Leitrim.'

She laughs. 'And if it doesn't happen in Battlebridge, then it doesn't happen?'

'Exactly. Dull, dull, dull, if you ask me.'

'It's not. In fact, it's a lot more interesting than I'd expected, though the committee doesn't really need a full-time secretary from what I can see. Not yet anyway. They just thought they did.'

'First one that bad, was she?'

'There wasn't too much work. She just wasn't bothered doing any of it. But because I've some time on my hands I'm to help out with researching one of the radio programmes.' She smiles, still pleased that Patrick suggested she get involved. The memory of Aunt Josephine's photo and rifle badge, and a fresh curiosity about that old photograph of Cumann na mBan women at the table, has stayed with her. The flat black-and-white of the picture seems to have concentrated the past, made those strangers more fascinating and their blood a richer stock. If only it were possible to recognise the line of life as it's being lived. To understand it as the present rather than history.

'Don't tell me you're on the *Rising Curtains* documentary, you lucky thing?'

'No, not that one.' Lucky thing indeed, to be spared Brian O'Toole's pontificating on how 1916 and the subsequent War of Independence transformed Irish theatre. 'It's the one Robert Ryan's presenting about the women who took part.'

'Oh, well, never mind.' Michael lowers his voice, but not by much. 'I bet Patrick wanted you to keep an eye on Ryan. He's a lazy sod.'

'Michael Brennan!' she says, mock-scandalised. 'And Robert Ryan the crowned king of Ireland!'

'All that housewives' choice stuff? Blah, blah. Ryan's only interested in getting his mug in front of the television cameras, these days. Brian says he couldn't give two hoots about radio any more. Why do you think he got himself moved out here? He should be in the GPO with the rest of them.'

'Either way, I'll be back with you in a few months, answering phones as if I'd never been away.' But she knows it won't be the same; it never will again. She has a hand dipped into the past, into lives so different from her own, and she's not sure she wants to return to transcribing the fragile chaos of the living.

'I think they're watering down the drinks.' He pulls a face.

'You're certainly testing them very thoroughly.'

'Ha-ha,' he says. 'Droll.' He scans the room. The rest of *The Kennedys of Castleross* production team and actors are arriving and the noise level rises, dips, rises again. 'Hey, look,' he says, 'there's Vincent Dowling!'

'Who?'

'Never mind.'

'Michael!' There's a long whistle and Brian appears around the side of their booth. 'The hills certainly are alive in here this evening,' he says, glancing around the busy room.

'We saw *The Sound of Music* the other night,' Michael explains.

'I brought Anna last weekend.' Anna has been singing 'Do-Re-Mi' ever since and on Monday Maria rather worryingly heard her ask Mrs Halpin if she owned pinking shears.

Brian turns to Michael. 'I suppose you're dying to be introduced to Vincent?'

'Yes, please! Wait here, Maria, won't you?'

'I can't stay long. Eve asked me to meet her, but if she's not here in a few minutes I'll have to go.'

Her booth is next to a green-tinted window. A lone bird flies across the car park, its concentrated shadow flitting in and out of the lights. She leans back against the high seat. Some find the not-day-not-night atmosphere soothing, and the Club's green windows are often blamed by those who arrive at lunchtime and stay on into the evening. What freedom, to be able to suspend allegiance to the clock. The noise from the bar reaches her as a background hum. It's pleasant to sit there alone for a minute and listen to the sounds of Friday-happy people. Chatting, drinking, smoking, waiting for the music to start. Enjoying the anticipation of how the evening will bring them together in the green fishbowl. Voices strike up, so close that they must be sitting in the booth behind.

'Widow, I heard.'

'She's young for it. What happened?'

'No idea. TB, maybe?'

'Anyone we know had a try?'

'Not that I know of.'

'She's pretty enough. I might give it a go myself in that case. Seeing as how the shop's already open.' He laughs. 'You know what they say about widows.' His voice rises towards the end, the word smoothed like soft butter onto bread. *Wih-doze*. 'Twice the fun for half the effort.'

Maria looks outside. The bird has flown away. She picks up her lemonade. Tiny bubbles rise and pop as they hit the surface. It's getting flatter as she's watching it. She slips out of her booth and walks to the bar where there is a message board next to the counter.

'Can I get you a drink, Maria?'

She turns around. Patrick Keady.

'No, thank you, Patrick. I'm not staying.' She scribbles a note and presses it into the corkboard until the edge of the tack against her thumb hurts.

'Are you sure? Just to say thank you. We're all very pleased with your work on the committee over the last few weeks. How are you getting on in Robert's office?' He has one hand in his pocket and seems more relaxed than usual. She registers his smile as a throb low in her stomach, a sensation that is both familiar and new. And you're another one, I suppose, she thinks. Another one with an easy eye. *Wih-doze* has burrowed under her skin like a tick.

'I was just leaving,' she says, bitter at having to think badly of him but what other way is there to think? He's a man, same as any other. He sways from foot to foot as though he wants to put himself between her and the door. To distract her from the life that is calling her away.

'Oh, that's a shame. I was hoping to hear all about it.'

'There'll be a report at the next meeting.'

'Of course. Tuesday morning, isn't it?' She knows he's trying to keep her there, to continue the pretence that chatting together in the Club is something they do. Just her and him, talking. Just because they can, because they want to. For no reason.

'Yes.' She glances over his shoulder.

'At nine fifteen?'

'That's the time you requested.'

'Well,' he says, his eyes telling her that the finality of her tone has made him feel foolish, 'you mustn't let me keep you, Maria.'

'Nor I you,' she says, a fury she can't explain rising inside her.

'I wasn't in any hurry.'

'Really? Don't we both have family waiting on us?'

His smile disappears. He inclines his head, but says nothing for a beat, two, then moves to one side so she can walk past.

She has one hand on the Club door when she finds herself turning around. She closes her teeth to trap the words that want to rise from her chest into her mouth and out, to pour in a bilious rage round her feet. Patrick has moved to the bar so he doesn't notice her cross the width of the room. She sidesteps the little clusters of people that have popped up now that the seats are all taken, and rounds the edge of the booth by the window.

'Hello there.' The taller one smiles, his mouth a thin slit. He raises his pint by way of greeting. 'Look who it is. Would you like to join us?' His hair is dark and slicked back into a gleaming DA. The leatherette squeaks as he slides over to make space for her. He pats the seat next to him but she ignores him and looks from one to the other. The smaller, younger one isn't smiling. As she leans forward over their table he stares up at her. The shadow of his Adam's apple shifts nervously in his neck. The twist of desire she felt when Patrick smiled at her hasn't faded. She knows what that ache means and hates herself for it.

'Michael thinks I threw the page away, but I didn't.' She's almost spitting the words. She leans nearer again. Could touch his lips with her tongue, she's that close. The neck of her blouse gapes open in a heavy, deep V but she knows he won't dare drop his eyes from her face. Ash falls from his cigarette onto the sticky table top as she says, 'I have it still. And I saw you write it.'

CHAPTER NINE

The memory of his shocked face, the bump in his throat, sustains her during the bus journey home. The face reflected in the smoky window is smeared and unfamiliar. It appears and disappears, a plane of light coming into focus, then slipping away again. Every time it appears, it is smiling. Yet by the time she has walked up the dark shadows of Appian Way, through the Triangle at Ranelagh and up to Redoubt Terrace, the glory of her victory has faded. Was that the sort of war Eve talks about? A pointless victory in what was no more than a stupid skirmish? If it is a war, the opposing armies are unclear, shifting around until the very moment in which they declare themselves.

She wonders if Patrick Keady would be on the side of those sniggering fools. And him with a wife waiting for him at home, a shimmering creature in her evening dress, and those shivering children tucked up in their little beds. She doesn't like to think of him as he stood there in the Club, the light in his eyes as though there was a secret in the air between the two of them. She had wanted nothing more than to breathe in that secret, to take it as close to her as her own skin. The effort of not-thinking this thought is confusing her more than anything else.

'Mummy! Look!'

Maria has learnt to recognise the smell that launches itself into a jig in the porch as Mrs Halpin's heavy-handed dollops of Guinness Yeast Extract. 'Hello, sweetheart. Are you allowed open the front door by yourself?'

'Of course. Chuzzlewit is helping me.' She dances backwards, the cat tucked under her arm, like a newspaper.

'He doesn't look comfortable like that.' Maria shuts the door and follows the child down the tiled passage and into the kitchen, surrendered earlier in the evening to the starchy steam of long-boiled potatoes and stewing beef.

'He's fine. Look!' Anna drops the cat and twirls around, one hand pulling out the edge of her skirt. 'Ta-daa!'

'What?'

'This! My apron. I made it.' Maria finds herself giving the curtains a quick, nervous glance. 'Mrs Helping found the material in her workbox. It's called gingham. We sewed it together after the repairman in the lane fixed her old Singer. He said there's plenty of go in it yet,' she adds, in a confiding tone. She curtsies, the apron held wide at her sides. Pinched between each forefinger and thumb, its blue and white chequerboard pattern is distorted.

'And we started to read a book in Irish from the Late Mr Helping's collection but it's very hard. He had lots of Irish books.' She shrugs. 'He used work in the glue company or something.'

'An Gúm, Anna.' Mrs Halpin appears from the pantry. 'Hello, dear. He worked for the Publication Scheme, in O'Connell

Street. Mr Halpin's job was to arrange the Irish translations of the classic novels.'

'How lovely, to be able to read at work.'

Mrs Halpin frowns. 'He took it very seriously, let me tell you. Poor man was working on *Scéal fá dhá chathair* when the Lord saw fit to take him.'

'What's that?'

Mrs Halpin looks down at Anna, her eyebrows raised. 'Well? Do you remember?'

'*A Tale of Two Cities*.'

Maria smiles. 'Sounds like you've had a busy afternoon, Anna. Gather up your things and say goodbye.'

'Will you not take a cup of tea first?'

'No, thank you.' Maria is suddenly bone-weary, the Club far behind her. Winter is in the air all around them and, though it's just gone seven, it feels too late to be outside. 'Hurry up, Anna. It's bath night.'

'I'll be two shakes of a lamb's tail!'

'Tell me, Maria, have you met that Eamonn Andrews yet? Such a charming way about that man, I always think.'

'I've never even seen him.'

'Really?'

'It's a very big place. But I promise as soon as I do I'll ask him for an autograph especially for you.'

'Oh, go way out of that!' Mrs Halpin gives a pleased, girlish giggle. 'Anna tells me you're not doing all that copying work any more?'

'Copytaking. No, not for now. I'm secretary to the committee that's organising the programmes for the fiftieth anniversary of the Rising.'

'For the television?'

'And radio. I'm helping out on making one too,' she is aware of the proud note in her voice, 'about the women who took part.'

'Oh, I see.' Mrs Halpin sniffs. 'That Constance Markievicz and so forth?'

'Well, not just her. Close on ninety women were involved during the week itself.'

'I'm sure it was nothing like that many.' She sounds sceptical. 'In our house we didn't talk about the Rising much because the subject got Mam so furious.'

'Why?'

'My father never missed the races, never. He went out to Fairyhouse for the Grand National on the Easter Monday and it took him half the night to get home. Mam was beside herself, not knowing where he'd got to. With so many army men at the races, it turned out all manner of madness had broken out in town.' Mrs Halpin looks at the curtained kitchen window as though impatient for a play behind it to begin. She turns back to Maria. 'Do you know Tess McDermott? She lives in number thirty-nine?'

'No.'

'According to Ada, Tess was up to her neck in it in one of the garrisons. Marrowbone Lane, I think it was. They were forced to surrender, of course, and you can be sure not one of them had an explanation or what-have-you for all the trouble. Mam used to say those Cumann na mBan women hadn't a ladylike bone in their bodies. And she wasn't the only one thought it neither. There was plenty said shooting wouldn't be a good enough end for them. There was an article in the *Sunday Graphic* a few years later, during the war – I remember her showing it to my father. *Trigger-happy harpies*, Irish women were, it said. And the bishop told us how awful it all was, how we should be at home helping our mothers with their brasses. He was right too. That was our place and I for one was glad to know it.'

She folds her arms under her bosom. 'But don't take my word for it. You go call on Tess McDermott and ask her for yourself and you'll see what odd fish those women were. You'll recognise her from the street, I'm sure – she's such a little thing – and,' Mrs Halpin points at her mouth, 'her teeth are all at sixes and sevens. It's a mystery why she doesn't get a set put in like any normal person would.'

Anna buckles her satchel. She has her coat on, her gingham apron an untied cape over her shoulders. She fluffs the sides back, then stands in front of the two women expectantly, looking from one to the other, as though she's waiting for something.

'What?' Maria says.

Mrs Halpin steps forward and ties the apron strings in a bow under her chin. 'There you go. What a fine lady you are! Will I be seeing you both at ten Mass on Sunday? Anna helped me do the flowers this week and she has them as good as you'd see in a painting.'

'I'm sure we'll be there.' Maria passes Mrs Halpin her weekly envelope.

'Bye, Mrs Helping, bye-bye, Chuzzlewit.'

The yeasty smell follows them to the door. They are a few steps into the bitter chill before Maria looks back. The front door is nearly closed, Mrs Halpin a dark shape with the light of the hall behind her. Her grey hair is set in rollers once a week, and coins of light shine through the firm curls.

'Mrs Helping?' Anna says. 'What was it happened your daddy? Did he die in the fight after the races?'

'No, Anna love, he did not. He lived a long and healthy life.' Mrs Halpin shakes her head and looks at Maria. 'Though he never went near Fairyhouse again. The horses, he said. Lying there right in the middle of O'Connell Street – where the flowerbeds are now – and broken glass all around them.' Her expression is troubled and she looks lost in her past somewhere as she adds, 'Glittering, he said, as though they had diamonds sprinkled on their coats.'

CHAPTER TEN

Maria locks the door of the flat and creeps down the stairs. The house is quiet. The lads must be out, the nurse in the top bedsitter gone to work. Next to the shared payphone is a ledge where the long-forgotten letters live. Aerograms, crammed full of *dears* and *with love froms*, and unpaid bills wait in silence alongside the handbills for cheap tailors and parish jumble sales for the Black Babies. Every evening as they make their way up the stairs, Anna begs to open one. 'We don't get any for ourselves,' she argues, 'so we could pretend they're for us.'

The street reeks of coal fires. Maria hasn't paid any attention to number thirty-nine before. A gingerbread red-brick same as the rest, it is tattier than most, tucked away down the far end of Redoubt Terrace, where the street turns a corner in on itself. Redoubt Terrace makes three and a half sides of a rectangle. A pedestrian path leads out of the fourth side and into a gloomy high-walled laneway that runs down to Ranelagh. When they first moved to the street in August, the air sat still and heavy and wouldn't move through. There were days when Maria was sure she was taking the same breath in and out. The backs of the houses are different, though, with long narrow gardens easily whipped by the breeze. Mrs Halpin, a canny observer of good drying weather, claims she'd never get a screed of washing done otherwise.

There are evenings when Maria stands at their window and wonders if Redoubt Terrace is closing in on her stealthily, compressing her life until it is no bigger or more real than the cardboard doll's house. She shakes herself when this happens. Don't be daft.

As high as the first floor in jagged clumps, the hedge of number thirty-nine has leeched out across the garden gate. Moss and weeds coat the dirty tiles of the path. What in Mrs Halpin's pathway are lines that stride confidently to the front door, here are nothing more than the cracked creases of a torn and faded map.

Maria pauses just before the front step. Two up and one down. All seems dark behind the nets and whatever other curtains are pulled tight behind them. No wonder Mrs Halpin sounded a bit sniffy about you, she thinks, looking at the tarnished door brasses and the black paintwork peeling from the doorframe. Mrs Halpin is a woman for whom façades matter. Anna has told her about the glazed cotton cover that will hang over her front door in summer.

'It's stripy and hangs like a sheet but it has holes for the knocker and doorknob,' Anna said, 'so I'll be able to come and go, all summer long.'

'I'm sure you won't still be getting minded by Mrs Halpin then,' Maria replied. 'I know you like her and she's been very kind, but it was only ever to be for a little while, not for ever.'

'Oh, but I will.' Anna nodded, a wise head on young

shoulders. 'Yes, sirree, Bob. Sure, isn't she after telling me so herself?'

Maria feels suddenly foolish. What is she doing in the dark on a stranger's doorstep? She has no right to call here on a whim, with no more than street gossip as her source. She turns to leave. And then she remembers reading the minutes Eve gave her of the 1916 Programmes Committee meeting weeks before. Eve had tried to hide how she felt when her voice went unheeded during the discussion about the radio documentary – the very one Maria is helping out on – but Maria had recognised the troubled look on her face. Understood what the turn of Eve's mouth meant. Maria has sat through several of those meetings by now, and she no longer thinks Eve's descriptions of many of the participants to be unduly harsh. The most galling thing of all is that Eve's suggestion at that meeting was a great one: *Women Rising* would have been the perfect name.

'The role of women?' That idiot Hugh Clarke had laughed at the most recent meeting. 'How to make tea and sandwiches under fire, that sort of thing? And while we're talking about sandwiches . . .' he continued, taking his watch out of his waistcoat pocket.

'We weren't,' Edna Corrigan replied, without looking up from her notes.

'Edna and Robert,' Patrick jumped in, 'perhaps you'd update us as to how *The Women of 1916* is coming along?' As Maria transcribed their comments, she noticed Patrick gave her a curious glance, as though she were a plant on his desk that had just asked for a drink of water.

'Good, thanks, Robert,' Patrick cut across Robert's detailed description of the narration he was preparing for the documentary. 'That all sounds very promising. And Maria's working on that, too, now, aren't you?' Patrick said.

'Well, there's a lot going on in my office that requires secretarial attention as you can imagine.' Robert's self-deprecating smile was that of a man who receives more post than Santa Claus. 'We're trying to trace a number of Cumann na mBan women to set up some interviews and she's helping out with that, checking addresses, death registers, that sort of thing.'

'Come-on who?' There was a popping sound as Hugh Clarke extracted his pipe from his mouth.

'It's pronounced *kom-en na man*, as you well know,' Eamon O'Mara retorted.

Patrick was swift to interject: 'The Irishwomen's Council. It's all in your briefing notes, Hugh.'

'The participation of women was against Mr de Valera's wishes,' Mr de Valera's namesake added, to no one in particular.

'The dead ones won't be much help, surely,' Hugh Clarke said. 'You've taken that into account in your searches? Eh, Maria?'

Now, on the grubby step outside Tess McDermott's door, Maria recalls the exchange. She hadn't replied, just transcribed the stupid comments. Such ignorance deserved to be recorded. Eve is right, she thinks. They're as bad as each other.

With the fiftieth anniversary of the Rising looming, it seems dozens of books have been written about it. Patrick bought a selection for the committee. Maria has got into the habit of taking one with her on her lunch break, and the more she reads, the harder it is not to find an uncertain kinship with the women involved. What were they doing other than trying to shape a different existence? To own their lives and those of their children, both born and unborn. And yet, for all that, history doesn't seem to have recorded them as it has the men. Their ambitions were not made safe for her generation, for Anna's. Countess Markievcz became the first woman elected to the House of Commons although she never took her seat ('Typical,' Hugh Clarke commented), yet for the most part the women disappeared back to their hearths after the rebellion. Did the blood of childbirth thin their conviction? Was it by their own choice or was it a life pushed upon them?

She knocks. Once, twice. A faint blur of light glows through the ginger-beer glass of the fanlight. There is no sound of footsteps, or a key turning, yet the door is suddenly open and a small hand appears around the frame. A light from behind slicks over a single milk bottle standing to attention on the doorstep.

'Hello,' Maria says. The door creaks open, the gap slightly wider. 'Excuse me, but are you Mrs McDermott? Tess McDermott?' She smells the rich sulphur of coal dust and camphor and something else, sweeter, fainter.

'Who are you?' The woman looking up at her is tiny, birdlike. Her hair is high on her head, piled in a loose bun. It is the unnatural colour of stewed tea, and the contrast between it and her ghost-pale skin makes Maria think of the pictures in Anna's Ladybird book Snow White and Rose Red. Her cheekbones are high and wide, hollowed underneath. She wears a man's frayed cardigan open over a stained housecoat.

'My name is Maria Mills. I live down the street . . .' she points into the dark '. . . in number four.' Her voice is faltering. Even allowing for the passage of fifty years, Mrs Halpin must have it all wrong. This tiny woman bearing arms? Maria experiences a sudden pang for the simple routine of the copydesk, for the familiar spaces it left in her head.

'Whatever you're hawking, I don't want none of it.'

'No, it's nothing like that.' Lavender, that's what the smell is. She must have moths. 'I work in Telifís Éireann and—'

'No.'

'Honestly, I'm not trying to sell you anything, it's just that we're making a programme about the 1916 Rising, and I'm trying to contact—'

'No!' Her voice is raised this time. The door shuts so quickly it is as though it was never open. 'Can't help you' slips, muffled, through the keyhole.

The faint tinge of lavender in the air fades and she is alone again on the doorstep. She shivers. It's unsettling, the stench of dead leaves slowly decomposing in this silent, uncared-for garden. Right, Maria says to herself, a hiding to nothing. Thanks, Mrs Halpin.

'*Here!*' And then a second shout, 'Take this, will you?' She shrieks and jumps as something solid hits her back. She whirls around, her heart pounding. An *Evening Press* lies at her feet. The newsagent's lad has pedalled past in a dark blur of satchel and cap. It's just a boy, she tells herself, one hand pressed to her chest. You fool. Maria stands on the broken lines of the path holding Tess McDermott's newspaper and wonders what to do next.

'You're not the paper boy.' She's tugged forward by the door as it silently opens.

'No.' She twists her hand to slide it back out of the letterbox. She stands up again. 'I didn't want to leave your paper on the doorstep. It's so damp out, it'd be ruined on you.'

'That boy is some skite,' Tess mutters. 'Bloody hours late again.' Maria glances past her into the hallway. Unlike Mrs Halpin's house, the air that comes from behind Tess isn't much warmer than that outside. A dark staircase rises into blackness, a tatty runner of carpet like the rungs of a ladder up it. The hall is empty of furniture. Black and white floor tiles skitter-scatter towards a light that shines from a room at the back. Anna would love a hall like this, Maria thinks, looking at that floor, just waiting to be skated on in stockinged feet. There are none of Mrs Halpin's hatstands, whatnots, shopping baskets and fern holders. None of the ever-moving bicycles, empty boxes and strange odours that constantly trip them up in their own shared hallway. There is a heavy emptiness that makes Maria think of ghost stories; tales of bricked-up cellars and secrets carried to the grave and beyond.

Tess extracts the *Evening Press* Maria had jammed into the letterbox. Her fingers are thin and twisted. Sore-looking red bumps rise from the waxy sheen of her knuckles. 'Who did you say you are?'

'Maria Mills.' Is that who she really is? She doesn't know. Do you know who *you* say you are? she wants to ask the witchy figure.

'And you're from Telifís Éireann?' The words escape from narrowed lips.

'Yes.' That much she can be sure of.

'I don't know nothing about anything. I said so already.' She sounds cross again. This woman is all sides.

'Yes. I know. I must have misunderstood who you were. I'm sorry to have bothered you.'

Tess turns her newspaper over. There is a large photograph near the bottom of the front page, a man and woman together.

Maria can't make out the caption but even upside-down the beautiful, curling mouth of Elizabeth Taylor is easy to recognise. A velvet gown exposes her vast *décolleté* and a fur wrap slips over one shoulder. A collar of diamonds owns her throat. Maria thinks of the picture on Patrick Keady's desk. Of the immaculate coil of hair and the expensive dress. Of the tale of happiness it must tell and him wanting a photograph to capture it.

Tess McDermott lifts the grainy print to rheumy eyes. 'So that's what happened to you,' she says quietly. She touches the man's face as if she could smooth the hair back from his forehead. In the light behind her, the thick ink of the headlines stands out against the salmon-pink page.

'I beg your pardon?' Maria says.

Tess lowers the newspaper. 'Him, there.' She turns the caption to face Maria: *Star of movie* The VIPs, *Elizabeth Taylor, and its director Anthony Asquith arriving for a private party at the Shelbourne Hotel. Mr Asquith is the youngest son of the late Liberal MP H.H. Asquith, Britain's longest continuously serving Prime Minister.* 'Just a tot, last time I seen him.'

'Where was that?'

'When I was in service, in Cavendish Square.' For the first time, Maria hears the familiar trace in her accent of sounds pushed into each other by the tides of the Thames. Her eyes are gleaming. 'I remember him got up just like a little man. Waiting in his doorway to be taken out on a ride.'

'You were in service with the . . .' Maria glances back at the caption '. . . the Asquiths?'

'No. Across the Square with . . .' She pauses, blinks. Collects herself. 'Don't matter. Makes no odds now.'

'I thought I recognised your accent. I lived in London for years.' Maria tries to grab at any stray thread that may unravel anything in this curious woman's story. 'I worked near Cavendish Square for a while. On Mortimer Street. Do you know it?' She hears herself gabbling but doesn't care – she'll say anything. 'If you go down Cavendish Square towards Wimpole Street it's the—'

'Mortimer Street?'

'You know it?'

'Mortimer Street.' Tess rolls the words around her mouth like a child with a boiled sweet. 'What number?'

'Ten.'

'Is that side all done out in doctors' places still?'

'Pretty much, yes. A few looked to be in flats, but mainly it was surgeries.'

'The way the houses are all squashed together, like they're leaning over their own railings. As if they was friends gossiping at the fence.' Her mouth is still narrow but her face is a kaleidoscope. 'I liked that.' A shifting bulge roams around the old lady's cheeks, batting from side to side. Maria remembers Mrs Halpin saying something about Tess's teeth but it's impossible to see them: she keeps her lips so close. The too-dark hair aside, there is a faded quality to her as though she is not quite real. A wisp who, once sighted, will vanish into the mist.

Maria would do anything – anything – to keep this woman on her doorstep, to keep her talking. She wants to reach into the carousel of her memories and send it spinning around. 'Yes,' Maria says. 'I know what you mean. I used be a secretary in a doctor's there.'

As she speaks she sees Tess glance down at the paper

between them: *Bread Strike Threatens Dublin* cries the main headline. Maria watches her face change as she reads it. They are returned to the present, to silence. Tess clamps her mouth shut until her lips disappear and a flush suffuses her cheeks. The hurdy-gurdy has ended, the lights clicked off by an unseen hand. Once more they are two women facing each other on a doorstep. Tess refolds the paper until only *Threatens Dublin* remains and she turns into the dark mouth of her hallway.

'Wait, Mrs McDermott. Can I talk to you? Please?'

Her neighbour has had enough talking.

Maria's breath mists in the air and forms a fine damp halo around her head. She touches one cold hand to the other. Her fingertips are numb – she must have been gone ages. She feels as though she is waking up only to find herself in an unfamiliar, threatening place. Anna is a good sleeper and rarely ever wakes once she nods off. But still. She only meant to pop out for five minutes, to introduce herself and make an arrangement to meet Tess McDermott another day. She imagines the phone ringing in the hallway downstairs and Anna waking up, eager to answer it only to find herself locked in, her mother disappeared into thin air.

Overgrown bushes on both sides make the path narrow and airless as a coffin. Branches stretch out and touch her shoulders as she hurries towards the gate and the street beyond.

A thin finger touches her face and she shrieks. 'No!' she cries, and grabs the gate. *Hurry up*, she curses herself. The latch is stiff and rusty, she has to tug it up first, then drag the gate open. When she's on the far side she looks back. 'You fool,' she whispers. The finger is nothing more than a bony branch waggling at her in the night air. Tess McDermott's house has returned to silence. It has receded into darkness, Brigadoon swallowed by the mists for another century.

She turns to run but a sound on the street nearby stops her. Was that a scrape of a heel? A spark from a match? She pauses and listens to the silence. Her heart is thumping; she can feel the ache of it in her chest. She can hear it, louder than anything else. She runs back down Redoubt Terrace, tripping over her feet as she glances behind, over and over. What on earth was she thinking of, leaving Anna like that? But the street is quiet. The only other movements are the inky shadows thrown by the trees in the breeze. And yet when she is back at her own house, her numb fingers fumbling with her latch key, she is certain of one thing: when she first walked up Tess McDermott's path, she had left the gate open behind her.

CHAPTER ELEVEN

His voice. That was what she noticed first. His confident tone snagged something in her. It was the light, bantering way he addressed the other secretaries; spoke to the site managers coming and going from the office; even chatted with the boss, a stony, irritable Scot.

In the few weeks she'd been in London she'd realised how diffident Irish voices sound, her own as bad as the worst of them. It was as though, she thought, we've all agreed we're not really that bothered. Our voices are as unassuming as our expectations. *Ah, sure what harm. Go 'way with you. It's grand.* She preferred the sharp finality of the English accents in the office of Mulholland & Sons Builders. She liked the way syllables banged and crashed, that final *g* slung overboard into the Thames.

It was only when she heard his voice at the office door that morning that she found she had been listening out for it. Maria glanced up from her desk. He was on the other side of the typing pool and staring over the heads of the other girls straight at her. He held her gaze across the office until she blushed and looked down at her page. Her hands hadn't stopped obeying the dictation pouring into her headphones but her fingers had stupidly slipped one key to the left. *The order*, she read back, *was confirmed by telephone on July first inst., however the materials received qwew bir owe rgw ieswe.*

'All the girls have an eye for John Mills.' Gretta leant over from the next desk. 'Go on, don't deny it,' she continued, with a sly, pink-lipsticked smile. 'I was beginning to wonder if we'd ever see some life in you, Maria Power.'

He tipped an imaginary hat to Gretta and she giggled. But when he glanced back over his shoulder, it was Maria he looked at. His stare fuelled her for the rest of the day. The thought of his face made her fingertips feel cold and her stomach warm. It made her jittery in a way she didn't understand and hadn't expected. They'd all had pashes in school – it was a constant topic of conversation: Dean Martin, Eddie Fisher, Gregory Peck. The names changed with the seasons. A few unambitious girls fancied the grocer's son, a boy described as *not all there* by the nuns, and *to be avoided at all costs*, though such an instruction was no barrier to their pale, imaginary affections. Maria had understood those schoolgirl crushes for what they were: cardboard cut-outs whose job was to keep her heart right, to warm it for its eventual inhabitant. But such placeholders cannot keep strong for ever, and by the time she moved to London, their celluloid charms had long since worn thin. The girl at the desk in Mulholland & Sons Builders was nineteen and fervently hoped it was no more than a matter of time before she would be allowed cross the mysterious border into the promised land of marriage.

'Mulholland & Sons Builders.' Gretta's sing-song answer

distracted Maria from staring at the agonisingly empty space John Mills had left behind him in the room. 'Supplies and orders section. Can I help you?'

He was outside. Waiting. Just for her.

He took her arm and walked her down the road. 'I used to think you Irish would be all red hair and freckles,' he said.

'Hardly any of us are.' She smiled. 'Most of us look like me.'

'No one else could look like you,' he said, and halted so suddenly that she had to as well. The man walking behind was forced to stop short, so as not to bump into their backs. He cursed as he overtook them but John ignored him.

'Sorry,' Maria said, to the man's back, embarrassed, her apology a whisper.

And that was the start of it, she thinks. In the blink of a cold eye she had become a twenty-three-year-old woman standing over her baby's cot, feeling every breath that the baby took. She loved it, that she used to know every second of her baby's life. Nothing could happen to Anna without Maria being the instigator, the caretaker, the owner. But now that tiny baby is six and at school and losing her London accent, and Maria no longer has access to every minute of her day. The cot has been stripped bare.

Maria is sitting in a sheltered corner by the side of the television building, on her usual bench. A book from Patrick's 1916 collection is next to her but she's not bothered with reading today. Instead she has been watching her breath haw out in front of her into the cold January air. During the Christmas holidays she had realised that she is happy at work, that it suits her. It feels longer than four months since she first sat on this bench and that, too, makes her happy. She can feel herself slowly exhaling into this life. It is 6 January, Little Christmas. Tradition has it that women go out for the evening together on the sixth, leaving the drudge of Christmas and the unending work of looking after their families behind them for an evening. Aunt Josephine used to celebrate *Nollaig na mBan* despite always protesting at what nonsense it was.

'We're meant to believe that women's servitude deserves only the one night off in a year, are we?' she'd mutter, and Maria would feel terribly, stupidly guilty for her part in ensuring Aunt Josephine spent every other day in domestic slavery. (Eve, needless to say, has planned a celebratory assault on several unsuspecting public houses.)

Michael appears in front of her, squinting. He is shielding his eyes with one hand, as though he's not used to daylight. He sits down next to her and offers her a cigarette, which she refuses. 'You sure?' he says, 'I've got loads, my sister's a nurse. The patients give her ciggies as a thank you.' Maria shakes her head. He sits next to her in silence for a moment, opening his mouth then shutting it again, an uncharacteristically hesitant manner that reminds her of Eve's friend Bernie.

'Are you all right, Michael?'

'Yes, but are you?' He blushes and jams his hands into his coat pockets. 'I didn't want to ask when anyone else was around but I thought, when I heard about the Sea Gem last week, that the news might have upset you. Reminded you, sort of thing.'

'The see what?' She has no idea what he's talking about.

It is his turn to look confused. 'But isn't that – I mean,

wasn't that the rig in the North Sea your husband was working on when he, um . . . the Sea Gem? It exploded just after Christmas. I was on the desk – the reports took up my whole day. Fourteen men were killed.'

She turns her head away and looks across at the cars driving in and out of the car park. Tyres slick through puddles and winter sunshine glints against chrome headlamps and windscreens. The flashes shine in a code she cannot understand. Not see: *Sea*. Of course. She's being stupid. Keep track, Maria, she warns herself. You're up to your neck in lies. Keep track or you'll be the one doing the drowning. She looks at him and wonders does he suspect anything. Could he have sniffed out the lies that hide beneath her story, like a dead rat under the floorboards? Months before, on the morning she'd run up the corridor after him, she had felt a tangential tie between them that she still can't put a shape to. Does he feel it too? She has no way to ask, no language to put on it.

She lays her gloved hand on his arm. 'Come on, Michael, we'd better get back to work.'

Hugh turns a small silver object in his hand. 'This one must be a mistake, surely?'

Maria consults her list. 'Toffee hammer. Taken from a sweetshop on South Anne Street.'

'Bloody looters.' He throws the hammer back on the table and takes his pipe from his pocket. All painstakingly catalogued by Maria, the table is covered with objects posted in by the public in response to the advertisement for 'relics and keepsakes of the 1916 Rising'. The 1916 Programmes

Committee are rummaging through them, like shawlies at a parish jumble.

'Anyone need a light?' Eamon picks up a matchbox holder. He turns the box to show both sides: Thomas McDonagh's picture is on one, Patrick Pearse's the other.

'Please don't move things around too much,' Maria says. 'I've put them in order and when you've chosen the ones you want to use I've to return the rest.'

Eamon flicks through the June 1916 edition of the *Catholic Herald*, published with its first five pages blank in protest at censorship. 'Are the categories you've adopted those of the saints?' he asks. Patrick, who examined everything on the table in advance of the meeting, looks puzzled. 'What do you mean?'

'Category one, body part. Category two, piece of their clothing, category three, an object touched by them.'

'We've no fingers or toes, if that's what you mean.' Patrick turns to Maria. 'Have we?'

'Of course not.' She smiles. 'Though we do have three locks of hair, purporting to be from . . .' she consults her list '. . . Éamonn Ceannt and Joseph Plunkett. Well, we've two Plunketts, but they're different colours.'

'Shall I be mother?' Robert Ryan has picked up a tea cosy. Knitted in thick green wool, it is stained a muddy brown around the spout hole. The label says it was knitted by a prisoner in Frongoch Internment Camp, Wales. Maria imagines a faceless man sitting on a pallet bed, his elbows stuck out in a laborious knit-one-purl-one, slowly making a cosy to take the place at his table that he had been denied.

Keith Kirwin unfolds a large sheet of paper. The top half is completely blank yet the bottom half is densely printed, beginning *The Irish Republic is entitled to, and hereby claims, the allegiance of every Irishman and Irishwoman*. It is the bottom half of the proclamation issued by the self-styled Provisional Government of the Irish Republic and read by Padraig Pearse outside the GPO at the start of the Rising. Its seven signatories were later executed by the British government as traitors. The Minister for Education has announced that schools must read aloud the *Forógra na Poblachta* on the fiftieth anniversary of the Rising and are to display it prominently from then on. Of much more interest to Anna, he also declared an extra day off school at Easter.

'Relic my backside.' Keith snorts. 'Copies of this are everywhere. Yanks buy the tea towel ones as souvenirs.' He spreads out the page, which is creased at the folds and yellowing. The type fades towards the bottom.

'This one is different,' Patrick says. 'They weren't able to scrounge enough type to set the entire document in one go so printed half at a time.' When the British Army got into the GPO after the surrender, he explains, the Proclamation was still up on some sort of makeshift press and this half-declaration was one of many run off by an enterprising RIC man who touted them as souvenirs.

'Sometimes I think that was the entire business all over,' Patrick says quietly to Maria, 'a half-risen Rising.' She glances nervously at Eamon but he is poring over the table, happy as a child at Christmas, and didn't hear. Before the meeting began Patrick told her he was concerned that the true job of the committee was to create an illusion; a charade of kinship with an uncertain past. It would be meaningless, he suspected. She had said nothing but looked at the table, wondering how much more real their work could possibly be. These postcards and belts, tea cosies, photographs and objects were more than relics, more than keepsakes. They had honest meaning in the lives of men and women just like her.

'I can't stay for the rest of the meeting.' Keith throws down a photograph of a group of young men in Celtic Revival dress. 'It's the last day of shooting tomorrow and I'm up to here.'

'Best of luck,' Patrick says, but Keith has already shut the door behind him.

'You've done a great job with this lot,' Robert looks at Maria and waves at the clutter on the table, 'the cataloguing and so forth.'

'Thank you, Mr Ryan.' She pinks at the unexpected compliment.

'Why don't you pop along to the shoot tomorrow?' he says. 'Just for a while, mind. Go to O'Connell Street, have a walk about and see who you meet. We haven't enough interviews for *The Women of 1916* yet.'

Maria is delighted. This is the first time in weeks he has asked her to do something interesting – something *active* – in relation to the work of the committee. In the two months since she moved to his office, Robert has fallen into the habit of treating her as his secretary. Dolores' hours seem to be a secret shared only with him, and she is regularly out sick. On the occasions that Eve passes by and Dolores' desk is unoccupied, she laughs and says, 'Let me guess: I've-got-one-of-my-stomachs has got one of her stomachs?'

Everyone takes their seat and the meeting begins. Maria pulls out her notebook. Her failure a few weeks before to get Tess McDermott talking has left her dispirited. She had resigned herself to her involvement in the documentary being no more than taking a list of names for a walk in every phone directory and death register in the country. And now a second chance! She'll do it right this time. Go to the shoot, find interesting real stories and people. Across the room the table lies abandoned, the neat rows of relics and keepsakes in careless disarray. But what harm? Can't she sort it all again later on?

CHAPTER TWELVE

I t is the morning of the final day of filming on O'Connell Street and the mounted British Lancers are scheduled to charge in ten minutes.

'Jesus Christ, can you not clear the bloody pavement?' Keith Kirwin tugs his hand roughly through his hair, thoroughly exasperated. 'Get those bloody gawkers moved back!'

'We had no idea so many people would come down to watch. If they're not on the road, there's nothing we can do. Our permit doesn't cover the pavement.' From their base near Nelson's Pillar, the location producer – a small, sallow man whose name Maria didn't catch – looks up and down O'Connell Street. People are three and four deep as far as Parnell Square. The producer gives a long, low whistle. 'It's going to be a headache for the edit and that's no lie.'

'A pain in my backside is what it is. If I wanted a crowd, I'd have bloody well hired one.'

A runner told her earlier that *Easter Rebellion* has ninety-three speaking roles and at least two hundred extras. And that's not to mention the three hundred-odd members of the defence forces, some of whom are waiting around the corner dressed in British Army uniforms.

'How are my Lancers?' Keith shouts to the runner.

'The horses are fecked from all the noise,' he replies. 'Excuse me, Mr Kirwin, sir.' The men, too, the runner had whispered to Maria, are fecked from all the waiting around. Made nervous by the crowds and the cameras, they have begun to rag each other about the British uniforms.

'Bloody bystanders. Get them as far back on the pavement as you can and we'll shoot tight,' Keith says. He bites his left thumb. His nail is already chewed so low that the touch of his own mouth must hurt. She knows that sting, knows how comforting yet disheartening it can be. The producer is right, though: between the TV aerials, the cheap signage, the cars parked everywhere and the newly built Liberty Hall looming, as Keith groans, 'like bloody King Kong over the job lot of them', on Eden Quay, *Easter Rebellion* is going to be a problem to edit, that's for sure. 'You can be sure this many people didn't show up the first time.'

'They did, that old lad over there told me.' The producer waves his cigarette in the general direction of the Grafton Savings & Building Society, temporarily shut because its staff are outside with everyone else. 'He told me he was here on the afternoon of the Tuesday and it was just as busy. Only difference . . .' he offers a cigarette to Keith, who shakes his head '. . . was that there were more children knocking about then, what with it being a school holiday.'

This production, the runner told her, is said to be the trickiest job Keith Kirwin has had in his three years as a television director. Maria glances at him again. His thumb back between his teeth, he certainly has the look of a man who is finding this mercurial mix of actors, amateurs and animals almost impossible to manage.

Maria wanders off among the people lining O'Connell Street. The more elderly they look, the closer she hovers. But nobody seems interested in the reconstruction of history. Rather, it is an exciting break in routine, fodder for fresh anecdotes for weeks to come. From the snatches of conversation that reach her, young and old together are in match-day mood.

'It's a great day for it altogether.'

'You've not eaten your sandwiches already? They were to last us the day.'

'What will they do with the cars? There weren't all them cars in those days.'

'They just cover up a bit of the camera so it doesn't see them.'

'That fellah over there, the one next to the one with the camera. Is he from the Telifís too?'

'That frowning fellah? He is for sure, I'd say.'

'We wouldn't have been let walk around with our hands stuffed into our gobs like that in my day, let me tell you.'

She came with ill-formed hopes of overhearing people reminiscing, that she could somehow paddle in memories that would be flowing as easily as the Liffey under O'Connell Bridge. And yet all that is washing around her is gossip and petty squabbles, in-jokes and complaints about the cold. She sees a man about her own age with a small boy on his shoulders. What will today become for that boy? she wonders. An anecdote for his own grandchildren fifty years from now about the day he saw the Rising being filmed for the television? *Oh, for sure*, she imagines him exclaiming, *it*

was just like 1916 itself. Everyone there said so. Yes indeed.
Swear to God. Except it isn't, in every possible respect. And
here, on O'Connell Street on a cold Friday morning in January
1966, how can it ever be? She moves on. The sun hangs low
and bright and the earlier rain has the road glistening like
greasy glass. This, too, has caused Keith to sigh and curse.

'Have a walk about and see who you meet,' was what
Robert Ryan said. But now that she's here with Clerys behind
her back – *Last Week of the Winter Sale! Pop By for a Seasonal*
Bargain! cry the posters – she's not sure how to get started.
She looks at the GPO across the road. It has the solid, dignified
air of an elderly lady told as a girl never to heed her looks
because they would desert her in time.

'Hello there,' she says, to a woman standing next to her.
'Have you come to watch the filming?'

'I have.' She nods furiously. 'I've been here for an hour so
as to get a good view and I've not seen sight nor sound of a
famous person.' She takes out a handkerchief and blows her
nose. 'And I'm after getting a cold now too.'

'What filming?' replies the elderly man she tries next.
Standing alone at the edge of the pavement, his eyes are
bloodshot and watery. 'I'm waiting on the twelve.'

'The buses are off until the filming's over. The street's
closed to traffic.'

'Is that what's going on? I thought there was a big queue
right enough. I can't see a thing since I sat on my glasses. Is
the stop on Eden Quay open?'

'All the quay stops are, as far as I know.'

'Show me up there, will you? I've to get the bus to my
daughter's but with all these people mucking about I'll be
over on my oxter before you know it.'

'Well, I . . .' But he has already grasped her arm and is waiting for her to move off. He is tall and his hand is tight on her elbow. 'Of course,' she says, feeling like a tugboat pulling a coal ship out to sea. 'With pleasure. My name is Maria.'

'Peadar O'Brien. Good to make your acquaintance, young lady.' He gives her elbow a squeeze by way of handshake. His coat is unbuttoned despite the cold. A few paces further on, he coughs, stops, thumps his chest, starts off again. This is all one movement, his transitions smooth as the well-practised rhythm of a dance.

'This old chest of mine,' he says, but his voice is kindly, as if speaking of a friend. His shoulders roll forward and his old-man belly is a soft, distended shape through high, belted trousers. He must have been handsome once, she thinks. His collarless shirt looks clean, but grey and thin from washing.

'Mr O'Brien, had you no interest in staying for the filming? It'll be very exciting.'

'For the Telifís, is it? I have not. I wouldn't have one of those filthy things in the house, even if I could see it. They'll be the ruination of Ireland.'

'Well,' she says, 'I know not everyone agrees with the programmes, but—'

'The priest said as much to us Sunday just gone. *I Love Lucy* or somesuch. Is that from the Telifís?'

'Yes.'

'Father Dwyer said he had seen it himself and it's a desperate corrupt yoke. And whatever else you might hear about Father Dwyer, and him maybe a bit too fond of a sup of porter, he's a wise man.'

Their voyage takes them past Nelson's Pillar and Maria blinks in the sudden shift from glare to shadow. It's months since she and Anna stood at the top and gazed at the summer city laid out around them. She remembers Anna's excitement, her arms spread wide and the sun shining on her London-pale face. How with just one turn of their heads they could look from the peaty mountains to those tall chimneys by the sea. Then the steps down. Twisting round and round, Anna dizzy and giggling. Maria looks at the dark coats and hats of the people moving all round her and Mr O'Brien on the street. Ants, she thinks. I am one of the ants now. We all are.

When they emerge from Nelson's shade she says, 'But, Mr O'Brien, the one they're making today isn't like that. It's a history programme, a series about the Easter Rising.'

'Sure wasn't I there myself? I have it all,' he taps the side of his head with his free hand, 'up here already.'

'You were there? I mean here? At the GPO?'

'I remember it like it was yesterday. A sight clearer than yesterday, if truth be told. Just back there at my bus stop is where we were made line up by the British.'

'What happened?' What a bit of luck to meet someone who was there! Actually there! She is delighted with her good fortune at finding a story so easily.

''Twas one of the leaders gave us the surrender order. *This is the beginning,* says he. *The leaders will be executed but you men can carry it on.* He nearly escaped himself but . . .' He pauses and shrugs his stooped shoulders. But he didn't escape. He tried to, but he didn't. His shrug tells her this; no words are needed. It's what happens in a war.

'And what about you?' she asks.

'We were told to put our weapons down and then we were put into lines. An officer went up and down taking every man's name. Then we were brought round the back. There was a patch of grass there. Near the back of Clerys, it was, long gone now. All night we was left lying there, and if you moved even a twitch you got a whack of a rifle, or stripped of your clothes, right down – begging your pardon, young lady – to your underthings.

'I remember a lad standing just down from where I was in the line. And the British officer stops in front of him, and says nothing, not a bit, then walks on. And after a minute I leans forward and says, "Why didn't he ask your name?" and do you know what?'

'No.' Maria is transfixed.

'"He doesn't need to," he goes. "That man is my brother."'

'What a story!'

Robert Ryan is going to love this. Maybe she does have an ear for researching after all! She had been worried it would be prurient, rude even, to be scavenging around in people's lives, deciding what was worthy of interest and what was not. But it's not like that at all. It's fascinating. Every person here on O'Connell Street is a palimpsest of truths and lies, of stories and memories.

'It's not a story, young lady,' he retorts, 'it's the truth.'

'Yes, sorry. But how sad to see families against each other like that.'

'Against Our Lord it may be to see brother pitched against brother, but families know that war has its own way. A fight will break a household but it will unite a people like nothing else. They were fools, the English, if they thought that crushing the Rising would see an end to it. It did the opposite. It gave us back our conviction for fighting.' They have reached his bus stop. 'This mine here, is it?' He drops her elbow, his voice raised above the rough cries of the engine.

'Let me help you on,' she says, as he slowly lifts one foot then the other onto the platform. She gives his back a gentle shove.

'Thank you, young lady.' He doffs his hat.

'Come on now, Peadar O'Brien,' the driver says. 'We're waiting on you as always.' He leans forward and gives Maria the once-over. He winks. 'Trust you to find the best-looking woman to help you, eh? You're his prettiest yet, love. And there's him says he can't see a hand in front of his face!'

Holding the rail inside the platform, Mr O'Brien half turns to face her. 'I'll tell you one thing those Jews out in Telifís Éireann don't know.' His body rumbles gently in rhythm with the bus. 'They can put their pictures on it, but they'll never show those days as they really were. The smell of fire was everywhere on us. I could smell it off myself for weeks afterwards. It was as though the whole of Dublin was on fire.'

As though he were her child, Maria watches him slowly take his seat in the bus. She waits in case he turns and seeks her out. She wants to see his face again, to see if some trace of his tale has been cast on his features. But he sits on the far side and her view of him is obscured by a woman with a suitcase on her lap. The pressure of the old man's grip is still on her when the bus pulls out and leaves a strange lull in traffic, the coincidence of calm that can unexpectedly happen in busy city streets. She has one hand on the low Liffey wall. The river splashes below. It glitters in the sun, the water rich with the spilt jewels of mermaids.

Maria walks slowly back down O'Connell Street. Peadar O'Brien is right, of course. Keith Kirwin's programme could look like it, sound like it and, if it were possible, smell like it, but it would always be an imposter. A moment of history remade, time recreated for television. A story retold is always a different story: hindsight throws different shadows, creates a play of light and shade that didn't exist the first time. Yet why do we insist on stories being treated as though they are insects trapped in amber? Caught for all eternity, a fixed curiosity for future generations. More relics, she thinks.

She rejoins the fringes of the crowd a few yards from where the *Easter Rebellion* crew are stationed. Seagulls shriek their banshee cries overhead. Beach eagles, Anna calls them. Maria decides to have a quick peek into Clerys before getting her own bus. With a story as good as Mr O'Brien's under her belt, it's been a great morning's work.

Filming must be about to begin. The crew are shifting from foot to foot, looking jittery. From the expressions on their faces, it's going to be a long, cold day. Keith Kirwin's lips move in a low-voiced prayer. From around the corner can be heard the click of hoofs, whistles and 'Whoa there, wait up,' from Irish boys in English uniforms. Written on the slate is the name of this episode: 'Will we win, do you think?'

'Christ,' she hears Keith mutter, 'I bloody hope so.' He moves forward and nods at the assistant director to raise the megaphone.

'Everyone! Back as far as you can and remain silent, please. Mounted charge on the GPO, scene one, take one. Filming in five and four and three and two and one and – *action*.'

Hoofs strike sharp in the otherwise silent road. The man dressed as the lieutenant colonel leading the charge of the British Lancers has a scarlet tab at his collar and cap, two shapes shining as bright as blood. The camera tracks them tight. The horses hold their heads high, and the men's faces are set, determined to fight to the death.

She watches as Keith lets his breath out slowly. The sun is a touch warmer now and the breeze around them is clean and fresh. His shoulders visibly relax. She overhears him whisper to the producer, 'To hell with the TV aerials. We'll fix them in the edit. This is going to be good. Very good.' He shakes out his hands, a man enjoying a surge of conviction in his own ability.

'It's going to be perfect television.' The producer nods vigorously because perfect television, as they both know well, is better than life.

And with that, for the second time in fifty years, shooting begins on O'Connell Street.

She eases off the cape. The prices they're charging, even in the sale! Her own coat will just have to do until next winter. Her fingers edge each shining button through. It's Donegal tweed and what on the mannequin looked a dappled, purplish colour is a hazy mix of greens and blues. She runs her palm over its slight burr. It looks spun from heather and brackish mountain streams. Her own coat is lying in a chair, its arms wide and the frayed lining exposed. The assistant stops fiddling with the overhead wire and walks over. 'How did you get on? Isn't it lovely?'

'It's not for me.'

'Will I see if we've anything else?'

'No.' She blinks back the unexpected sting of tears. 'It's fine. Thank you anyway.' Clerys is hot and her own coat, bought for her by John years before, is heavy, sticky against her neck when she puts it back on. John hadn't liked the red coat she owned before this one, she remembers. Too short, he thought. Too bright. She remembers that day in the Lyons Corner House, when all she could stomach was toast and tea but she hadn't told him why. She had been waiting for the right moment. She wanted to create a perfect memory, one that would ensure her child had the right, the most loved, beginning to its life. Only before she could say anything, he had got annoyed. A man across the room was staring at her legs, he was sure of it. The coat: that was the problem. It was common-looking. And she felt tired suddenly, unsure of herself, and stupidly blurted out about the baby.

They should get married, he replied. The baby was a sign that they should get married. The relief of it! She had been so eager to get rid of 'Power', what good had it ever done her? And sure who could feel lost with a solid name like Mills to keep them tethered to the world? They left their tea unfinished, and went to choose a ring and a new coat. He insisted on the coat. She'd need a new one, he told her, for when she started showing.

Maria hands the cape to the assistant, a woman about her own age. Her skirt is strained tight over her stomach and the flat Germolene pink of her lipstick makes her teeth look browner than they probably are. The woman smiles sympathetically. 'Pop back when the spring modes come in. Whatever's left of the winter stock might take a final drop then.' There is a smear of lipstick on her front tooth, which Maria sees but doesn't mention. Yet even as she nods and leaves she knows that later on she will think of that kind smile. She knows she will wish that she had felt less done-to in that moment, and had told her about the lipstick.

It's late morning by the time she gets the bus to work. It's odd to be out in Dublin at this time, almost as though the life of the city can't exist during the week because she herself is always five miles away. The worker bees might be busy in their hives but the bus is chock-a-block with women who have been shopping in town. Many have young children in tow, their faces pressed against the windows. Next to her, a grubby toddler licks the rail of the seat in front as his mother leans across the aisle to light her friend's cigarette.

As they chug through town she remembers the red-as-cherries buses that bore down on them through the fogged London streets in winter. The afternoons when she was one of these women, and would bring Anna anywhere that took her fancy on the map. The museums in South Kensington, a walk on Primrose Hill, the zoo in Regent's Park. As long as they were home in time to have John's dinner ready for him it didn't matter how they spent the day. As Anna's mark on the kitchen wall got higher and higher, John didn't always come home in time for dinner. So they stayed out longer. As far as Kew Gardens, Richmond, even. They would get on the Tube and count how long it took to rumble in and out of the tunnels, then smile at each other when the soft brightness of daylight welcomed them back above ground. Then home, just in time for Anna to have a quick supper and get ready for bed.

On many evenings during the previous year Anna would fall into an exhausted, day-stained sleep and Maria would sit at the table and wait, wondering if John would be home or not. The night he doesn't come home at all, she promised herself, will be the night before the trip to Brighton. Even if it's snowing, it won't matter. Anna can throw pebbles on the beach and have an ice-cream on the prom. They'll sleep in a room with a view of the water and stare out until they're convinced they can see France. Sit late by the window and tell each other silly stories. And listen, listen hard to the steady promises of the sea.

Her office is empty and the door to Robert Ryan's is ajar. 'Ha, ha,' she hears him saying. 'It must have been a truly fascinating stage in your career. Tell me, did you ever play opposite John Gielgud? . . . Really? And now do let's talk about your latest picture, which has them rolling in the aisles, I believe . . .'

He must be rehearsing an interview for his radio programme. His questions and the interviewees' answers are scripted. The interviewees – the majority of whom just want to tell him about their latest picture and little else – will never see this script. But it's a game they know how to play and it's surprising how easily Robert's interviews trot neatly down their pre-prepared path. Maria hears him stop mid-sentence and pour himself a drink – a large one, it sounds like – and light a cigarette. She removes her typewriter cover and folds it as noisily as she can.

'So,' Robert calls through the open door, 'did the filming go well?'

'It's still going on, as far as I know. I saw Mr Kirwin just as they stopped for lunch and he looked happy.'

'Was he biting his nails?'

'Um, no, I don't think so.'

'Then it was doing all right. Did you meet anyone useful?'

Maria begins to tell him about Peadar O'Brien. After the first few sentences she moves through to his office. To her own ears Peadar O'Brien's story sounds wonderful. It's so honest, full of colour and detail. And the part about the volunteer and his British soldier brother! She feels absurdly proud of her find.

'GPO?' Robert says. 'Hmm, they'll all tell you that.'

'What do you mean?'

'You'd fill Croke Park with the men who say they were in the GPO that week. Did he mention a wife? Sister?' Robert asks. 'It's women we're after, really. You know we haven't enough yet for *The Women of 1916*.' He sighs with the effort of issuing orders. 'Still, though, he might be useful. Get his details to Research before you do anything else. Let them look into his claims.'

'Claims?'

'Is he on the phone? If not, drop him a line today. Got to move quickly, especially with these old boys.'

'I didn't take any . . . his details.'

'What?'

'I'm sorry, Mr Ryan, I didn't realise.'

'So you thought what? We'd use what *you* say he said?'

'I'm so sorry, I didn't think of it. I thought you wanted me to go there just to talk to people and write it up afterwards. I can type up his story for you now. I remember it all and it'll only take me a few minutes.'

'Why on earth would I want your account? I don't even care about his, for God's sake. You were meant to get information, contact details for people we could follow up with. It's not worth the paper it's written on otherwise. For Christ's sake,' he waits a beat before he says her name, as though he's not entirely sure what it is, 'Maria, what a waste! It's not as though you've no work to be getting on with.' He lifts his glass. 'Take that face off you and fetch your notebook. I've a pile of letters need doing. They all need to get out today, mind.'

Maria walks back into the outer office for her stenographer's pad, trying desperately to steady her expression. The humiliation! First, harassing an old woman on her doorstep for nothing, and now this. She wants to crawl back to the copytaking unit and hide under Hilda's desk, sobbing like a lost child. A bloom springs down the back of her slip and under her arms. From the inner office she hears the distinctive click of Robert's phone. He doesn't usually place his own calls. He must be calling Eve to give out about Maria, to ask for another secretary! How embarrassing. Or – no, please, not! – complaining to Patrick Keady. She blushes again, worse this time.

'I'm really so sorry, Mr Ryan.' She returns to his office. 'Mr O'Brien said he's a regular on that bus route, so I could go back and see if he comes along again. Even at the weekend – I don't mind.'

'Don't be ridiculous. Stick with this stuff.' He puts the phone down and gestures at a tray of papers waiting to be filed. 'It's more your line of work. Now let's get started. Time may not be worth much to you, but mine has been wasted enough.' She sits on the hard chair facing him across the desk and picks up her pen. She has long known that he prefers the view when she sits with her legs to one side, so she always makes sure to tuck them as far out of sight under the chair as she can.

'First, Eugene Gilbert,' he says. 'You haven't lost his address, I take it?'

'No.' Point made, she thinks bitterly. You can stop now.

'Dear Eugene,' he leans back in his chair. 'Thank you for your letter of the whatever-it-was, Maria, inst. I regret to inform you that the Programmatic Advisory Panel did not . . .'

He dictates, she writes. It is a rhythm. A messenger sticks his head around the door with a note and Maria imagines how peacefully productive the scene must look, that all is right in the world. He doesn't notice that she's leaning so hard on the biro that the spark-blue marks of her shorthand score the page.

Her penance is this hour of dictation followed by two hours of typing. Only when Robert returns to the office from the Club to sign his letters does he grant her an indulgence. He pushes himself back from his desk, pats his Club-filled stomach, puts on his hat and leaves the office.

Maria has never cut a day's work in her life. But within minutes of his final admonishment – will she be sure not to miss the bloody post boy – and her final assurances that she will not – that she has never once missed the post boy – she is on her way out of the door, feeling schoolgirl-bold. Courage drains from her as she passes the security hut by the exit to the main road. Go back, she tells herself. Don't look for trouble. Stay until five. Pretend it's a tea break, and so what if you take your break at the gate while wearing a coat and scarf? So what if your typewriter cover is on?

But she doesn't go back and she knows why – and she knows why it doesn't matter if it gets her into trouble. She tried to be someone else, someone more interesting, more ambitious than she really is, and she has failed. And all she wants now is to go home. To see her daughter, to hear about school, about Chuzzlewit's superior, almost-human abilities. She needs to absolve her stupidity in the pure waters of Anna's perfect, unconditional love.

The empire-bright sun that had shone that morning over the British Lancers as they charged down O'Connell Street has dropped away and a wintry grey occupies the laneway that leads up from Ranelagh Road. Shapes shift and twist in the shadows and make her jump. As always they find their true forms: a dog, two cats, discarded sweet wrappers rustling in the breeze. At the top of the lane she turns right onto Redoubt Terrace.

'"The length of a cock's step",' Anna quoted Mrs Halpin the day before. 'That's what you notice in the daylight by the Feast of the Epiphany.' It is the length of nothing, as far as Maria can see.

'Help!' A small, dark figure stands on the other side of the entrance to the laneway but further back, almost at the corner where the two lines of houses form a right angle. And again, 'You there! Help!'

'Hello?' Maria calls, cautious. The shape moves closer and comes to a stop under a yellowish pool of streetlight.

'I remember you,' the old woman says, her thin face ghoulish under the sulphuric glow. One hand holds a woollen muffler close to her mouth. It is two months since she sent Maria home with a flea in her ear and she hasn't seen her since. She looks even more ethereal now than she did then.

'Are you all right, Mrs McDermott?'

'There's something wrong upstairs. I heard a thump and a cry but now there's nothing.'

'Did you phone for a doctor? The gardaí?'

'The house isn't on the telephone. I've knocked on either side but there's no one home and then I saw you in the laneway.'

Maria follows Tess up the path to the door, stumbling over cracked tiles that have lifted from the ground. Tess leads her into the hallway. 'Stay here,' she says. In the dim light the faint, ghostly glow of the chequerboard tiles reminds Maria of the religious pictures Mrs Halpin has pinned around her house, the Holy Family's halos throbbing luminously in the dark. The wallpaper's flower pattern climbs thickly up the walls, as crammed as the hothouses in Kew Gardens. Maria imagines touching it only for her hand to continue through the wall into a dense undergrowth beyond.

With a click it becomes an ordinary hallway. Dim, uncared-for and empty, but nothing more.

'This way.' Tess walks ahead up the stairs. 'Mr Owens has the flat above mine.'

Unlike Maria's, Tess's house hasn't been partitioned into flats. Mr Owens lives alone in the rooms upstairs and Tess downstairs. The no man's land of the bathroom on the return is shared. Watching her clip soundlessly up the stairs, Maria can see she is a lot less frail than she had assumed. She is aware of the click of her shoes tapping the dirty brass runner rails and her own puffing as she hurries to keep up with Tess.

'Mr Owens?' Tess taps once, twice. 'Mr Owens?' Nothing. 'It's Tess McDermott again. From downstairs. I heard a noise. Is everything all right?' The resounding silence is not the Sandman's soundless lullaby. Maria shivers. There is a dense weight to the quiet that she recognises.

'What was the noise you heard?'

'A shout and a big thump like furniture falling.'

'And there's no spare key anywhere?'

'I don't know nothing about keys.'

Maria tries the handle. She sees his foot first. Then the entire body, which lies on the floor next to the narrow bed. His right foot is hugely swollen, the skin taut, mottled purple and white. A heavy, high-backed armchair lies on its back on the wooden floor next to him. Broken springs and stuffing leer at them from slits ripped in its underside. A slight breeze flutters the torn net curtain. The room is freezing. It smells of dust and mouse. Tess's mouth falls open and Maria can see how broken her teeth are; ancient standing stones in her gums.

'Mr Owens?' Tess reaches out and touches his hand. 'A goner,' she says, a crack in her voice, 'you poor man.'

'What happened him?'

'Heart, I'd say, from the colour of him. He had enough bother with it, I know that.'

Something crunches under Maria's shoe. A rosary. She rolls the soft, dark wood of the beads between her fingers. Jesus and his cross are tarnished, made black from age and use. A crown of thorns winds around his tiny forehead.

'What do we do?' Maria looks at the stranger's face. He is wearing pyjamas, his coat on over them. Despite having all three rooms of the first floor, it appears that he lived in this one alone. Yet the grate is empty and dark, the dresser that served as his kitchen has only a few cups and plates on it. The room smells of neglect, dust and loneliness, of a life lived away from the shelter of others. Yet you were a baby in your mother's lap once, she thinks. What jump was it brought you from her arms to this room? There aren't words for how the sight of his body makes her feel. Or if there are, she doesn't know where in herself she might go to find them.

Tess plucks a blanket from the bed and drapes it over him. 'We'd best telephone the gardaí,' she says. 'There's nothing we can do here. Are you on the phone?' Maria nods. 'Good. Run home and ring the station in Rathmines and ask them what we're to do, then come back and we'll wait downstairs.'

An hour later the ambulance has been and gone, Mr Owens

with it. His flat is empty of him, the door left open. Moonlight shines through the open curtains and lands on clothes on the bed and the stained seat of the chair, now back on its four legs. Flakes of paint from the ceiling dust the floor, pale and soft as snow.

'You never get used to the sight of death, no matter how many you see.' Tess pours another long nip of whiskey into her teacup. 'He's not the worst I seen, though, not by a long way.' It is impossible to know where Tess is looking: her eyes skitter around like a bird after a worm. 'But to think of him up there in a bad way for God knows how long. And me down here and not hearing a bit of it till the end.' She shakes her head.

They are downstairs in the kitchen at the back of the house. Maria realises Tess must sleep in the front room, the equivalent of Mrs Halpin's parlour. Compared to the blank chill of the hallway, this room is stuffy, more of a junk shop than a kitchen. Every surface is covered. Unwashed crockery, clothes and papers litter the table. A china cat's broken head – a sight that would horrify Anna – guards an unruly stack of books. Like Rapunzel's unfinished ladder, knotted threads spill from an open workbasket to the floor. A brassy glint of some jewellery shines, half hidden under a newspaper that lies beneath a discarded cardigan. With a single sweep of her arm, Tess shoves it all to one side. The cardigan and everything under it slides off the table and onto the floor. Maria goes to pick them up.

'No, leave it,' Tess says, sharp. 'I'm not very tidy in my ways, but they're my ways and I keep to 'em.' Next to her teacup on the table is a copybook of the sort Anna uses in school. It is lying open, a pencil waiting in the gully between the half-filled pages. She slaps it shut and pushes it away from her, saying, 'I done enough tidying to do me my whole life.'

'When you worked in Cavendish Square?'

'I told you that afore, didn't I?'

'Yes.' Maria realises her hands are shaking. Her head seems to be working at a delayed speed. 'What did you mean, he' – Maria points at the ceiling and blushes – 'wasn't the worst?'

Tess lights a cigarette. 'I seen a woman who took her own life. That's a sight set to haunt you.'

'*What?* Where?'

'In Holloway.'

'Holloway-the-*prison* Holloway?' Maria splutters, thinking that maybe Mrs Halpin was right after all.

'I was in there in '09,' Tess replies, then takes a long sip from her cup. She is more garrulous than Maria had thought she could ever be. 'And I was being moved from one division to another. I wasn't well but they made me walk it anyways. Those metal landings would make you desperate dizzy because you could see through them to the ground, and all the clanging that went on, too. A door to a cell was wide open and the guards were fussing and making a commotion. And I looks in past them and there she was, hung with strips of her own cape from the bars. The posh ladies was allowed keep their own clothes, see.' Tess lifts her cup. Pink roses wrap around it, even up the handle. They look fragile against the thick knots of her knuckles. 'I was stood there, staring in – I'd never seen anything like it. Green fabric it was, so it was as if she were strung up by a rope woven from grass. I was so weak I thought I was hallucinating. But it was real. When I woke up the next day and the memory of her was still there, I knew there was no denying it.'

'Who was she? Did you know her?'

Tess looks down at her hands. Her wedding band is loose and up as far as her knuckle. 'Not really.'

Maria sips from her cup. She's never had whiskey before and Tess's generous nips are hitting her like a hammer wrapped in a kid glove. She had hurried to Mrs Halpin's to telephone and tell them ('He's been taken ill. Anna, I said I'd wait to see if I can help. I won't be long, promise.') before returning to Tess's flat to wait with her for the gardaí. Maria runs her hands over her forehead but the fingers touching her face don't feel like her own. With every sip her brain feels more blurred. The day that started in sunlight on O'Connell Street might have happened to someone else many years before. Maybe she has fallen under some sort of cruel spell and is destined never to sleep again but to live one long, hard day for the rest of her life. She recognises this trapped sensation from her dreams, every fibre of her body straining forward but her legs remain trapped in sleep's quicksand, and she can go nowhere.

Double R's rudeness is a lifetime before. Triple R, she thinks as the whiskey rolls hotly down her throat. She closes her eyes but sees Mr Owens's folded body on the floor, his face now jumbled up with Peadar O'Brien's, whose ghostly clutch she feels on her elbow still.

'Mrs McDermott?'

'You'd do as well to call me Tess. I'd say we're past the formalities, wouldn't you?' She taps her cigarette into a chipped wooden eggcup painted to look like a chicken. The bird's beak is a thin, reproving line and one round eye is scratched out.

'All right, then. Tess, why were you in prison?'

'Throwing eggs.'

'You were sent to prison for throwing eggs?' Confused, Maria looks at the chicken. Its single black eye stares coldly back.

'I pegged a constable right square on the forehead. Fell over like a tree in a storm, he did.' She looks at Maria's face and adds, as though it would explain everything, 'We used hard-boil 'em first.'

'Did he . . .' Maria hesitates '. . . was he badly hurt?'

'Out cold for a while. But even if it had just bounced off his uniform and he'd kept it for a sandwich it wouldn't have mattered. That magistrate would've pinned anything he could on us, he was that sick of having our colours in the dock. I was unlucky, that's all. I was only trying to break a window. The constable got in the way.'

'Your colours?'

'Suffragette colours. And what of it?' Tess pours herself another generous whiskey and tops up Maria's teacup without asking. A faint, stale tinge of lavender dusts the air. 'If this is about your what-do-you-call-it for Telifís Éireann, I told you afore I'm not the person you want. I put all that behind me when I left London.' Her mouth is set and the bulge of her tongue moves against her cheeks. 'I'm after telling you about that time in gaol . . . Well, I don't know why I am, it must be the upset after seeing him upstairs, but it's my tale and you can't have it.'

'I wasn't asking because of the radio programme. I'm not involved in researching it any more.' Maria takes another drink.

'Why?'

'I made a hames of it. I should have stayed in the copy office.'

'What's that when it's at home?'

'A fancy term for taking dictation.'

'And what happened?'

'I didn't understand what I was meant to do.' One tiny chance, she thinks, to show I could do something, that there was more to me than a phone and a pen and a typewriter.

'So you don't want to do it – what was it? – again?'

'Researching. It's not my decision.' Her head feels dull and sharp all at once, her legs made of lead. 'But,' she drinks, then chases the taste down with another sip, 'I didn't realise I'd enjoy it, but I did. I liked trying to find things out, to unravel knots. It was more interesting than transcribing the reporters' phone calls. In the copy office we've just to write words down and we're not even meant to notice whether any of it makes sense or not.'

'Sounds like one of them Ouija boards.'

'A Ouija board, Tess, is exactly what I am.' She raises her teacup in salute. She's so tired, she knows she should leave, collect Anna and carry her home. Yet she's rooted to the spot. This cramped, overcrowded kitchen has become hungry grass to her, and even though she knows it will starve her, it's impossible to break free from its spell. She asks, 'Why did you join the suffragettes?'

'None of your business.'

'Sorry. You're right, it's not,' Maria says, and then again, 'Sorry.' Nothing is her business. Robert Ryan was clear enough on that.

Tess's frown suggests she was anticipating an argument. 'You give up easy, don't you?'

Maria says nothing and Tess continues, 'It's not as though I just showed up one day and put my name to it. That's not how it works. You can't always decide what's going to matter to you.'

'But isn't that one of the few things you, I mean, whoever,' Maria shakes her head, as if the words need oiling to come free, 'can decide?' When everything on the outside is beyond control, aren't beliefs free to own?

'Forcing yourself to believe something is a lie. This country's seen too much of that already. It catches you out, mark my words.'

'What about everything it took to get the vote? Were the suffragettes right to do what they did?'

Tess shrugs. 'For everyone together, I suppose. For each of us in ourselves, in our own lives with our own childer, the sacrifice is too much. Sacrifice sounds like a pure word, but it's not. It's filthy.'

'So good is good if it's for the common good?' Maria stumbles through the sentence.

'If you can stand by your actions after the battle is over and for the rest of your life. When you can't . . . well, that's when it goes sour.' She holds Maria's gaze. There is a warning in her face but a buzz in Maria's ears drowns everything else. The noise appears to be coming from inside her head and her thoughts are butterflies in a summer garden, dancing just out of sight.

Tess says, 'Did you ever go to a fairground and play that game with the pea and the three cups? Where you have to guess which one the pea is under?'

Maria nods.

A sticky summer's evening in Primrose Hill. The sun hung heavy on the horizon for what felt like the entire night. Engine noise and the reek of diesel and stale beer from the fairground. Sweat on her slip and her hand tucked into John's trouser pocket and his fingers slipping up her skirt when no one was looking. 'Yes,' she says.

'Well, that's what it's like. You'll spend your days lifting cup after cup and every time you'll be sure you've got it. But you'll not find it because it's not there.'

Maria glances at the ceiling, befuddled. A perfect truth flutters, ever-shifting, just beyond her grasp. She says, 'I hope Mr Owens wasn't in too much pain.'

'Poor divil. He wasn't the type to ask for help. Loneliness is worse in a man, somehow, I don't know why. Men take life harder than we do.'

'Yes.'

'Though it's us live it harder.'

In the centre of the mantelpiece squats a shiny brass travelling clock with a photograph on either side. A young Tess and her husband on their wedding day are to the left, a little boy by himself to the right.

'My Daniel.' Tess follows her gaze. 'He died a soldier with the Irish Guards and a brave one. I don't care who knows it.'

The heaviness is moving up from Maria's legs through her body with every passing second. 'What happened to him?'

'He was on leave in London and a wall collapsed on him during an air raid. 1943 it was, and him having survived so much in the war already . . . It was an insult to him to go that way.' She swallows the last of her drink. 'I was done with London after gaol. Didn't go back for years, till my husband Paddy wanted to – he was a cooper, see. Then Paddy got a position in Guinness's and we came back here again. Danny was four then, a London boy through and through.'

Maria nods, thinking of Anna's sing-song vowels, her Bow Bells speech. 'I'm sorry you lost him, Tess.'

'He thought he was unbeatable. But none of us are. And the little bastards can get you even when the big ones don't.'

Feeling Daniel's big eyes heavy on her, Maria stands to leave. The junk-shop kitchen sways around her. It is even fuller than it was earlier. Tess's belongings seem to be replicating. The jewellery Tess shoved to the floor winks a brassy eye up at her. She can just about make out now that it's a brooch, with a shadowed blur of another lying next to it. Maria closes an eye and the duplicate vanishes.

When they say goodbye, whiskey warms the air between them. Maria looks up at Mr Owens's window above their heads. The curtains are open and the window is a wide, dark howl. 'Sure you're all right, alone here like this?'

'I was always alone, even when he was there.'

Maria has the oddest sensation that the house will disappear into the heartland of a fairy kingdom and that she will never see Tess again. She puts a hand on the gate to steady herself. The path is bouncing under her feet.

'Maria?' Tess is a grey blur in the doorway. 'History makes fools of us all. You'd do well to remember that.'

CHAPTER THIRTEEN

A blade, sawing through her skull.

Macushla! Macushla!
Your red lips are saying
That death is a dream
And love is . . .

the voice continues to rise,

> *. . . for aaaaaaye.*

One eye opens but the other is stuck. Her tongue seems to be glued to the roof of her mouth. Slowly she turns her head. Two eyes stare into her one; a small nose almost touches her cheek. Anna's face is curiously abstracted. The song is so close to Maria's face it is as though Anna is breathing it – 'love is for aaaaaaye' – straight into her mouth. Maria's stomach turns uneasily at the smell of milk on Anna's breath and the white flakes that have dried on her upper lip.

Then awaken Macushla,
Awake from your dreaming,
My blue-eyed Macushla,
Awaken to staaaay.

She takes a step back and finishes with a flourish, her mouth an exaggerated O. She throws her arms wide and drops into a low curtsy. The gingham apron is a cloak round her shoulders.

'Anna?' It comes out an arid whisper. 'What are you doing?'

'Serenading you. That's what it's called. Mrs Helping played the record of the song until I learnt the words. It's by a famous singer.'

Her brain is tight. Is this what whiskey does to a person? And Tess must have done this more than once. 'Pass me that water. No, two hands.'

'Here. He's called John McCormack, and he's safe in the arms of Our Lord.' As if the singer was in front of her, Anna takes a step back and drops into another reverential bow. She raises her hands to her head to fluff out her badly ringleted hair. The curls droop like streamers at a long-finished party. 'He's a count, you know,' she adds. 'It's a bit like being a king or a prince.'

'He's a count of the Vatican.'

'Papal counts are the most superior kind.'

Maria sighs. 'Mrs Halpin?'

Anna nods. 'She heard him sing years ago, at the . . .' she takes a breath worthy of the tenor himself before launching herself into the next words '. . . Eucharistic Congress.' And with that she pirouettes off, through the door that connects the bedroom to their kitchen and sitting room.

Maria's head is pounding. Anna's calendar is pinned on the wall at the end of the bed. The square for Saturday, 8 January has been decorated in crayon with a pattern of wands and stars, but Maria can't remember why. She aches with a tiredness that is beyond sleep.

Anna calls through, 'I think that was in olden times. Mrs Helping says when he opened his mouth it was as though God Himself was issuing forth from his very lips.'

Maria slumps back against her pillow. From the other room she hears the sound of the doll's house being lifted onto the table and the spitter-spatter of the furniture being tipped out to be rearranged. Anna's still singing, her *rs* long and thickened, unwittingly imitating the high whine of Mrs Halpin's old record player.

> *Macushla! Macushla!*
> *Your white arms are reaching,*
> *I feel them enfolding,*
> *Caressing me still.*
> *Fling them out from the darkness,*
> *My lost love, Macushla,*
> *Let them find me and bind me*
> *Again, if they wiiiiill.*

Maria closes her eyes and listens. Her head is heavy against the pillow. She is sweating and uncomfortable, even though her cold nose tells her the bedroom isn't warm. It feels as though the bed is listing under her, trying to tip her out onto the floor. Too tired after her whiskey-soaked sleep to move, she just lies there with legs made of lead and her eyes closed, thinking of Tess's words about her soldier son. And, listening to Anna's long-ago song of loss, she drifts off.

She wakes in London.

Francis is a big baby, with thick black hair on the top of his head, like a pom-pom. At least, that's how she imagines him, now and for ever after. But she doesn't see him. He is born dead. And yet how could he be? Hadn't she felt him moving about inside her all that morning? They take him away immediately. John sees him for the longest shortest moment: long enough to notice how healthy he seems, long enough for his heart to break at the black hair, the ordinary everyday perfection of his baby fingers and toes. She is hoarse, deranged from shouting at the doctor and the nurses for an hour that it's going wrong, that it feels wrong, but they wouldn't listen.

'Hysterical Irish,' one said, sourly loud, to another, determined that she overhear. The doctor allows John to see his son. But not her. The words that come out of her mouth then are shocking, even to herself. They may not even be words. She doesn't know. She is beyond language.

'There we are,' the doctor comments coldly. The pure metal ping of an emptied syringe landing in the tray echoes in her ears as she is dragged down, down and deep under the ocean. She bumps along the bottom of the seabed, where mermaids, their seaweed hair dragging free, tug at her legs and their scaly mother-of-pearl fins brush over her wet, salty face. She gasps, swallowing great draughts of icy water. At first she panics and tries to push her way through water that quickly becomes heavy as quicksand. Then she stops resisting. Yes, her dream body thinks, yes. Give in. This is the end. And she opens her mouth and flings her arms wide. She begins to float upwards, bursting and lifeless and empty.

'Mummy?'

'*No!*' She breaks through the surface of the water, gulping and gasping, not knowing if she's awake or asleep.

'Mummy! I've been calling you. I can't find anything to eat.'

She's in her own bed. Francis, she thinks. *Francis*. 'Was I asleep?'

'For ages.' Anna puts her hand out. 'Please get up, Mummy. I don't want to be late.'

'Late?'

'The panto! It starts at two. That only gives us . . .' Anna counts on her fingers '. . . four hours.'

Of course. The crayon marks on the calendar are because of *Cinderella*. A pal of Michael's in the Eamonn Andrews Studios passed on two spare tickets. Anna has been looking forward to it all week.

'The Gaiety is at Stephen's Green. It won't even take us half an hour to get there.'

'You said we could go to the playground first, remember?'

'Yes.' Maria smiles, suddenly terribly grateful for her child's demands. 'Of course I remember.' The ringlets Mrs Halpin put in Anna's hair have turned to frizz overnight: she reaches out and gently tugs the most unruly of the twists, noticing for the first time that Anna is wearing her duffel coat. The *Cinderella* tickets are folded and carefully tucked into one of the toggles.

'Why are you laughing, Mummy?'

'Nothing, sweetheart. Now, can I have a hug to help me get up, please? A big, big, squeezy one.' Her milky breath hot on Maria's cheek, Anna's arms are the line that pulls her, dripping and heavy, from the ocean.

Just before they turn from Redoubt Terrace onto the laneway Maria looks over at number thirty-nine. The curtains of Mr Owens's room are as she left them the night before. Where is he now? She didn't think to ask where his body was being taken. The downstairs window is screened by heavy nets on the inside and an overgrown bush out front so she can't be sure whether Tess's bedroom curtains are open or not.

The night before hangs around her, heavy as a blanket draped over her shoulders. Mr Owens, the gardaí, Tess, her son killed by the wall . . . even the long-ago, long-dead London constable and the hard-boiled egg are all rattling around in her head, whirling and twirling in a sweat-stained tombola. But it wasn't a dream. And whatever else may or may not be true, Mr Owens is still dead.

Maria blushes as she recalls what had happened with Mrs Halpin when she finally collected Anna. 'The poor man.' Mrs Halpin had crossed herself repeatedly. 'He was a martyr to his health. Lord have mercy on his soul!'

Maria swayed on her feet. The cold air had hit her like a cuff to the side of the head. 'The gardaí said they'll contact me if they need me. S'formalities and whatnot,' she slurred.

'Are you all right?' Mrs Halpin hauled her arms up and fastened them tight under her bosom. 'That Tess McDermott is a fine piece and no mistake. She's after getting you half mithered with drink!'

'No, no. I mean, maybe, yes. I don't know. A bit.' Mrs Halpin's clock struck ten. Was that all? She was sure it was much later, deep in the bitter heart of the night.

'Will you not let Anna sleep here tonight?'

'No, no, 's fine, thanks. I want to take her home. So sorry, so sorry.' Maria was aware that she was repeating herself yet couldn't stop. No sooner had she spoken than she felt the need to say the words again. That sliver of truth about the world continued to evade her net, no matter how wide she cast it. Something vital, always wriggling out of sight.

'But right you were, Mrs Halpin, about Tess McDermott. S'was a suffragette.'

'Didn't I tell you so?'

'But not here, that bit was incorrect information, Mrs Helping. Halpin! Sorry. In London, not here. And information has to be accurate. 'S not worth the paper it's written on otherwise, so I'm told.'

'Ada is never wrong. She's been elected to the Committee of the Irish Housewives Association.' Mrs Halpin had bristled. 'And it was her told me that Tess had claimed herself a military pension. The gall of that woman.'

Maria bounced off the doorframe and on into the front room where Anna lay asleep under a tartan travel rug. The imitation coal light of the fire was on, an illusion of heat unmatched by what radiated from a single electric bar. She bundled her up awkwardly, noticing suddenly how heavy she had got from all these months of Mrs Halpin's meat and potato dinners. Anna's hair fell back from her face in tight sausage-thick rolls.

'I know Friday's her hair-wash night, so I did it for her. She told me,' Mrs Halpin sounded scandalised, 'that she'd never had the ringlets before.'

The two women stood on either side of the threshold, the child between them. 'Delighted she was, with her new curls.' Maria tightened her grip. The forced, uncomfortable twists in her hair made the sleeping face look like that of a much older and unfamiliar child.

'Prefer if you didn't.' Maria heard herself slur and coughed to cover it up, wondering why such anger was building inside her about the ringlets.

'Sure, what harm? We had the time. I'll do them again another day, I told her. Are you sure you're all right, Maria? You got a desperate shock, I'm sure.' Mrs Halpin looked down at Anna's sleeping face and touched her fingertips to the child's temple. 'She missed you this evening, right enough.'

'Missed her too.' Maria turned to go, unsteady on the path. She tottered down Redoubt Terrace with Anna held close in her arms and the bitter smell of singed hair all around them.

The park is cold and she has forgotten her gloves. Her hands sting at the touch of the pole. 'Harder, Mummy, harder,' Anna calls, as she twirls by on the Witch's Hat. Maria cringes again at the memory of that conversation. Something is clanging through the haze, jumping up and down in her mind, desperate to attract her attention. She closes her eyes. The January air is soothing, a snow queen's kiss on her eyelids. She sees a golden shape pointing at her from under yellowing newspaper and Tess sweeping an arm across the clutter of the kitchen table, shoving the mess away to make space for their teacups. She sees the brooch fall to the floor, the brassy glow of letters curling around that distinctive shape.

Relics and keepsakes.

Maria's eyes open again. A golden rifle. Identical to the one she had played with in secret in her aunt's bedroom. She knows exactly what it is and what it means. Tess has lied to her.

'I'm a witch, I'm a witch, and you can't catch me,' Anna

chants, her face a laughing blur as she whizzes past. 'With my magic hat I'm always free.'

Anna stares at Cinderella, transfixed. Broomstick for a partner, she is waltzing around the scullery, singing to herself. Plucky and sweet, she twirls her patched sky-blue skirts, blithely oblivious to the devilish character lurking in the painted shadows behind her. Because there, and determined to prevent her exchanging her broomstick for a living, breathing prince, is none other than the Evil King himself! Sooty-faced and thin-lipped, his exaggerated moustache-twirling makes Maria think of Brian O'Toole and his silly scarf.

'I've been waiting for love for my lifetime,' she sings, hugging the broom to her body. 'For for ever and for a day.'

Anna tugs at Maria's sleeve, concerned. 'It's too soon to be *for ever*, isn't it?'

'Don't fret, the *for ever* bit isn't just for the end.' Maria smiles. 'Here, have these.' She passes her a little poke of mint creams that Michael sent with the tickets. Anna takes one and carefully tucks the bag into the pocket of her tartan pinafore. At her request, they're dressed in their best rig-outs (last year's raspberry-wool patch-pocket dress for Maria; new for-Christmas outfit of pinafore and white pussy-bow blouse for Anna) and are going for a cream tea afterwards. Maria smiles at the thought of how often, and in what great detail, Anna will relive this afternoon – sure to be billed as the Best Ever Afternoon of My Life – later on. Anna reaches across the padded armrest and clutches Maria's hand between her own. And in the plush red velvet of her seat, their hands clasped, she is gloriously, giddily happy. She's got away with it. She has a job – such as it is, she thinks, flushing again at the memory of Robert Ryan's harsh words – a home and this perfect child. When she finally gets the courage to tell Anna she's going to arrange a replacement for Mrs Halpin, everything will be just right. It's all been worth it. They're safe.

'Look out!' the audience screams, and Anna kneels up on her seat.

'What's that you say, boys and girls?' Cinders pauses mid-twirl and turns sweetly to the audience, her arms outstretched. 'Look out? For who?'

'The Evil King!' hundreds of voices chorus.

'But I can't see anybody here but me! Where could he be?'

Despite the piercing screams from all round them, which sharpen the lingering darts of Maria's headache, she can't help but laugh at Anna's face. Her eyes are wide, she is bubbling with excitement. Maria watches her with pride as, loud as she possibly can, Anna shouts up at the young woman on the stage, 'He's behind you!'

CHAPTER FOURTEEN

The few sounds echo loudly because they escape from silence: a turning of pages, the whispers of librarians, the squeak of her shoe against the high shine of the parquet floors. There is even something in the air of the National Library: the Reading Room has the reverence found in churches, a weight that demands respect. Maria inhales again, this time picking up the faint aroma of a meaty soup.

'Another one for 1916, eh? People can't get enough of the Easter Rising, these days. Will anyone still care in another fifty years? That's what I want to know.' The man behind the orders desk has receding wiry red curls, his clown-like appearance exaggerated by the flower in his buttonhole. He looks younger when he smiles: a child imperfectly impersonating the grown up they would like to become. He pushes a request slip and a pencil stub across the information desk. 'Write down your name with the titles and numbers of the volumes you want, then take a seat.'

'Is there somewhere I'd get a list of the women involved?' It sounds silly even to her own ears. Is she really expecting to find Tess in the archive, caught red-handed in black-and-white? Perhaps neatly shelved – the notion of Tess being tidy makes her smile – in a catalogue of now-forgotten handmaidens to the revolutionaries.

'*Only* women?' He couldn't sound more surprised had she asked about volunteer animals. Seditious budgies maybe, or rabbits armed with rifles. 'Hmm.' He clicks his teeth. 'I can do you any number of lists of casualties, right enough, though it's men and women together.' He takes a breath and rattles off, 'Apart from those executed afterwards, there were sixty-four insurgent casualties, a hundred and thirty-two soldiers and police and approximately two hundred and thirty civilian deaths.' The secretary within her admires the efficient disinterest of his information. 'The names of the insurgents and those of the military and police are recorded, needless to say, but there are no official lists of the civilians, so I wouldn't be able to help you there. There were well over a thousand wounded, but no archive.' He tut-tuts at the carelessness of previous generations. 'The hospitals might have publicly available records of the wounded. I know the Jervis Street Hospital treated plenty.' He takes the still-blank slip and pencil out of her hand. 'James Crawford Neil, one of our own, died there. He was a library assistant, same as myself.'

'What happened to him?'

'On the Easter Tuesday he went across the city to get home, even though everyone knew to stay away. He was trying to avoid Sackville Street – as it was at the time – so he went up Liffey Street. There were children looting a shop – the looting was desperate by all accounts – and when he tried to stop them he was shot by a young lad with a stolen air rifle. And do you know what?' She shakes her head. 'He had written a book of poetry – it was published not long after. *Happy Island: child poems*. We've a copy in the archives. One moment, please, sir,' he says, to someone behind her in the queue of those eager to be off their feet and tucked in behind the desks.

'The woman I'm looking for wasn't a civilian. Or a casualty. Where would I find information about Cumann na mBan volunteers?'

He has completed her request slip before she's finished speaking. 'I'll get you started with this lot and we'll see how you get on. Find yourself a desk.' She wonders was he listening to her at all. 'You'd do better,' he whispers, 'to choose one that isn't too close to the wall.' He nods towards the seats nearest the large cast-iron radiators, most of which are occupied by elderly men. 'They come in out of the cold for a read of the papers. They won't bother you, but when it warms up in the afternoons it can get a touch whiffy.' He turns away. 'Somebody will be with you in a moment, madam,' she hears him say. 'Please complete a request slip while you wait.'

Maria chooses a single desk near the door to the stone staircase. The reading stand attached to the desk waits, empty and expectant, in front of her. Every time the door opens, cold air curls in around her ankles, which must explain why this side of the Reading Room is under-occupied. The room is horseshoe-shaped, and grey winter light putters in through the dome nearly fifty feet over her head and through narrow windows set high in the walls. Dimpling cherubs in plaster smile benignly down at her.

'Here's enough to be going on with.' The assistant is at her side, his arms full. Maria begins with *The Sinn Féin Rebellion Handbook*, published by the *Weekly Irish Times* in 1917. It is full of lists: casualties among the military, the Royal Irish

Constabulary and the Dublin Metropolitan Police; lists of burials in the Dublin cemeteries; a list of all the insurgents who were later executed. These lists are classified by cemetery and each ends with a short note as to the number of bodies interred *whose identity was not clearly established*, and the hospitals where they died. If they weren't identified by 1917, presumably they never were. She shivers for those long-dead unknowns. Identity is a shifting, shadowy thing, easily lost for any of us. And when lost, it can be gone for ever. She finds something hypnotic about the lists of the dead and, almost without realising she is doing it, reads through them.

She begins with the victims interred at Glasnevin Cemetery *whose deaths occurred as a result of bullet or gunshot wounds arising out of the rebellion*. The list includes several persons who were trampled to death by crowds in the streets. Names, ages, last known addresses. Some of the ages are given in halves. Her heart turns at an age given in quarters: a poignant attempt to extend in print what never could have been in life. There is an eighty-two-year-old from Rutland Square, a young man from Daisy Market, a woman from the South Union Workhouse, an unnamed twelve-year-old boy shot in Baggot Street. She passes by Sainsbury, George P. (9½), from the South Circular Road, newspaper editor McIntyre, Patrick (38), shot by military in Portobello Barracks. Were Fennell, Thos J. (24) and Fennell, Rose (23), of 20 Upper Buckingham Street, brother and sister or man and wife? What was Foster, Jimmy (2 years 10 months) doing out of his cot in Manor Place? Who was holding him when he died? She thinks of Mr Owens on the floor of his cold home and alone at the moment of his death.

These pages are a map of Dublin's dead. What would it be if every last man, woman and child could jump up, alive-alive-o once more and link hands? Forge a human wall around the city and protect each other from harm, for ever and ever, amen. Maria puts the book to one side. Tess is never to be found in those lists of long-dried blood. She resumes her search for the living in an illustrated history of the Rising. Patrick Keady has lots of similar books, but she hasn't seen this one before and opens a page at random.

A photograph shows a view of Sackville Street and along Eden Quay. It is taken from a high angle, presumably the roof of a nearby building, and dated 5 May 1916. A dull, brackish wash of sepia renders everything lifeless. Daniel O'Connell's statue stands alone in the foreground. An exposed chimneybreast is a broken spine on a wall; all five storeys of the house it once heated are gone. On Eden Quay over to the right, tiny figures – ants! – are frozen in movement. Even the Easter clouds to the top of the picture look like smoke hanging high above. And, of course, just edging out of sight on the right, there is the Liffey, where the British gunboat *Helga* (the very thing that caused the destruction the photograph has captured) was stationed. The statue of Daniel O'Connell frowns from his untouched monument. He is trapped up on his plinth, forced to watch and powerless to stop the squandering. Look, his cross stone face seems to say, you called me the Liberator because I won Catholic emancipation from the British for you by peaceful means, and what have you done with your inheritance?

She works her way through the books until her head aches. Statistics and strongholds. Hard-line positions and surrenders. Bodies abandoned where they fell in St Stephen's Green and the firing continuing over them. The British officer who, blithely oblivious to the siege, wandered into the GPO and demanded a twopenny stamp. The four fresh battalions of Sherwood Foresters, who were docked in Kingstown and marched to the city centre, many of them presuming they were walking towards the muddy trenches of Ypres. The majority of them had never once fired the rifles they carried, and Percy Place is said to have been haunted by a soldier since that day.

Every statistic is a person, a story. Each one a different Rising. She thinks of Peadar O'Brien, face down all night on a patch of grass. One of the books reproduces the front page of newspapers from 1 May 1916. *SMASHING UP THE IRISH REBELS*, blares a headline. That was how the blood and sinew of Easter Week reached the readers of the *Daily Express* over their breakfast: *Notorious Countess Captured* and *Column of Troops Sent to Retake a Provincial Stronghold*.

It is touching closing time when she reaches the bottom of the pile. At least her journey home will be shorter than usual today. She didn't ask Robert Ryan's permission ('Why should you?' Eve told her. 'Double R's not your boss, even if he Double T thinks he is.'). Dolores has appeared every day this week, so Robert didn't fuss when Maria said she was on a half-day.

'Make sure you let Personnel know, won't you?' Patrick had said, when she asked for the afternoon off. 'Are you, um, doing anything nice?'

'Just a message for a friend,' she replied, unwilling to share her quest with anyone.

She looks from the wooden panels lining the walls to the domed ceiling overhead. Over the course of the afternoon the light has changed from a smudged grey to black. The room is finally warm and has become stuffy. All around her, heads are beginning to nod. She hears coughs and snorts, the occasional light snore. Her own eyes feel heavy.

'We're closing in ten minutes.' The library assistant appears at her elbow. 'Have you found what you were looking for?'

'No, not really,' she says, forcing her eyes open. His tie has migrated under his left ear and the chrysanthemum in his buttonhole is drooping. 'But thank you for your suggestions,' she adds, not wanting to seem ungrateful. She has told herself that she wants to find out why Tess has lied about her involvement with the Rising; that her interest is founded on nothing more than personal curiosity. But there is more to it than that, and she knows it. She wants a story, something meaty, with provenance, to bring back to Robert Ryan. She dislikes herself for it; a cat desperate to present its owner with the bloody carcass of a sparrow.

'It can take a while,' he says, 'to find what you want. I always tell people, you have to be patient. It's not as though we can make the world appear before you at the flick of a switch.'

'No, of course not.'

'But,' he says over his shoulder, as he leans over to shake the man at the next desk awake, 'I do find people often don't really understand what they're looking for until they start searching.'

With a few minutes left she flicks through the last book. *The Tide That Turned* is a collection of personal accounts of the Rising and the War of Independence. Assembled from interviews done in 1927, it was privately produced in 1947. Was the editor waiting for someone within its pages to die? she wonders. She skips through the first few chapters, each a whistle-stop tour of Easter week. *The Women of Marrowbone Lane* is the last in this section. A sentence zips past her like a bullet and she flicks back to the first page of the interview. She looks about quickly to check the librarian isn't hovering nearby, before giving the spine of the book a hard, flattening crack.

Chapter Ten - The Women of Marrowbone Lane
A personal account by Cumann na mBan Volunteer Eliza O'Mahony

Fighting inside four walls, that was our error in 1916. By the time it was a war, we knew better, make no mistake about it! A war should be fought in God's own open air, and spread out all round, not held in a number of fixed spots. I was stationed at Marrowbone Lane, under the command of Joe McGrath. He was a man I knew from working at Craig Gardner, the accountants in town, where I was after being a telephonist for two years. At first some of them didn't believe the surrender order that came a week into the Rising, they thought it was a forgery to lure us out into a trap. But we got word that it was real right enough and that Boland's Mill, Jacob's Biscuits, the South Dublin Union and the Green and ourselves were to lay down our arms, that there was after being parlay with the British to surrender. Joe McGrath told us to escape quick as we could. 'Toor a loo boys,' he turns to us, 'I'm off.' And away he goes! It was a Sunday I remember, there had been talk of a priest coming up later to say Mass and give us Communion. But never did he arrive.

We were marched through the streets, people outside and watching us pass by. We got the odd cheer to be sure, but mostly shouting and spits. There was rotten food and worse thrown at us. Dog's abuse they gave us, and us after trying to do nothing more than take our country back from the brutaliser of our people. The separation women were the worst of them, throwing the filth of their chamberpots at us and them bribed to send their husbands to be killed as King's soldiers!

The five-minute bell clangs. Eliza O'Mahony's account skips around in time, travelling from surrender backwards to the day she entered the Marrowbone Lane building, then forwards again to 1919 and beyond. Maria skims the rest of the page. Between the awkward shifts in time and her meandering writing style, Eliza O'Mahony is likely to bump into herself going backwards, slap-bang in the middle of 1921.

. . . and so there I was, stood at the window, watching down into the street and all I could hear was the clack-clack of gunfire in the city centre. It seemed to me at the time that I spent the entirety of Easter there. On the Monday, or maybe the Tuesday, we saw the Irish Times, *and it said that evilly disposed persons had disturbed the peace and that the situation was well in hand. Sinn Féin was after rising in Dublin, it said, and the rest of the country was quiet. It made it sound like nothing at all, but when you'd be out in the streets like I was, taking messages from one command to another, I heard a different story. It was a Bank Holiday weekend, you see, and people were coming back into the city and the story was getting told over and over and it getting stronger every time.*

What those rags that passed for newspapers wouldn't have told you is the bravery of the volunteers. We were all over them then, for the first few days at least. I witnessed some sights that would bring you tears of devotion. Here's one of them:

I was passing Stephen's Green on my way with a message to the Arts Club when I came across Johnny Murphy, a young lad whose mother was well known to us all. Some knew her by reputation and some by trade, if you get my inference. Johnny Murphy would have been no more than eleven or twelve at the time, and he swinging his revolver as well as any man. 'Liberty Hall's after been blown into smash,' he said. 'No!' went I, fearful because I had my mind set on a lad who I knew had been there the day afore. Liberty Hall was the heart of that week, despite how it's remembered. ''Twas empty though,' he told me. It was true, what he said, though it wasn't always easy to know what was true and what wasn't. All week long, rumours spewed around the city. Whichever way you turned, you got a new one. Countess Markievicz was arrested in George's Street and shot in Dublin Castle. The Germans had landed in Balbriggan. The Liffey is aflame. All sorts.

'Whatever man was your daddy would be proud to see you,' I said, knowing he'd square up to grown men twice his size, and that revolver huge in his hand. He'd walked the length of Lower Baggot Street in the valley of the roofs, he told me, looking the three floors down to the street and keeping his hand steady and pointed the whole time.

Near the end of the week I was sent on a message to the Cumann na mBan women in Camden Street. They were tending wounded who couldn't get any further out of the city. I had an order for them, so off I went over the walls and down the back laneway where the flower-sellers keep their barrows. It was dark and I tripped over a few times. Cats and dogs, I soon saw, is what was under my feet. Lumps of fur just left there on the pavement for us to fall over. There wasn't an animal left alive in all of Camden Street.

The house stank like a butcher's slab in summer. I gave over my message – an order to move out by the next morning and a new address to collect more billycans that had been made over into bombs – and was off about my business. I was walking up the road, glad to be outside in the air and feeling safe because it was so dark. I don't know how, but the boots of the soldiers were lost on me until I heard a shout and faces looming out of the dark! They began to shout, one or more running after me but I ducked into the side street. As I passed a doorway at Camden Market a hand reached out and pulled me into the porch! Jesus wept, I nearly died. 'Shut up,' whispered a woman's voice from next to me. 'We won't hurt you.' I stood quiet as a mouse until the commotion had passed over. I heard a soldier run past, then stop on the pavement. He couldn't have been more than a few feet away from me. I didn't dare breathe until I heard him curse and move on.

'Dear Jesus, you're just a child!' the second one said when she got a good look at me. It was a Cumann na mBan volunteer like myself next to me, her gun held by *her side. I was near on eighteen but looked closer to thirteen. 'I am not!' I said but realising all the time that she had saved my life. The cheek of her, I was thinking, she wasn't far off as small as myself. 'Who are you?' she said, realising we had the same uniform on. I nodded over towards the direction of Camden Street. The curtain was twitching. 'Eliza O'Mahony, I had to give a message.' 'What's the business at Stephen's Green?' she asked me next. Her voice was all mixed up. With one word she sounded as British as the soldiers, the next as Irish as myself. 'We're holding up good,' I said, thinking about young Johnny Murphy swinging his revolver like a man. 'Indeeden we are.'*

'We're doing it right, Tess,' the woman who had pulled me in said to her pal, and then she whispered to me, 'Go on, get out of here.' I didn't need to be told twice. This being the Thursday we'd had the best part of the week at war, and being quick on your feet is the best way to stay out of trouble. Just before I set off, 'What's your name?' I said to her.

'Lily,' she said. 'Lily Byrne.' I never saw her again, but during the war, in 1920 it must have been, I recalled her name and it was a source of further pride to me

'I'll take those from you.'

As if shoved through time by Eliza O'Mahony herself, Maria is propelled forward fifty years. She lands at a desk in the Reading Room. The one-minute bell is clanging, the library assistant's hands are extended.

'Yes, of course, I'm sorry,' she says, flustered. He takes the pile from her desk as she grabs *The Tide That Turned* from the reading stand and quickly gulps down the last few lines of Eliza's account.

> *because Lily was a clicker girl who took a British soldier down a lane that he never saw the end of. All blood runs red, I know, but blood spilt in the cause of Ireland is spring water when it falls on our scorched land, and long may it nourish us. God have mercy on our souls.*

CHAPTER FIFTEEN

I n the background is the familiar hum of an office. Maria hears the typewriters, shrill peals of other phones. Voices, an occasional laugh. She has no idea what the Public Record Office looks like, but she's sure that the woman's world must mirror her own. Right down to having its own version of Robert Ryan. 'Long death or short death?' the official asks.

'Pardon?' If only death were available in variants. She thinks of John, a non-death.

'The first name you enquired about died in 1962. Long death includes parents and next of kin, if known, and costs two and six, payable by postal order or cheque in advance. Short doesn't, and costs one and six. Long takes a week by post, short is two days if we receive your request by noon.'

Another hiding to nothing, Maria thinks. Eliza O'Mahony and her memories are buried, so whether the woman Eliza had met really *was* Tess McDermott, she will never know. Mrs Halpin refers to the dead as being safe in the arms of Our Lord and Maria imagines a white-bearded, white-robed figure with a tiny, garrulous Eliza O'Mahony perched on his knee, a single bony finger poking him in the chest.

'And the second woman?'

'We've no record of her at all, but that's not unusual. Thousands of records were destroyed when the Four Courts burnt down.'

Maria sits at her desk, her typewriter carriage empty in front of her. The words of the woman in Personnel who hired her rattle around in her head. *Essentially secretarial.* That's me, she thinks.

'Maria!' Dolores closes the door to Robert Ryan's office behind her. Her beige skirt is as figure-hugging as her beige jumper. And Dolores has, as Hilda has often commented, such an awful lot of figure to hug. Pale stockings and beige court shoes give an overall effect of an unexpected nudity. 'I've got one of my stomachs. Robert said you'd take care of this lot.'

'What lot?'

Dolores' hands are empty. Her nails are short, varnished a deep coral pink. 'Oh, look at me! Give us a mo.' She opens the door just wide enough to slip back inside. Maria can see that the blinds are almost closed. Thin slats of watery light run across the floor. His low rumble, beloved in homes around the country, is followed by a giggle and a 'Now now,' from Dolores. Chair castors squeak and groan.

'How could you not want to know the whole story?' Michael pouts and lights another cigarette. 'Spoilsport!'

'Yes, Maria.' Eve dunks her biscuit in her tea. They are in the canteen. Eve has insisted that Maria join them. 'What happened next?'

'Nothing. She came back.'

It was ten minutes later and Dolores was wearing one earring and her frosted hair listed to one side, but Maria decides not to mention this and just says, 'Then she gave me all her dictation and off she went.'

'Is that what they call it?' Michael sniggers.

Maria is surprised at his tone. 'You sound like you admire her for it!'

Eve dunks again. 'Why shouldn't we? She's getting what she wants, isn't she?'

'How on earth could he be what she wants?' Robert Ryan is round and rude and thinks secretaries are typewriters on legs. Machines, with keys waiting to be pressed.

Eve shrugs. 'Maybe she likes him. Even if she doesn't, maybe what she sees in him is getting time off whenever she wants, and she's having her own fun somewhere else.' Eve swishes a finger around the inside of her cup to scoop up the soggy crumbs.

'What age do you suppose she is?' Maria asks.

'Late thirties?' Eve guesses. 'Though she's still good-looking. And while we're sitting here, you can be sure Dolores is in Switzers café with her shoes off under the table and a magazine in her hands.'

'But that's . . .' Maria hesitates '. . . that's no better than selling herself.'

'So?' Eve licks her finger. 'Better to sell yourself than give yourself away for nothing.'

'Isn't he married?'

'Course he is.' Eve is burrowing about in the depths of her handbag. 'They all are.'

'Ahem,' Michael says.

'Present company excepted.'

A waitress clears the table, and as Maria rises to leave, Patrick looks up from a table of executives across the room. Eamon O'Mara is sitting to his right and she recognises the boredom in Patrick's fixed, neutral expression. 'Right, you two,' she says. 'I'm getting back to work. 1916 won't commemorate itself.'

'Do you know,' Michael grumbles, 'I think I preferred it when you stayed at your desk during break time.'

'I don't believe you.' Maria smiles at him.

'Quite right too.' He stubs out his cigarette. Eve closes her compact and snaps her bag shut. 'I'm going to phone Alicia to arrange our next outing. Bernie's going cold on me, I know she is. Won't you come with us, Maria? I need another person.'

'Eve, you know what I think about all that.'

'You could come along just to support me. You don't have to believe exactly what I believe to do that, do you?'

'I wish you'd let *me* go!'

Eve rolls her eyes at Michael. 'You can have a pint whenever you like. What's the point in having you with us?'

'I'd be showing my support!'

'You'd be finding someone to drink with, more like. Alicia would have my guts for garters if I showed up with a man in tow.'

'Maybe I should start my own campaign. A campaign to be allowed campaign with the campaign for pints. I bet you'd let me sign up then!'

'Maybe you should.' She laughs. 'Though it won't get you anywhere. You'll never break me down.'

'I think you're being very unfair.'

'Michael, honey,' Eve pats his hand, 'you don't know the meaning of the word.'

He slips his hand out from under hers and picks up his cigarette case. The movement is gentle yet quick. Maria remembers the note. Eve knows nothing about that day, about his tears. She can be so blinkered sometimes! Of course he understands: he knows what it means as well as she does. More so.

Maria returns to her office. She is less sure now about the objections she raised that night in the Chopstick. The image surprises her, but out of nowhere she thinks of links: links in a chain. Yet where that chain starts and ends she has no idea. Dolores' missing earring; every lipstick stain that Eve, Alicia, Bernie or Mary-Anne leaves behind on her glass; every time she speaks in a meeting and the committee look around for the source of the sound . . . they are all connected and she's beginning to believe that they all – somehow – matter. But if that's true, how can she continue to ignore them?

As before, the door opens silently and the thin face appears around the frame. She is pale today, with high spots of colour in both cheeks. 'It's yourself.' Tess coughs. 'I suppose you'd better come in for a minute.' She pads back down the hallway to the kitchen. The room seems fuller than the previous week, if that's possible. More papers, more sewing, more used teacups. Tess goes to put the kettle on the hob and Maria stares at the floor around and under the table. She swishes her foot about but the brooch is gone. Whether it has been removed or just buried in the general mess and detritus it is impossible to tell. Her foot nudges a book, some sort of hard-backed ledger with a dark marble-effect cover. A handwritten page protrudes from a foil-blocked edge and, written in a tidy copperplate script, the date *1909* is just visible.

'What are you doing down there?'

'Nothing! I mean, I dropped this.' Maria jumps up, holding her hankie. 'I noticed the curtains upstairs are closed.'

'The landlord was in this morning. He's the place cleared out – I've never known him move so fast. It's to be let again from next week. He has it in the *Evening Press* from tomorrow.'

'Did someone come to collect Mr Owens's belongings?'

Tess snorts. 'A cardboard box horsed up into the attic, that's where they've gone. I suppose you'll be wanting a cup of tea?'

'Thank you, yes. I've a few minutes before I've to get Anna.'

She tells Tess about Eve and her quest for a pint. About Alicia and her stubborn solidity.

'My, but that's a good one.' Tess sips from her cup. It's the colour of tea but doesn't smell like it. 'I'd say she makes those ratty old barmen go spare!'

Maria feels a childish flush of pride at making Tess laugh, at impressing her. 'It put me in mind of you and your hard-boiled eggs, Tess, only it's small fry, really, compared with being in the suffragettes.' Now that she is in her kitchen, feeling the restless energy that flows from Tess despite her size, she feels a desperate need to be worthy of her. To be a true inheritor of Tess's struggle. She wants it for Anna. She wants it, she understands suddenly, for herself.

'And your friends, they go all round the city? They'd do better to have a larger gang and pick a different few each time. That'd be the safer way, mark my words.'

'It's the city centre mainly. They've been out as far as

Blackrock, and I think Eve has plans for Drumcondra and that direction next month.'

'There was a woman I knew once, Nellie . . . She'd have been right in there, I'd say, swinging her fists around when she got refused her drink.'

'Was she in the suffragettes?' Tess had fought for something once, so why shouldn't she be able to make her understand that they are on the same side? Fighting for freedom, for women: it's all the same when it's the fight for the right to be the person you know you should be. Go on, Maria urges herself silently. This is why you're here. Be brave, for once.

'Or,' she takes a deep breath, 'was she in Cumann na mBan with you?'

Tess's jaw is set tight. 'You'd do right to remember what I told you before. I don't know what you're talking about.'

Her palms sweating, Maria persists: 'Did you meet a woman called Eliza O'Mahony in Camden Street during the Rising?'

'Never heard of her.'

'How about Lily Byrne?'

'Lily Byrne?' Tess's face pales, her tongue racing behind her cheeks. She stands up. 'Lily Byrne,' she repeats quietly. Maria rises, too, and they stand facing each other in the kitchen, their hands by their sides. War is different: isn't that what Peadar O'Brien told her? It has its own rules.

'I want you to leave,' Tess says. 'I'm not who you think I am.' She knots her hands together. Her ring is trapped on her finger; it slides up to the arthritic lump of her knuckle before falling down again. 'Don't be making me someone I'm not. My past is my business and, for the life of me, I don't know why *you* want to get hold of it. Fifty years since the Rising, who's to care? It's a number, it means nothing. The dead are dead. Grass grows over both sides equally.'

'But, Tess—'

'No!' Tess is walking down the hall to the front door. 'Now, for the last time, go away and leave me alone!'

Maria has failed again. Hot, angry tears come from the back of her eyes. She really believed that . . . What? That she had the power to force the truth out of Tess? That it would simply spill like clean water across that dishevelled kitchen?

Tess opens the front door. Foggy air is waiting outside. Secrets everywhere. Life is a straitjacket of secrets. She catches a last glimpse of her face as the door shuts. It is that of someone who knows how to fight a long fight. Who knows that it's not anger that wins battles, but tactics.

It is the face of a servant.

CHAPTER SIXTEEN

Anna stirs her cocoa first clockwise, then anti-clockwise, and says, 'You never told me I was named for a saint, Mummy.' Four twists each way: it has to be the same in both directions or it won't count and she'll have to start again. 'Ooh, whirlpool!'

'Most of us are in one way or another, there are so many saints. There's even a St Maria now.'

'Were you named for her?'

'No, I was named after my own grandmother who I never met. Maria Agnes Power, her name was. St Maria is a new saint.'

'St Anne's not new. She was Jesus's granny. Look.' Anna puts down her cup and takes *A Child's Treasury of the Saints and Martyrs* from her schoolbag. She raises the book as carefully as the parish priest in the Church of the Holy Name raises the sacrament. The cover illustration is of a beautiful young woman with tortured eyes and a soft blur of light around her dark hair. She has a lily in one hand and a sword in the other. 'Miss Thurston said I had permission to bring it home for the night. Wait,' as Maria reaches over to take the book, 'are your hands clean?'

'That was nice of her, and yes.'

'She says I haven't enough knowledge of the saints.'

'I see.' The book must be intended for the mother, not the child.

'If I die before my time, does that mean I won't get into Heaven?' Her face is troubled: a crease runs across her forehead.

Maria can read fear in her eyes, the bewilderment that comes with realising there are more doors in the world than can ever be opened. Maria takes her hands.

'Anna, that's just not true. Of course you will. You're a good, kind girl and that's what matters to God, not whether you know the names of saints.'

'Just say there's a test?'

'In school?'

'In Heaven.'

'There won't be. Heaven is for people who have done good things for each other, not people who only get high marks in tests.'

'Will Daddy be there?'

'All the good people will be there.' Maria hoists the child onto her lap. 'And I think you're the best person of all. What? Why are you upset?'

'You shouldn't say that, that you think I'm the best.'

'Why not? It's true.'

'It makes children get big-headed, to talk to them – I mean,' she shakes her head, confused, 'to me like that. Mrs Rogers said so to Mrs Helping, I heard her.'

Old biddies, Maria fumed inwardly. 'I had an aunt who used to talk that sort of rubbish. She claimed I'd get notions – delusions of grandeur, she called them – when my father told me I was doing good at my lessons.'

'And did you get the – what did you call them? – the lusions?'

'Delusions. No. And do you know why? Because she was wrong. Now, come on, show me the page with St Anne. I bet she's the smartest saint of the lot.'

'It's hard to be a saint. You have to be really, really holy and do good works when you die as well as when you're alive. Yes, sirree, Bob,' Anna whistles under her breath, her good humour restored, 'there's a lot of work in sainting. Miss Thurston said that being a nun is a great thing and any of us who are lucky enough to be chosen by God should be grateful for his calling.'

'Wanting to be a nun or a priest is called having a vocation. But, Anna, I think it's important to do whatever makes you happy.' She says it lightly, as though happiness is easily caught. As though it is anything other than a rare bird that flies high overhead.

'Mrs Helping's sister is a nun. Sister Helen, she's called, but everyone calls her Sister, not just Mrs Helping. She minds the black babies in the Missions. We're saving silver paper into a big ball for her.'

'What will she do with it?'

Anna considers. 'Maybe it's for the babies to play with.'

'Did you show Mrs Halpin the book?'

'Of course. This afternoon I read from St Anthony to St Eithne out loud without stopping.'

'That's a lot of saints.'

'Yes. My throat was parched but she said to offer it up.'

These words give Maria a pang. It is partly fear that she leaves her child with such an influence, and partly self-loathing that she leaves her at all. But what else is she to do? She can't not-work, because then she will have no money. Poverty would be a worse crime to inflict on Anna than Mrs Halpin's beliefs. This grandmotherly kitchen-sink style of care won't hurt Anna for ever, whereas poverty could destroy her.

The best thing is to face up to it and find someone else. Anna needs proper friends. Ones who aren't pensioners. Or cats. She has been avoiding it for far too long, ignoring every fresh Mrs Helping anecdote instead of using it to strengthen her resolve. Should have held out that time for someone younger with other children, she thinks, forgetting how desperate she was at the time. Just arrange it gently, she reasons, put an advertisement in the paper with Eve's address on it so Mrs Halpin won't suspect, should she spot it. Make it a smooth slide from the care of one to the next. Yes, that's the best way. Mrs Halpin is a good woman, and she's giving Anna the attention she would heap on her own grandchildren if only she could. Kindness in return is the very least she deserves.

'Mrs Helping told me she has a devotion to St Jude.' Anna shows her an illustration of a cross-looking, bearded man clutching a picture of Jesus to his chest. His eyes are black and flames flicker around his head. When she turns the page a Mr Onions *In Memoriam* card falls to the floor. She returns him to his page. 'She gave me this to mark the page. St Jude is the patron saint of lost causes.'

Maria crosses to the window. Its curtains are a warring couple: though a sharp pull reunites them, they quickly separate again. Condensation drips down the glass, falling in uneven lines around the greasy smears made by Anna's fingers. The paint on the frame is chipped, the wood damp where it has been exposed. She tugs the curtains anyway.

Redoubt Terrace is quiet at this time of the evening. She looks in the direction of number thirty-nine. The compulsion to uncover whatever Tess is hiding hasn't faded in the days since Tess threw her out of her house. If anything, it has burrowed under her skin. And how rude the woman was to her, too! If only she could have found the brooch on the floor. It would have made a liar of Tess, that's for sure. Maria puts her hands to her forehead and pushes the skin up and back. The grooves under her fingertips run deep as tram tracks. The touch of her own flesh feels unfamiliar; her hands are those of a stranger. Someone new has taken residence beneath her skin, someone she doesn't always recognise. 'What is happening to you, Maria Mills?' she mutters, yet immediately afterwards she's not sure whether she spoke the words aloud or not.

Out of the corner of her eye she notices a blur of movement on the pavement below. A shape standing in the fringes of a nearby streetlight moves away until it is swallowed by black. Dark hat, dark coat. He moved too quickly – impossible to tell who he was. She yanks the curtains again, harder this time, willing them to stay closed. It is springtime, yet she has the strangest sensation that the world is drawing in on her.

'Bedtime, Anna,' she says, trying to keep her voice steady. Anna carefully tucks in Mr Onions so he is face to face with St Jude, and when she closes the book the lips of the two men meet in a perfect dead kiss. 'Go and brush your teeth, love. Make sure to leave the bathroom door open.'

Her hands against the window, she cranes her head in both directions. Nothing. No one. *Stop it*, she tells herself. Everything is going fine. It's been seven months since London. Stop it.

But. The thought digs in and won't leave. *But*. There had been a man standing on the street outside the house. She is sure of it.

CHAPTER SEVENTEEN

She didn't get a wink, she'd swear, but the alarm that hauls her from a sweaty, disturbed sleep tells her otherwise. During the night she had padded to and fro from bed to window and back again. The moonlight fell in a pillar between the gap in the curtains and lit a translucent path across the room. There was nothing moving out in the inky blackness. The trees and their bone-thin branches were barely visible. The dense shape of next door's blue Austin drowsed peacefully under its tarpaulin. Even the dirty stop-out cats were home in their baskets, their dirty stop-out dreams flickering with mice soaked in cream. Standing at the window, Maria felt she was the only person still awake in the land. The only one alive in Ranelagh, in Dublin, in Ireland. The stout sky had thinned to a milky dawn when she'd left the window for the last time and climbed back into her bed. The touch of the sheet was so cold against her feet it could have been wet.

And then the Westclox shouts and the day begins.

Dolores doesn't appear that morning, and Robert donates

her work to Maria to do on top of her own. 'Here,' he says, 'get this lot sorted while I'm out.' And with that the housewives' choice runs his hands across his hair, eases his waistcoat over his paunch and is gone.

Her fingers fly across the typewriter, to and from her notebook, spin around the phone dial. The in-tray to the left of her typewriter diminishes as the out-tray increases. There is a 1916 Programmes Committee meeting this afternoon but the prospect of the working day leaking into home-time keeps the meeting tidy and focused. Patrick tells her before it starts that he plans to push them through the agenda, 'as though it's the single ladder out of a burning building'.

Eamon's concerns are aired and duly noted; Hugh's retorts are acknowledged and parried; Keith Kirwin is congratulated on getting another episode of *Easter Rebellion* successfully edited.

By the time the 1916 Committee rise to leave for their 1966 homes, another twenty pages of her notebook are ready to be typed up the following morning. 'We've really got the hang of this.' Patrick shoves his papers into an untidy stack. 'You and I.' He looks at sea, cast adrift by the unfamiliar cartography of his own emotions. Maria suspects he is used to living life in a line: this happens, then this. A, B, C.

'Yes.' She chooses to misunderstand his meaning. 'Four o'clock is a good time for a meeting.'

'Em, yes, I suppose so. Unfortunate that Robert couldn't make it. Where did you say he was?'

'I didn't, because I don't know.' Maria stacks cups and tucks chairs back under the table.

'Right, yes. I see,' he says, looking at her. His expression is one she recognises. It is that of a man who feels a jump inside him, a sensation that is sharp and unexpected, and all the more real for being so. He stands up from the table and flushes. 'Maria?'

'Yes?' She is distracted too, flustered by the thump of her own heart. Oh, Lord, she thinks. He's not going to? Is he?

But before he can there is a tap on the door. Eve's head appears. 'I'm heading off now. We're meeting Alicia at— Oh, hello, Patrick.'

'Oh, bugger,' he says. He's dropped his cigarettes under the table. 'Excuse me,' he mutters, though it's unclear whether he's excusing himself for swearing or in order to drop out of sight to pick them up. Maria moves to help him but Eve grabs her arm.

'Come on, we've to go.' She propels Maria out of the door, with a farewell over her shoulder as they go. The door shuts over a muffled 'Goodbye' from under the table.

'I've to pop home first,' Maria protests, only partly grateful for the distraction. 'I promised Anna I'd have tea with her. I'll catch up with you in town later on.'

Eve frowns. 'You're not going to back out, are you? I've a bad feeling again about Bernie. She was very vague when I dropped by her digs last night.'

'I said I'd be there.'

There is a tightness across her shoulders, brought on by a day at the typewriter and aggravated by the prospect of rushing to the bus. And there is something else she has to do. She's put it off too long already. It can't wait any longer.

'It's Maria.' Her lips are pursed to shout through the letterbox. 'Tess? I know you're there. Please answer.' The rectangle of the letterbox frames her view, like an oddly shaped television set. On this set, the picture is unmoving. The dusty shapes of the hallway, a faint sliver of light from the passageway that leads to the kitchen. The volume is turned down but the jaunty hum of music tells Maria that Tess is listening to the radio. The light disappears suddenly. The hall gets dimmer and dimmer and— 'What do you want now?' The door opens swiftly. 'Here to hound me again, are you? Leave me alone.' Tess is sweating. Her skin is the colour of blotting paper and her eyes are far back in her head.

'Tess?' As she looks at her, Tess's eyes begin to swim and the lids flutter.

'Tess!' Maria reaches in and grabs her arm just as Tess falls. She holds her awkwardly for a minute, half in and half outside the door. Tess has fainted, head back, mouth open. There is no weight in her. It's not much more than lifting Anna. Maria averts her eyes from the sight of her open jaws. It feels oddly prurient to be looking at Tess's exposed, broken teeth. The pink and scarlet lines of her narrow throat are more affecting, more disconcerting, than the grubby edges of the thin, old-fashioned bloomers that Maria notices when she lays her on the single bed in the front room of the house. Her forehead is hot to Maria's touch but she's shivering.

Maria piles all the blankets she can find on top of her and goes into the kitchen. There is a bottle of aspirin high on a shelf and she takes it, a mug full of salted water, a bowl and a cup of tea laced with a generous shot of whiskey into the bedroom. There seems to be only one pillow so she rolls up a blanket and packs it in behind Tess's head. Then she reaches down and lifts Tess up by the armpits as if she were picking up a toddler. A furred smell comes off her, sour milk and stale clothes.

'Here, rinse with this one first.' Tess winces as she swills the salted water. Maria asks, 'Shall I get the doctor?'

'No need.' It's a whisper. 'My throat's scarred, makes it worse. Be gone in a few days.' She sips the tea. Drops of sweat shine on her forehead and her bun is loose and greasy. 'I'll be fine.' She's lying back, facing the ceiling. Maria kneels next to her, her head bent. 'You go about your own business now, Maria Mills. I'm fine.'

'Let me stay with you, Tess. Please – just for a short while?'

Without turning her head, Tess reaches out and touches Maria's hand. 'I was thinking to myself after, what of it matters now?' She leans back again and closes her eyes. They are silent for a few minutes until Maria notices her breathing has got deeper and more regular. The whiskey and aspirin must be working. Maria looks at the fingers now wrapped around her own. From the knuckle to the nails they are the waxy white of old potatoes but from the knuckle down they are pink and warm. Her hands are the size of a child's. An exhausted, overworked child.

Maria's foot nudges something on the floor. *A Gentlewoman's Journal*, says the front, the debossed gold foil dull with age. She puts the notebook back but the veined marble pattern of the cover stares at her, willing her. *Go on*, it whispers, *you know you want to see what's hiding in here.*

Tess is fast asleep, her head fallen to one side. Maria's heart thuds as she takes up the book again, lifting it more carefully this time. The pages are thin, the ink faded. She opens the book at random, and kneeling next to Tess's bed, all propriety gone, begins to read.

She has no idea how much time has passed when Tess gives a twitch in her sleep. Her arm joggles Maria's hand and the book is sent thudding to the floor. Maria quickly kicks it away, embarrassed. Tess mutters but doesn't wake up. Maria looks at the thin figure bundled up under the covers and feels horribly ashamed. She should have stopped herself reading, but she hadn't. She should feel guilty. But she doesn't. She prods at the thought, as if it were a bruise, but there's nothing. No throb, no pain. It's incredible to think that this irritable, dishevelled pensioner is the same person as *that* girl: a young woman whose heart and spirit leapt up dancing from the pages.

She feels the itch of wanting to know more, and although she can never tell Tess what she's done, Maria feels both closer to her, and yet – tantalisingly – even further away. She gently tucks Tess's thin hand under the blanket. There are plenty more pages waiting to be read, but she is already late and can't take it up again. She stands. Time to go.

CHAPTER EIGHTEEN

The Whitechapel graveyard is as full as an emigrant's suitcase. Generations of London Irish for ever asleep together, packed in any old way. Her breath frosts in the cold of the death tenement. A row of houses share a back wall with this shabby end of the cemetery, a soot-barnacled terrace with a ragged gap in the middle where a wartime bomb must have stolen an entire house. Above ground the cemetery is empty, apart from the curate, John, herself and baby Francis in his white cot-coffin. The curate (Irish, of course, aren't they all?) has arranged the hasty burial in a quiet corner of the cemetery. He's not really meant to, he says. Strictly speaking, he's not permitted to officiate at a burial service for a baby who died like that. According to the teachings of the Church, the baby hasn't lived. Human rubbish, is that what you mean? Maria wanted to know and John tugged at her arm. Will she not be quiet? The curate skulks around shame-faced, he must be afraid the parish priest will jump out from behind a headstone, sharp-eyed and mean as a crow. A lot of them are like that. Lives lived as monuments to themselves.

She is leaning against an old gravestone and John stands to one side. Her back aches, the empty bag of her womb contracts. The barbed-wire sting in her breasts reminds her that her body has yet to learn that the baby it aches to feed will never be hungry. The stone is brutally cold and damp under her hand, but soft on the top and to the sides where a mantilla of green moss tumbles over it. The inscription is weathered and faded and she can't make out much, just the date *1854*, then further down, *beloved*. While the curate hurries through his few prayers, Maria stares dumbly up at the house to one side of the gap; it can't be more than thirty feet away. A young man at an upstairs window looks down. V-neck jumper over a shirt. Slicked hair shines like a halo as he stands still as a photograph. He has one hand raised. At first she thinks he is waving, an odd, half-finished salute, but then she realises he has one hand on the glass, his palm pressed firm.

With all her cracked heart she wishes she could be in that bedroom. Leaning into his back with one arm wrapped around him, her other hand inside his shirt and nothing else in her mind but the thought of the body underneath the fabric. To be sheltered from her own life by his and wanting nothing other than what was breathing hard against her. To be ignorant of the pathetic Irish woman cowering in the graveyard below.

As the curate reaches his hasty, embarrassed end, she looks at John but his head is turned away and she can't make out his face. Not being able to see him clearly makes her angry.

She can't tell if he, too, is burning up inside with pain and fear and rage: if he is only half breathing. His best suit is shiny as a bus conductor's from pressing. At the sight of the dry sheen of his lapel, a splinter of ice lodges itself in her heart. Deep and sharp it goes, as if shunted there by the Ice Queen herself. He has it, too, she knows. A coldness that froze black in him the moment he saw his dead son. Somewhere in the dark, scrubby bushes a cat taunts them with its awful baby-cry. Maria looks back up at the house. The man is gone.

She comes to with a jump. The side of her head hurts – she must have banged up against the window. Where is she? Has she missed her stop? She swipes at the condensation on the glass with her glove until the lights of the city centre resolve themselves into familiar buildings. Westmoreland Street, D'Olier Street. The windows are closed and the bus made airless by smoke. A ghostly face looks back at her. She was asleep for no more than a minute, though it feels like a year. Baby Francis is back once more in her private crypt and the effort of waking up fully is that of hauling a wreck from the ocean floor.

The rough fabric of the seat scratches her legs through her stockings as the bus bumps along O'Connell Street. She jolts down the stairs, wanting nothing more than to turn around and go home. To be able to slip into her bed next to Anna's and listen to her daughter's soft breath. To lie next to her as she owns the world in her sleep. As Anna skips up mountains and dances over enchanted lakes, pulling plumes of coloured water behind her like ribbons. As she spins so high on the Witch's Hat that she whirls off down the rainbow and the yellow-brick road. That is all Maria wants. To be next to that dream life and let the dark of the night take away her sins.

Nelson's Pillar looms ahead through the streetlights of O'Connell Street. Eve and the others will be waiting – and cross, for she is late – under Clerys' clock. It's cold and damp but it's Thursday and the payday money is willing to be spent. She wants to stop people and shout into their faces: *How do you not realise, how can you not know what suffering went on so that you and I could ramble around the city tonight, all equal in the demands we can put on those who govern these streets for us?*

Apart from a light burning high in the top floor of the photographer's studio next to O'Connell Bridge, the darkened shop façades are closed up so tightly it is impossible to believe they will open again in the morning. A wind whips off the Liffey. Nelson must be chilly up there, she thinks. Lonely on his high, grey perch.

'Here you are!' Eve is stamping her feet, cold and impatient. Alicia has one hand jammed in her pocket, the other cups her cigarette. She nods a hello. Maria hasn't seen her since the night of the Percy French.

'Am I late?'

'Everyone's late.' Eve is cross. 'We'll give the others five minutes, then go without them.' She is unusually edgy, irritable.

They watch as Mary-Anne makes her approach down the street from the direction of Parnell Square. Her skirt is too narrow for her to build up much speed, and her hobbled legs wrap wildly around each other with every step. 'Sorry, sorry,' she pants, as she stutters to a stop outside Clerys. 'And Bernie's not coming, she said to tell you.'

'Why not?' Eve looks furious. 'I knew she was up to something! She'll hear all about it, the next time I see her.'

'And you wonder why she didn't tell you herself?' Alicia's low, even voice is a rare sound. 'Doesn't matter, come on. Let's go.'

Mary-Anne links Maria's arm for the walk up to O'Connell Bridge. Eve and Alicia are ahead. Eve is gesticulating, one finger pointed in remonstration at an invisible Bernie. Maria sees the shrug of Alicia's shoulders inside her coat. She is tall, nearly half a head taller than Eve, and broad with it. Alicia looks strong and ready and fearless, and Maria wonders should she feel more nervous.

'I couldn't tell Eve this, but it's Bernie's chap. He won't let her.'

'Won't let her what? Out at all, or out with Eve?'

Mary-Anne's answer is swallowed by the rumble of voices that greet them as they turn into the Grenville Arms on Eden Quay. Maria remembers how it went the time before, and just watches Eve for her cue. Eve is pint this time. Alicia a double port'n'lem, Mary-Anne a brandy and red, Maria a snowball. Drink and out, back into the sudden cold, the Liffey-soaked air of the city centre. The barman curses them from a height but they are gone, four women walking quickly and alone, each slipping into the shadows behind the out-of-service buses on the quays. Her mind is so fogged by the past that she follows the others without paying much attention. They regroup on the far side of O'Connell Bridge. In the next pub Eve tells Maria to be pint. She's nervous asking, desperately tries to imitate Alicia's solid calm. It's a relief all the same, though, to be spared the alcohol of another drink. Alicia is pint in the third place. The 'hit', as Maria notices Eve now refers to it.

'Can we be finished now?' Maria asks, when the third place

is over and done with. But Eve's having none of it. She's still cross about Bernie. It's just the Robert Emmet on D'Olier Street to go to before they finish up, she insists. Maria's had enough. She wants to leave town. Look in on Tess quickly, then collect Anna and go home. She is about to cry off but Eve's mutinous face is enough to make her stay. All right, she thinks. Just the Robert Emmet, then I'm finished. Another twenty minutes.

Mary-Anne is pint but she's nervous, hesitant in asking for her drink.

'What's that?' The barman cups a hand behind his ear.

'Guinness,' she says, her voice faltering. 'Pint. Please. Of Guinness.'

He laughs, 'That's a good one,' and waits for her to ask for something else. She says nothing, just stands there looking at him.

'Go on,' Eve hisses.

Mary-Anne whispers, 'Please may I have a Guinness in a pint gla—'

'Oh, for Heaven's sake, Mary-Anne!' Eve pushes in front of her. 'She wants a pint of Guinness.' It's the set of Eve's jaw as much as the challenge in Alicia's expression that convinces him.

'She's not getting it.'

'She's the customer. Give her what she asked for.'

'Give her the back of my hand, more like. Get out,' he says, and in a quick swoop gathers up their untouched glasses. Mary-Anne has already backed away from the counter so the others have no choice but to follow her.

On the pavement outside Eve is furious. 'You've been pint before. You've seen it done plenty of times. What's wrong with you?' Eve waves her arms around. 'That was useless. Worse than useless. We're going somewhere else.'

'Can't we be finished now? That was the last one.'

'We're doing another. That was a waste of time. He didn't care less and nobody noticed.' It was true: the barman in the Robert Emmet hadn't appeared to care. As they left the bar Maria noticed him turn to a shelf next to the payphone where dirty glasses had piled up.

'Hurry up,' Eve says. 'We'll go across to Mullerys.' Mullerys is around the corner from the Star Cinema; it fills and empties to the tidal flow of the film times.

'Mullerys? But it's always packed in there,' Mary-Anne says weakly.

'Exactly! Alicia,' with a glare at Mary-Anne's downcast expression, 'you be pint again.' From Eve's face Maria can see that this matters to her even more than she'd known. The planning, the scheming: if Eve fails in this, she will feel the loss in so much more. They walk in silence around the corner. Mullerys public bar is a long narrow room, with stools down one wall and next to the bar. Mary-Anne is right: the bar is at least two people deep. They have to turn sideways and sidle up to the counter.

It goes smoothly this time. 'Snowball, please,' Maria says. It's easier to gulp down than the spirits. She rarely drinks, and Mr Owens Night, as she thinks of it, has made her even more cautious about alcohol. 'She'll have a brandy and red. Double. So will I,' Eve interrupts, and Maria lacks the nerve to overrule her. The barman nods and turns away. Her mouth is bitter with saliva at the prospect of having to knock back such a strong, burning drink. She watches him sluice brandy from the optic into her glass once, twice.

Alicia asks for Guinness, Beamish, Harp and finally McArdles before he loses patience and shouts at them to go. On Eve's command, Maria tilts her head back and pours the brandy and red down her throat. It rushes to her stomach and head at the same time and she feels the room spin. They turn to leave but the final movie of the night has ended and the pub is suddenly even busier. Last to leave, Maria bumps against a man's arm. His pint of stout joggles and a creamy slug jumps onto his overcoat.

'Sorry, sorry.' She's dizzy and rubs at the stranger's sleeve with her glove. 'It'll wipe off.' She sounds like Anna caught with her paw in the bread tin.

'Come *on!*' Alicia tugs her arm. She stumbles forward to the door that leads into the street lobby. She gives a quick glance behind her, down the empty path briefly created by their exit. A woman is standing next to the man whose arm she bumped, her head turned in the opposite direction. Her dress is tight and cherry red and her Custard Cream-coloured hair looks cast in plaster. The door swings closed behind them and Eve shouts, 'Christ! Run!'

'Christ with you, is he?' There are four gardaí, one for each of them.

'Only place you'll be running, my lady, is Pearse Street Station,' a voice says, and she realises it is no longer Alicia at her side. 'Come on.' Maria feels a rough tug at her arm. 'This way.' Maria thinks of Tess and her hard-boiled egg and she laughs. She doesn't mean to, doesn't know it's coming from her until she hears herself and recognises the sound. 'Funny now, is it?' he says. He is the same height as her, though looks younger. A piece of lint is stuck to the underside of his chin next to a jammy rash of spots.

'Let me tell you what's not funny, shall I?' He has a Cork accent that turns every line into a question. 'Theft. Now, how's about that? You're not laughing now, I'll be bound?' He half walks, half tugs her up the street. Eve and Alicia are ahead. Maria can hear sobs from Mary-Anne behind them.

'Hush yourself now,' Mary-Anne's garda is saying to her. 'You'll get no sympathy for that carry-on.'

'We're walking to the station?' Eve's voice is loud, pert.

'Got a problem with that?'

'I'd sooner get a taxi.' That bright-as-a-button tone is back in her voice. Does Eve not understand what's happened? Or, worse, does she not care?

The brandy has landed uneasily on top of the snowball. Maria swallows hard, willing it to stay down. Dear God, she thinks. What have we done?

They are under arrest.

CHAPTER NINETEEN

She walks the remaining fifty yards up Pearse Street to the garda station in acquiescent silence. *In, out, in, out.* It is all she can do to breathe.

They are brought in turn into a room to give their names, then told to sit on a bench the shape and colour of a church pew. The wood is scored by cigarette burns. They sit in a line under the bright, unforgiving white of the strip lighting. Mary-Anne is crying. Alicia is impassive, watching the desk and the large sergeant parked on a stool behind it. The desk runs the length of the wall and reaches to the height of his stomach. It is L-shaped and, like a child in a high-chair, as Eve whispers, he has to raise a hatch to get in and out.

'Quite like a bar here, too, isn't it?' Eve says, looking at the sergeant behind his counter. Her eyebrows are raised expectantly, as though she is impatient for a performance to begin.

Notices are pinned on all the walls. Driving licences and passports, missing pets and contraband. A statue of the Blessed Virgin has been pinched from the church of St

Nicholas of Myra Without; a hundred pounds stolen by masked raiders in Sandwith Street Credit Union. The criss-cross interchange of life, of greed and desperation, of want and loss, has been printed and pinned to the walls. Maria reads every poster in turn, breathing through each one in an effort to force calm on herself.

'Got a cigarette?' Alicia asks him.

'No,' he growls in return. 'You?' There is a faint smile on her lips as Alicia turns her head away. 'Theft is a serious business, girls,' he says. 'Do you need a drink that much? Do your husbands know you're at this?'

'I don't have a husband.' Mary-Anne sniffles.

'You're not likely to find one, neither. Sure what man would want a girl who'd only be after his pint?'

'It's not the pint, it's the right,' Eve says. Maria puts a warning hand on her arm. This is not the time for Eve's speech. 'No, Maria! Let me continue.' Eve pushes away her hand and straightens up, her back ramrod straight against the hard slats of the bench. 'We have a legitimate claim and want to be heard.'

'Do you now?' He snorts, but there is no humour in his laugh.

'Yes. We demand the right to order any drink we like, in any establishment we like.'

'You've no such right.'

'We have. We are citizens of this country and we demand our equal rights.'

'Now let me get this right.' He shakes his head. 'You girls are demanding *drink*?'

Maria puts her head in her hands. It sounds so ridiculous. To think of Tess in Holloway and the poor wretch she'd told her about who hanged herself with her own cape, and God knows who else, what else . . . hundreds, thousands of other women, other lives. Their dignity and spirit and the true fight they lived.

'We're demanding the right to drink,' Eve corrects him.

'You're thieves,' the garda corrects her, his voice flat.

'We're protesters,' Eve says. 'Protesting against the shameful patriarchal—'

'You're thieves,' he repeats and points at a poster on the wall. *Be Vigilant! Don't Let Persons Unknown to You into Your Home*, it says, above a picture of an elderly couple peering around a door. A thin chain cuts across their faces, like a grimace. 'You're no better than any of these here.'

'That's not true!' Eve cries.

'Yes,' Alicia interjects, her voice softer than Maria has heard it before. Eve turns to her, her mouth open. 'Yes,' she says again. 'We are thieves. And you know it, Eve.' Eve closes her mouth as Alicia turns to face the garda. 'We stole tonight and we stole last Thursday and pretty much every Thursday before that for months. I can give you a list: every public house we stole from, every drink we ordered and didn't pay for.'

'You *can*?' Eve squeaks but Alicia ignores her. 'And,' she continues, 'I will go and pay that debt in each place now and without complaint.'

'Will you indeed?'

'Yes. On the condition that I can ask for and receive a pint of beer in each place and be allowed drink it if I choose to do so.'

'You're in no place to be laying down conditions.'

Alicia produces a box from her pocket. 'Cigarette, Garda?'

'Sergeant Joyce.' He lifts the hatch in his desk and walks over to their bench. 'Stand up.'

Mary-Anne jumps to her feet and looks at the front door.

'You must be joking, Missy.' He smiles the smile of the victor. 'Didn't your friend here just admit you've a string of thefts behind you?' He lights a cigarette. 'Feckin' women,' he mutters, as he leads them to a large cell in the basement of the station. It's cold and grubby but empty. Which, he points out as he shuts the cell door, is probably for the good.

'Stop crying, Mary-Anne!' Eve snaps. 'You're driving me mad.'

'Leave her alone, Eve,' Alicia says. 'You got what you wanted, didn't you?'

'I never asked for us to be arrested!'

'Are you sure? You don't seem that bothered. It's sure to get into the newspapers. Isn't that what you wanted?'

'Well, the publicity will help, of course it will. Women all around the country will hear about it and do the same. I'm going to get cards with *Your Pint Is Our Right* printed on them for women to sign and leave in the pubs after a hit! You know, Alicia, this could inspire an entire—'

'Eve, here's a question. Can you explain how the gardaí knew where to find us?' Maria cuts across Eve's nonsense. She has been silent since the cell door closed behind them. Now she straightens up.

'What do you mean?' Eve says, stung.

'Those four gardaí standing outside Mullerys, as if they were waiting. You were hoping this would happen!' Maria is suddenly sure of it. What else was Eve going to do? Go to every pub in the city – in the country – one by one? It had to end somewhere, somehow. Maria is stunned that she's never thought of it before. Eve has gone out every week in the hope of getting them into trouble. 'Damn you, Eve,' Maria says.

'You didn't, Eve, did you? Was it you told the gardaí?' Mary-Anne whispers, wide-eyed and scared.

'*What?*' Eve shouts. 'Of course not! Why would I?'

'Alicia's right. You want the attention, to get publicity for your stupid campaign!' Maria jumps up, shouting just as loudly as Eve did. Almost immediately she sits down again, embarrassed. What are they like? They were nothing more than four fools scrapping for drink in a room full of bored, drunk men who aren't bothered by the whole thing anyway. That's the true right, she thinks. The choice *not* to be there, *not* to take part. The right to believe it doesn't matter. She looks at the floor. She's been such an idiot.

'You don't believe I wanted us to get arrested?' Eve says. 'Honestly?'

'I do believe it. You're using us to get attention because you know it's a joke otherwise, a few women making fools of themselves all over town every Thursday. And believe you me, Eve, there's nothing new in that. There's women making eejits of themselves in this city every night of the week.'

'For God's sake, Maria, you should hear yourself.'

'Calm down, the pair of you,' Alicia says.

Mary-Anne gulps. 'Bernie,' she says.

'What about her?' Eve rounds on her.

'The driver in the Swastika she's doing a line with. She told me not to tell you, Eve, but he wouldn't let her come out with us any more when she told him what we were doing.' So that was what Mary-Anne was muttering about earlier, Maria realises.

'She *told* him? Stupid fool, what did she do that for? She knew not to tell anyone.'

'He's her boyfriend. She's bound to tell him everything.' Mary-Anne finds a hankie up the sleeve of her cardigan and wipes her eyes.

'But nobody knew we were going to Mullerys tonight. I hadn't planned to. I only thought of it when we left the Robert Emmet.'

'The pubs were all too close.' Alicia shrugs. 'Anyone could have followed us from one to the next. We should have gone to Duke Street, Grafton Street even, rather than stay so close to the quays.'

'It was that barman,' Maria says quietly. 'I've just realised. When we left the Robert Emmet, he must have phoned other local places to tell them.'

'The nuns are going to eat me alive when they hear about this.' Mary-Anne is crying again. 'Sister Benedicta will send me up to the parish priest. I'll lose my job.'

'That'd be the best thing that could happen to you.' Alicia blows a smoke ring into the air.

'What are you talking about? I'll never get another.'

'Nor should you. You hate teaching. You're giving out about it every time I meet you. Just because your parents told you to be a teacher doesn't mean you have to be one. Do something else.'

'Like what?'

'Go abroad. Stay here.' Alicia replies. 'It's up to you. That's the point.'

'Stop worrying, Mary-Anne,' Eve snaps. 'You gave your name in Irish, didn't you? The nuns aren't likely to twig it's you, even if they do read about it.' Mary-Anne wails again and Eve looks slowly from one blank face to the next. '*What?* None of you?'

A key turns in the door. Sergeant Joyce is back. 'Any of you girls have to make a phone call? There's a phone by the desk, one call each.'

'Me.' Maria stands up. It's after ten o'clock – she's more than an hour late already. Eve nods too. Mary-Anne shakes her head, appalled at the very idea of telling anyone what's happened or where she is.

'Later maybe,' Alicia says, and lights another cigarette.

He smirks. 'There's no *later* in this place. It's now or never.'

'Never, then.'

The payphone is a dirty grey and stinks of stale breath. Maria imagines the dozens of false claims and threats, of misunderstandings, tears and confessions that must pour into its grimy mouthpiece every day.

'Mrs Halpin?'

'Molly, dear, I've told you enough times. Is everything all right?'

'No, not really.' As she begins to lie she feels her throat tighten. Pain contracts in her chest and she breathes quickly so that she won't weaken and cry, won't find herself honestly asking for the older woman's help. 'I'm with a friend, and she's had an accident. We're at the hospital.'

'Which one?'

'Um, Mary-Anne.'

'I meant, which hospital.'

'Oh . . . Jervis Street.'

'I know it well. It's where Mr Halpin went for his appendix. Is she all right?'

'She fell. They think her leg might be broken.'

'Poor dear, what happened?'

'She tripped over a loose paving stone. Just down from

Clerys.' Maria is warming to her story: the more real she can
make it sound the more she might come to believe it herself.
'And she landed badly on the kerb – you know where they're
putting in the new flower baskets? I've to stay with her while
she gets examined but it's going to take a while. I don't know
how long I'll be.' There is silence from the other end. A soft
clicking comes down the line, a faint cotton-wool hum of
static. Maria inhales the rancid smell of the handset and feels
it catch in her throat. 'She'll need an X-ray. I'm so sorry to ask
you this out of the blue, I really am.'

'Hurry up there.' Sergeant Joyce leans across the desk and
taps the side of the phone with a pen.

'Mrs Halpin? Please? Do you still have that room made up?
Could Anna stay for the night?' The sergeant gestures at her
to finish up the call. 'Mrs Halpin? I hope it's not too much
trouble? And sorry again—'

'Hurry up!' The sergeant leans over with one arm
outstretched as if he's going to take the receiver out of her
hand. Maria moves to the far side, pulling the cord with her.
He can't reach her now without coming out from behind the
desk. She turns her back to him and speaks as quickly as she
can. 'If I have to stay with my friend all night, can you bring
Anna to school?'

'Of course.'

'Is she asleep now?'

'She nodded off on the couch. I had her there under a
blanket to wait for you. Poor love, she was very tired. I've put
a bar on.'

'Will you give her a kiss from me in the morning and tell
her I'm really sorry and I'll see her tomorrow evening?'

'Accidents happen, it can't be helped.'

'I am really sorry, though.'

'It's not your fault. She'll be fine. Maria?'

'Yes?'

'Mind yourself, won't you?' She sounds concerned, but before Maria can say anything else, can lie her reassurances, the phone is pulled out of her hand. He replaces the receiver and Mrs Halpin's last words are trapped in the handset, now damp and smeared with tears.

Back in the cell, Mary-Anne has stopped crying and is hunched up on the bench, her hankie twisted around her fingers. She has her handbag on her arm, whether for the reassurance of her possessions or because she assumes they will be leaving soon, it's hard to tell. She is pale still, but seems calmer. Alicia is leaning back against the bench on the far side of the cell. Her legs are stretched out, crossed at the ankles. She has taken a paperback from her jacket pocket and is reading quietly. There's no picture on the front, just the title, *Island*. Eve takes a seat to one side and closes her eyes.

'Who did you phone?' Mary-Anne asks. 'Your digs?'

'Bernie.' Eve's eyes are still closed.

'I hope you didn't have a go at her,' Maria says, without looking up from the floor. She squints at the tiles. They have a slight glint in them, the glare of the strip lighting overhead reflecting tiny slivers of quartz. 'It's not her fault.'

'I know it's not,' Eve replies. 'It's mine.' Alicia closes her book and looks up. 'I'm sorry,' Eve says. 'You're right, all of you. I did want something to happen, something that would bring us attention, would make it all bigger and matter more. I've been calling it a campaign but it didn't feel important, the way I thought it would.' She opens her eyes. 'And, Maria,

I should never have gone on at you to come along. I'm sorry, I really am. It wasn't fair on you, what with Anna and all.'

Maria nods but doesn't speak, and Eve continues, 'Do you remember the time we went to the Chopstick?' How could she not? Those priests chewing their food in silence. The atmosphere that hung like a grey winter cloud over the street outside when they left. That sense that they were all trapped in a world that would never change and never wanted to change. And that sad, leaden feeling she has come to know well since: the feeling that it doesn't matter how many times the Rolling Stones might perform, or however much people might come to enjoy the fresh filth that pours daily from radios and televisions into their homes, or wear miniskirts or drink pints. It's all a carney, a merry-go-round. Just because the view shifts, moves around, doesn't mean it isn't always the same.

'I said it was a battle.' Eve's voice is heavy.

'Yes.'

'I pushed you into this one, and I'm sorry for it.'

Maria looks up finally. The tear tracks down Mary-Anne's cheeks are a tell-tale line in her face powder and put Maria in mind of Michael's face that afternoon months before.

'Eve, you also asked me if I wanted my daughter to grow up in a country where she's the equal of men. Where her existence is the thing that makes her their equal, not whether she's as able or as qualified or as anything else about her.'

Eve nods. 'And I didn't understand,' Maria continues. 'No, more than that, I didn't believe it could be the way you said. I thought that change just happened, that Anna and her generation would know differently and the world would move on, with or without us. I thought it wasn't about me, that it can't matter what I put my name to, because what can one person do anyway? What was meant to be would just be.' How stupid she was, she decides, to have abdicated responsibility for her daughter's adulthood in that way. To think that providing safety and food and a roof over her head would be enough, that the future would somehow take care of itself.

'Yes,' Eve says. 'I remember, course I do.'

Maria meets her friend's eyes, her own full of fresh tears, and says, 'I believe you now.'

Tess already understood the truth of this, she thinks, remembering the life she had secretly gulped down just hours before. Tess has the heart of a warrior and Maria is no more than a grubby thief, quietly pawing through her secrets. She had sat on the bed, guiltily reading and re-reading the diary, skipping over months, years, in her haste, until the room turned to ashes around her. Where had the world taken the other women Tess had written about, she wonders? The suffragettes and servants, and the girl who defiantly said of prison, *I will go when I have to*. The story is but one tide hitting a single beach: it is impossible to know the full span of the sea or the power of its reach.

She looks down at the floor tiles. The sparkles are refracting through her tears; a glittering world lies hidden beneath the floor. When she squints, her tears make the tiny lights glow stronger. The diary began when Tess was working in Cavendish Square, and Maria stares at the floor and tries to picture its stucco houses as Tess must have known them: glowing white and high as the cliffs of Dover, the sun winking through the vinegar-polished windows. She transports herself there, too, into the heart of Cavendish Square, her arms outstretched. She forces herself to stay there, in the grass, living Tess's life through her words. Because in this basement cell in Dublin she couldn't be further from it if she tried.

CHAPTER TWENTY

23 June 1906

Something queer was going on, down below in the Square. Through the window of Miss Celia's bedroom – every blasted inch of the glass polished by my own cracked hands – I could see something wasn't right. Women poured in like soup, only when they got to the middle of the Square they stopped & bunched up close to each other. I went back to my bedposts. Whatever man carved those lumps didn't give a flying fiddlers for the maid who'd be cleaning them, that's for sure. Lick & a promise'll be good enough for you lads today, I said to meself, & I gave them an almighty slap of my duster.

Our attics are always freezing, but even in summer the fires are kept lit in the family's bedrooms. No wonder the Master's rich – he'll not spend a farthing on the staff. I was sweating like a pig by then. I gave it my best Mrs Judge voice & said loud as I dared, Should you hinsist on referring to it Tess, then the term is glowing. Came out a treat for once, good as the real thing. Shame there was no one else to hear it. After the bedposts was the lacquered cabinet. A bugger to shine, that japanned furniture. I gave the front legs a good rub, the back ones can shift for themselves. My forehead got a swipe of the cloth too, it still smells of lavender & beeswax tonight. I always keep the cloth in my hand, so that if Herself appears around the door I can be wiping something double-quick.

I was half leaning against the window – that lavender smell always makes me want to stand still for a little minute – & I saw the blur of moving outside again. I don't like to look out too far through those windows, what with being four floors up. But whatever was going on was so queer I made myself. Thirty or forty women down there by now and me with only my own air muffling the glass for company. I tried to count, but I'm slow at the numbers compared to letters. Nanna used say that letters are lonely fellows but put them into words & they are all great company & carousing for each other.

My breath bounced back off the window & reminded me of the mesmerist at the Variety Palace last week. Lord but that was a thing to behold! The air going dark then filling with spirits! The haze of them! It was like a miracle. There were mutterings behind us that she'd gone and swallowed muslin & was spitting it out into the air. A likely story! How could she do that, & her in a trance? I wiped myself off the glass and saw a pair arrive in the Square with a bolt of material clutched upright between them. I imagined leaping into the air & landing in the heart of the flowerbeds & I don't know exactly what made me do it but I turned on my heel right then & there.

Mrs Judge nabbled me next to the pantry but I said I needed the privy for my time of the Month so she let me go on. Betty comes along then, so I goes come on Betty, there's something starting up in the Square! There was no budging her though, said Mrs Judge would give us our suitcases on the spot if she caught us blah blah & on & on. That's Betty for you, too thick to know what's good for her. I shouldn't have writ that, Betty's my friend it's not like I got many of them.

Shawl over my head, I fell in behind two women at the back of the crowd. They looked at me all cautious first, but then they smiled I nodded back, friendly-like. When I don't know a person I won't smile in case I open my mouth too wide. The older of the two women was all pelerine & swanky hat, & what a hat! Purple & trimmed right round with lavender lace. A lace bow trailed down her back & swung like a kite tail. Imagine having that much lace to spare!

I stayed close behind Mrs Lavender Lace & we all shuffled forward as far as the pavement outside the grandest house in the Square. A chit of a girl no more than myself in a dress the colour of Miss Celia's emeralds dark purple hat ran up the steps to the front door. She looked like a bunch of violets. She hauled the bell-pull till the pavement fair clanged with the noise. As the peals died off, the sound of the bell sort of hung over our heads. Miss Billington & her friend unfurled the bolt of material taut over their heads. There was words on it, I could see the backwards shadow of the letters. That tensed everyone up, & they stood square, shoulder to shoulder, & me behind them. Even the babies gave over

their grizzling. The Butler opened the door. He didn't
turn to face the women straight away because someone in
the hallway behind was talking to him. Lady Asquith! &
her bent over, talking to a tot dressed like a man. Some
elbow grease had gone into her riding habit let me say.
A nurse hung about behind, waiting to take the boy out.
All at once the butler, the nurse, Lady Asquith & the boy
looked up. Votes for women, shouted Miss Billington.
Votes for women, screamed the women. Waaah, cried
the babies. Mother of Divine Jesus! went I.

The little boy-man's mouth fell open & the door got
slammed shut. Next – this was some Experience, & no
mistake – an Inspector appeared from nowhere & told
Miss Billington to sling her hook. All puffed-up with
himself he was & he had four Constables trotting behind
him like roast potatoes tucked around a joint. There's
no meetings allowed in the Square sneers Bucko to Miss
Billington & he'll have to take her in charge if she won't
clear off right this minute! Oh, goes she, that's very well
then, I am quite willing to be taken in charge. There
was something to her voice, you'd follow it anywhere. A
lardy Constable grabbed the banner but she held tight.
To & fro they reeled, but Fatty was no dancer. It took
three of them to move her, she turned herself to a lead
bolster in their hands. One clamped his greasy paw over
her face. Sweat came out on my spine just to see it, those
dirty hands on her mouth. I hid behind a tree as she was
dragged out of the Square & the biggest potato of the
lot shouted at everyone to be gone or he'd arrest the
bloody lot of us. But the Votes For Women! started up
again somehow & suddenly the banner was up high, the

bell was pulled again. A woman I heard named as Annie Kenny appeared & started the shouting again. She'd a voice that reminded me of the time Betty dropped a tray of crockery on the scullery floor.

More Constables tipped into the Square. The first woman they grabbed a hold of was pulled off the ground by the hair & given a slap across the face. That's for nothing so don't start, he sneered. Jesus, but I felt it with her, right into my bones. Her with a babby in arms too! Everyone ran in a thousand directions at once. I saw one woman, brown as a monkey-nut & with the arms of a washerwoman, land a policeman a real hook to the jaw. The Constable grabbed her but she kicked back till he couldn't hold her anymore & she ran off, spitting at him! Annie Kenny got pulled away, her arms pinned behind her till her shoulders must have cracked. Quick then, goes I to myself, move it girl or you'll have more than Mrs Judge to answer to. I legged it as far as the turn onto Clyde Street only who did I see at the far end but Miss Billington & two Constables & her fighting all the while! It brought tears to my eyes to see her struggling still, no more than if she was a terrier in a sack.

What you standing around for? a voice went. Don't you know the police don't care who they take a hold of? I jumped fair out of my skin. She had a maid's uniform on, same as me. Said they're all suffragettes didn't I know, like I was a halfwit. Cheek of her. She ran off then, calling over her shoulder that I'd know them from now on. We're the enemy, she said & she grinned at me.

Huge houses face onto Cavendish Square and I noticed then that on all four sides people were staring out of the bedroom windows. Like they were portraits of servants, stacked into rows & columns behind the leaded panes. Footmen, maids in dark uniforms & mob caps. Look at the cut of all of you, I thought to myself. Trapped crows, beating your wings against the glass. Then I had a worse thought, one that made me boil like a kettle, & it was this: I'm one of them! I'm a prisoner & I polish the windows of my very own cell.

Sweat was after pouring down me when I got back to the House & sneaked back upstairs. The carpets were waiting on the Chivers, the bedclothes begging to be shook, those buggering bedposts whining to be polished. Sod you all, I said. Back upstairs I stood full at the window & stared into the Square only it was empty as a widow's purse. & then I spotted the lavender hat. The pretty ribbon was ripped clean off & the lace was all a-tatter, bloody with summer dew.

7 November 1906

All evening Mrs Judge kept me busier than a one-eyed cat with 2 mouseholes to watch, yet now that I've made it as far as my bed I won't sleep. It's too noisy, what with Betty thundering away next to me like a pig in a pen. I've decided instead that I'm going to write the Happenings of This Afternoon in full, which will be a full explanation of hows I came about this cutting from the *London Evening News*.

Mrs Judge went spare when I reappeared that morning in the summer. She relieved me of seven sorts of shite for time-wasting-&-what-have-you, telling me my contango was coming. If I knew what that meant I might agree with her. I'm not thick though, so I kept my head down, did my work quiet & that was it for months. Yes Ma'am, yes Miss, yes Sir. Yes, Yes, bloody Yes.

It was our Half-Day today, so me & Betty headed out to the matinee in the Old Mo' on Drury Lane (Marie Dainton, then a chorus, then that fat female impersonator who sweats like a basted turkey). Betty was hankering to wait at the stage door. You're off your onion, I goes. Give us that page, I goes, & I'll write any autograph you like! But she's stubborn Betty, so I left her to it & walked towards Oxford Street. It was chilly but it kills me to go back to the House before I have to, so I was swanking at the hats in the shop windows when all of a sudden there was a tug on my arm & Oi! Remember me? I do for sure, replied I. You're the enemy. The girl pointed at the window of the gentlemen's outfitters next door & goes, Not your enemy, daftie, them next door. Ah, I says, I've got it now. Gave you your marching orders, did they? Course not, she goes. It's the MEN who shop there are the trouble, not the shop. Then she goes, Do you really not know about us suffragettes? We aren't allowed talk politics in the servants' hall but I pick up bits & bobs from newspapers when I'm lighting the fires. I thought suffragettes & suffragists were the same but she said that suffragists are all talk & it's the suffragettes who act.

Well, I've always been of a curious disposition. Nosy, some might say, so when she said let's go for a cuppa in the ABC at Oxford Circus I said rightio. I was bored was the truth of it, & the damp air was getting in on my chest. I'd nowhere to go till six, so why not? My body was itching inside my skin, like I was grown too big for my own wrappings. Minnie Craggs – such is what her name turned out to be – is a general with a Dr Morrison in Mortimer Street. He treats her very nice, she says. Good pay, a Half-Day every week & a full day every month. She lives out, goes by the Underground every day. The thought of those dark pits makes me shudder & I said as much. She said it was all right, if you keep your wits about you. Men with long arms & loose fingers down there, & she nodded towards her Downstairs Parts & said as how she's got sharp elbows. My face went scarlet!

After that day in the Square, Miss Billington & Miss Kenny were up in court, Minnie told me. Tenner fine each for assaulting the police. I'd be a long time putting my hands to that sum! Miss Billington is back inside now, with ten days left to go.

The memory of her struggling body jumped before my eyes so quick it must have been waiting just behind them. An ape's paw clapped over that pretty face & those grimy fingers touching her lips. But we won't pay fines, says Minnie & I gave a splutter: WE! Christ's blood. Have you been in prison, I asked her, but she said not yet. Her ma is sick & made Minnie promise to keep her nose clean till she's well again. Stands to reason. One of them has to earn.

I wondered if I looked like I didn't believe her, because what she said next sounded angry & it was this: I will go when I have to. You're an odd one, I thought. Most people want to stay out of prison, not go hurling themselves at it. She said the Women's Social & Political Union – I think that's what she called it – meet every Wednesday at four in the upstairs room of the ABC. They call it a women's social so they don't get chucked out. She took a tatty piece of newspaper & said Emmeline Pethick-Lawrence who wrote it could talk the coins out of your pocket. It was folded into a small square & the edges were all jagged: 'The struggle has begun. It is a life & death struggle. We appeal to none but women to rise up & fight by our side, shoulder to shoulder . . . We are not sorry for ourselves – the harder the fight, the better. What we are going to get is a great revolt of the women against their subjection of body & mind to men.' I've to be up for the fires in four hours. I meant just to tuck the cutting between the pages only I couldn't stop myself copying out the words with my own ink. I wanted them for myself; my own letters in my own hand. We share them now, me & Miss P.-L., whoever she is. Miss Billington must too. Are the letter-friends from the newspaper floating above her head, keeping her safe in the dark of Holloway Gaol? I hope so. God bless you, Miss Billington.

1 January 1907

Holy Mother of Divine, but that was a long one. I'm wiped as a rag. A dozen for dinner tonight & when it was finished the men took off for the billiards room quick as if they were trots & it was the privy. We could hear them braying from the servants' hall. There's a fog of cigar on my uniform still, all woody & sweet, as though there's a man hidden under the bed. Betty was horrified at the notion, even poked her head under for a look, daft thing.

Betty has this folding picture case & every night she
kisses goodnight to the photograph inside then tucks it
under her pillow. She does it all secretive-like but as if
she wants me to know. Ma's anniversary today, she said,
her old moon face all wobbly. I've asked her before not to
show it to me, but she kept at me to have a gander. If you
hinsist, I said in my Mrs Judge voice by way of reply &
took it out of her hand. Well, the cut of Baby Betty isn't
to be believed! She was by herself & squatting on top of a
wide chair that went up in a point at the back like a Red
Indian's Wigwam. The fabric had a pattern of fat flowers
& leaves, as good as being attacked by Regent's Park. Is
that you as a little one? I said, trying not to giggle at my
own cheek.

She patted her baby self on her solid, roundy head. Her
first birthday, she goes, & I let loose a splutter, thinking
she was going to say she was three, the size of her. That's
me & Mam together, God have mercy on her soul, she
says, dipping her head.

Here now, Betty, went I, what are you going on about?
For she was propped up on the settle alone, rammed
between two bolsters covered in flowers.

Wasn't her ma hidden under the blanket! The paraffin
Betty rubs into her hands left a smear on the glass & so
she wiped it against her apron. What? she goes, seeing
my face. Do you not have pictures of yourselves in
Ireland? Not with our ma hiding underneath us, said I,
& I took the picture from her paws again. Sure enough,
weren't two tiny feet sticking out from the Wigwam!
Betty's mother, hidden under a shawl, & Betty sitting
on her like she was a chair. I'd got paraffin on my hands

too, so I used the end of Betty's shawl to wipe it off. Imagine all Betty's family made into a room of furniture-people! All covered up & waiting for her arse to settle on them. Grannies bent over into beds, uncles & aunties shaped into kitchen chairs, her da a table for her to lean her chubby elbows on . . . I don't have a Father as you well know, she goes, very short with me. She grabbed the case & snapped it closed. Back with it under the pillow & her own head on the top. The Baby-Betty-pillow-Big-Betty sandwich made, she turned away & faced the empty grate. Nighty night, Baby Betty, I goes, but she ignored me.

I put myself to bed then too. I can't sleep though. My feet are ringing with tiredness & cold & my eyes are still stinging from the cigars. I feel bad now about being mean to Betty & her so lonely, I can see it in her.

There's the chimes! It's two in the morning in the 1st day of 1907. The 1st day of another year in this attic with Betty. What will happen? Nothing I suppose, same as the other years. Holy Mother but the thought of another same year as the last . . . I feel the blue devils themselves drop onto my shoulders. I asked Miss Celia the other day about the suffragettes, turns out she knows all about them & follows their doings in the newspapers even though the Master told her he'll horsewhip any woman in his family who gets involved with those dummy-mondames whatever that means. I haven't seen that Minnie Craggs again, but I hope I do because I've never got Miss Billington out of my mind. I did try tell Betty about it all, but she's not bothered. She don't want a vote, she says. Wouldn't know what to vote for.

Mrs Judge gave all us maids that new English Hymnal for our Christmas box. We're to occupy ourselves by reading hymns. Might as well be dancing with your ankles tied together. You got to be accepting of your lot in life, Tess Keating, she goes to me. I nodded & yes-Mrs-Judged, but what was in my mind all the rest of the day and since then is this: why? Why do I?

CHAPTER TWENTY-ONE

The trudge home from Pearse Street garda station took the last of Maria's strength but she couldn't bear not to walk, not to be out on the wingspan of the world.

And then with one whisper, one word, everything is over. The tick that has been living under her skin for so long, gorging itself on her blood, swells and bursts.

That word is her name. He has it in his mouth, is holding it, rolling his tongue around it.

She stops, one gloved hand on the railings of the house next to Mrs Halpin's. *Muh-reee-aah.* The same sweetness he used to give it, always, once upon a time. It wasn't loud, either. He must be close behind.

She looks at the black railings and slowly, carefully, drops her arm back to her side. Just yards ahead of her is Mrs Halpin's gate, and on the other side of it, her path, and at the end of the path, her clean front door. And behind the door: *Anna*. Anna and Mrs Halpin chatting, drinking tea, eating toast and marmalade. Anna, crumpled from sleep. Sure to be worried about her mother yet excited, too, to be having breakfast with Chuzzlewit, to have woken up in her vest and pants rather than her nightie, in a strange bed in a room other than their own.

Maria stares at the fine hoarfrost that lies across the bushes next to the gate. The world is sugar-coated.

'I said, good morning, Maria.' Maria has been awake for twenty-four hours yet her exhaustion, which seconds ago had been so complete – she'd felt like the very marrow of her bones had been sucked out in the night – sluices away in seconds. His accent is sharp as a sack of knives after all these months spent with cushioned Irish voices. She knows if she turns around the words will be there, hawed from his breath and gleaming like daggers in the cold March air.

So. This is how it is to happen. She swallows hard. Alongside the charge of fear is something else: *relief*. Relief that there is to be no more wondering. No more worrying or fretting about odd noises or shadows on the street. And now, she thinks, that other life will begin all over again.

Black overcoat, no hat. How handsome he is still! He's the same height as her, his looks the compact, sinewy sort. A crest of dark hair is greased back into a high wave above his forehead. He is thinner but it looks right on him; his cheekbones are high in his wolfish face. She wonders does his skin still taste of yeasty beer, fresh sweat and his own distinctive bitter-lemon tang.

'Tut tut, Maria.' He shakes his head from side to side without lifting his eyes from her. He smirks at the shock on her face, at her trembling lips. 'Isn't that a fine way to treat your husband?'

CHAPTER TWENTY-TWO

The connecting door to Robert's office is open; the room is empty, as is the office she shares with Dolores. Maria is made of lead. She has become a mechanical soldier, her limbs controlled by a key in her back. Her mind skitters about, desperate to land on something, on anything. She lowers herself onto the sofa. Her head falls down towards her lap, and she bends over as though broken in half. It's the first time she's sat here. She remembers Eve pointing the sofa out to her with a wink: Robert had asked that it be 'procured', as he put it.

She isn't even aware that she's swaying to and fro in the same gentle rocking movement she makes when she comforts Anna after a fall. An unholy screeching, the desperate, grasping wails of banshees, has been let loose inside her and she doesn't know how she will ever make it stop. Even though she is finally alone, she has to force herself to keep the noise inside. But it is not a good silence: it is the quiet that occurs just after Anna has fallen but before she registers how badly she has hurt herself. The longer the pause, the louder the scream that follows.

'So it was bad, then?' The words come to her on a waft of Miss Dior perfume and the sticky lacquer of Aqua Net hairspray. Dolores. She shuts the door and sits down beside her.

'What?' Maria doesn't lift her head. The effort to expel even this one word feels too much.

'I was there, I saw you.'

What on earth was Dolores doing on Redoubt Terrace this morning? 'You were *there*?' That doesn't make any sense.

'Yes. I followed you outside.'

'Followed me? But why?' Maria shakes her head as if to rid herself of her confusion. Her brain is a soda siphon that has been fizzed up until it's ready to explode.

'Fair play to you all.' When Dolores smiles, tiny off-white pearls peep through the plumped-up pink of her lips. 'I said as much to my friend.'

You all? She means *last night*. Thank God. Maria pushes her hair back, blinking as her palm brushes across her sore eyes. 'You saw us? In Mullerys?'

Dolores looks puzzled at the evident relief in Maria's voice and leans back against the cardinal velvet of the sofa. She crosses her legs and waits, a dowager beauty queen. 'We were in there after the pictures. Saw the whole thing. You're a dark horse, Maria Mills, and that's for sure! What else have you got up that sleeve of yours?' She half turns on the sofa so that they are almost facing each other, their knees just touching. Dolores' knees are broader than Maria's, her legs stronger-looking. She stares at Maria's face without speaking. She must see the seam of fear running deep inside her eyes because she frowns and says, 'Wait a second.' She returns from Robert's office with two cut-glass tumblers. 'Any port in a storm, I always say.'

'Port?' Maria says weakly, exhausted and still suffering from the spirits she'd had to drink the night before.

'Gin, in this case,' Dolores says. The edges of the glass feel solid in Maria's hand. She knows that if she pressed hard enough she could shatter it, could create a hurt in herself. She could own her pain, if she chose to. From her desk drawer Dolores takes a key to the office and locks the door to the corridor. 'This isn't one of Robert's interviews, Maria. If you want to tell me what's going on, then do. If you don't, don't.'

Maria does.

At no point in the story does Dolores look surprised, which Maria finds surprising in itself. And maybe that is why she tells her all of it. How she used to believe this life of hers started with Francis, with his slow birth and his quick death, but now she realises it had started long before that; she just couldn't see it because it was familiar to her, because she had learned to expect no more from her life. John didn't get handy with his fists exactly, nothing so *deliberate*. He got careless around her. Quick to anger, hard to calm. And he'd be so sorry afterwards, so penitent, whimpering for her forgiveness, like a pup who's done wrong but doesn't know any better. Then, a year after Francis: Anna. The sunbeam in a storm. So much can be overlooked, ignored, with a single glimpse inside the pram. Maria felt as though she were living in the cradle herself and looking up at the world fresh, through Anna's eyes. She was lost to the enchanted spell Anna's birth cast over her. And when you do that, it's easy to avoid the knotted, thorny adult world. That was when the fists had come a-calling. Not often ('Shouldn't once be enough?' Dolores murmurs), but where there's one dig there's always more, when the fist gets used to giving them. Easier to give. Easier to take, too, if you let them.

'And I let them,' Maria adds, her fingertips hard against the cut-glass. 'He told me once that I was the put-up-and-shut-up sort, and he was right. I was.' Losing Francis was her fault. She didn't know why or how, but she believed it. They both believed it, she was sure. It had to have been her fault. How could it have been otherwise? She was his mother; her job was to keep him safe. 'And then . . .' Maria hears herself relating the tale in the way Anna would tell a fairy tale. 'And then . . .' She pauses, wondering how she will know when she is at the last page. 'It wasn't about me, it wasn't something I could hide to myself any more.' Her words begin to slow down. 'She was only five – he'd have taken her childhood away from her. He'd have hurt her to get at me. I couldn't allow it, I just couldn't. He used to stay out very late, sometimes be away nights at a time by then, so it was easy to pack and go.'

'And he didn't know you'd moved to Dublin?'

'No one did. Even when I lived in Ireland, it was never in Dublin. John hadn't ever been here, and in the ten years I was gone I'd never bothered to come back once, what with having no proper family.'

She had left a note. Aunt Josephine Power had sent them the fare to the States, she'd told him. Josephine had been in Chicago the best part of twenty years, but had just turned seventy and was looking for help and companionship. 'I wasn't even sure he'd bother to look for us at all. And he'd no reason to come searching in Dublin.'

There are no what-ifs, no but-how-could-yous with

Dolores. She accepts what she hears. The words are just themselves. Dolores has no value to put on anybody's story, no judgements to make. Maria swallows the rest of her gin.

'Aren't you annoyed with me for lying to you all?' Maria asks. 'I expected people to be angry with me if they found out because I've been lying to you since the day I walked in the door. Or if not angry then at least feel so wrong-footed that no one would want to talk to me.'

Dolores shrugs. 'Why would I? As far as I'm concerned, it's your life. Do with it as you will. There's enough people out there dying to roll out your life, like it's a bolt of fabric. But your story isn't mine to unravel, no more than mine is yours. It is as it is.'

'Yes.' Maria stares at her.

'So you decided to say he was dead?' Dolores understands. Better a widow than a faithless wife. 'And Anna?'

'She's happier with a dead father who, I've persuaded her, she remembers she loved and who loved her. While he's dead, love can't change. He's more harm to her alive than dead.' She has never said these words aloud before. Maria has tried to teach her daughter honesty, yet their life is built on a lie. Her head drops to her chest again. This is her truth. There can be no undoing it. She has failed, completely and utterly. The warm current of Robert's gin has spread around her empty stomach and called up the memory of the drinks she knocked back last night. Of the pubs and the spilt beer and sticky glasses of spirits. Of sweat and cigarettes and cheap perfume. Men and women chasing happiness in the gaze of a stranger, not knowing or caring that the whole business is being conducted on the hire purchase.

'Dolores, I've done a terrible thing to Anna – will she grow up to hate me for it? Have I pretended it was all for her when it was about myself?'

'The second question only you can answer. As to the first, well, you didn't exist as a person before you had her. That's how she sees it – it's how we all see our parents. But you are her world and she is yours. Elastics stretch but they don't break. Where is he now?'

'He said he had some business to see to, apart from us. It's the sort of thing he always says. I was too shocked at the sight of him to ask anything else. He was acting strange, jittery. He's coming back this evening.'

Maria thinks of the box she made into a doll's house. The life she has tried to make has turned out as flimsy. No matter how she cuts and shapes and decorates it, there is no disguising how fragile, how exposed, it really is.

The handle on the door to the corridor rattles. 'What?' Dolores calls out.

'Messenger.'

'Busy,' she shouts, and when the handle continues to joggle up and down, she calls again, 'You heard. Beat it.' The handle falls still and an envelope addressed to the 1916 Programmes Committee slowly appears under the door.

Maria groans and pulls her hands through her hair.

'I'm going to be sacked, aren't I? Word must be out by now. What'll become of us? Theft is what the garda said we're to be –' she gulps '– charged with.'

'The barman said he'd never seen you before but he got a phone call to keep an eye out. I asked him after the fuss died down. "A group of women on the rampage", was how he put it.'

'That's what it will seem like to everyone. But it wasn't like that. It's not the pint, it's the . . .' She realises what she was about to say. 'Nothing. It's nothing.'

'What did you think would happen?'

'I didn't think. That's the problem.' It's so hard to explain. 'I wouldn't have any part of it for ages when Eve first explained it to me. She brought me along one time without warning me what it was about, and I was so annoyed that I said I'd never go again. But last night . . . I don't know, I wanted to show Eve that I'm on her side. That I believed her. I decided it couldn't be bad when it was for good overall.'

'I understand.' Dolores puts out a hand and gently pushes Maria's hair back behind her ears. Two pearlised bracelets bump gently against each other, their sound as soft as a caress. Maria wants to lean into her hand, to shelter in that strong palm until the storm is over. She closes her eyes.

'There are lots of ways to get what you want, Maria. That can be the easy part. Understanding in yourself what it is that you want, well,' she smiles, 'that's more difficult. Plenty of people think Robert Ryan's personality is as bitter as his gin, but I choose to think otherwise.'

Tears spill down Maria's face.

'The world's not black and white.' Dolores stands up.

'Not even in television?' Maria wipes her sleeve across her face.

'*Especially* not in television.' Dolores' smile is gentle. Her skirt has ruched up so she reaches behind and runs her palms down the curves of her bottom and thighs. There is an unselfconscious power to her that is hypnotic. 'Why don't you finish your drink, then rest here for a while? I'll lock the door behind me.'

'No, I can't. Anna is with me. I was too scared to let her go to school today or stay with Mrs Halpin, in case he came back early and found where Mrs Halpin lives. She'd get the fright of her life if she saw him.'

Dolores looks around as though waiting for Anna to pop out from inside a drawer or leap from the top of a stack of filing cabinets.

'Michael's teaching her card tricks in the copy room. He said he wouldn't let her out of his sight,' Maria says. 'I told them Mrs Halpin is sick and her school is closed because the heating broke down again.' She heaves her aching body off the sofa. 'I'd best go and find her. When you get the call from Personnel, will you tell me? I'd prefer to get my cards from you rather than hear about it from Hilda.'

Anna is stashed away in her office, exactly as Maria had once feared she might be. As she approaches the bend in the corridor she hears a familiar voice. *Patrick*. She had hoped to avoid him. She won't be able to bear it – to have to look at his face and say goodbye. The shame of it, knowing that he will soon be told she's been asked to leave the building and not come back. And worse, far worse: that she will soon be on her way to court.

'That sounds delightful,' he is saying.

'Yes, doesn't it?' replies a worryingly even-more-familiar voice. 'But I think we ought to shake hands on it, just to be sure, don't you?'

The two voices part, the best of friends. Maria waits just out of sight for a moment before catching up with one of them.

'For Heaven's sake, what are you doing out here?' She curses Michael under her breath. Christ's sake, what was he thinking of to let a child wander around alone? Anna turns from the glass window.

'Hello, Mummy! I was trying to find you. Michael told me where the toilet is and sure wasn't I a big enough girl to find it by myself, but I got lost and a man stopped and asked if I needed some assistance and I said yes, and when I told him who I was he said that he was a friend of yours and—'

'A *what*?'

'Friend,' she repeats, impatient in her excitement, 'and, Mummy, wait until you hear this! Patrick – that's your friend's name – told me he has three children and every Saturday – are you listening? – every *single* Saturday, he drives to Maid Marion' ('Mount Merrion, maybe?' Maria asks faintly, knowing Anna doesn't always catch soft Irish *r* sounds) 'to collect them and they go to a café for an ice-cream or a Coca-Cola! Every *single* Saturday!' She sounds outraged. The punitive regime she herself has been subject to has been royally exposed.

Collect them? Maria thinks. Is it possible that comment was intended for her, not Anna? And she recalls his smile at the photo of the children, then the picture of the woman in evening dress falling flat on his desk and him seeming not to notice, not bothering to pick it up.

'And he said that the youngest of them isn't much older than me and he thought they would love to meet me sometime. For ice-cream,' she adds, eager to stake her claim. 'He said there definitely would be ice-cream. We shook on it.'

'I see,' Maria says, breathing deeply in an effort to collect herself. 'Did you talk about anything else?'

'He asked me what I thought of the children's shows on the television but I said I've never seen them so I told him about the radio ones instead.'

'Lucky man. Come on, let's get you to the toilet and then we'll head back to the copy room.'

'Mummy? You shouldn't have lied to Michael. He asked me what was wrong with Mrs Helping because you said she is poorly. Only she's not, she's in the pink, I heard her say it to Mrs Rogers only yesterday. Lying's a sin.'

'Sorry. I'll apologise to Michael.'

'And to God?'

'To everyone, Anna. I'll apologise to everyone.'

What sort of apology should she give Mrs Halpin? How far back to begin, more like. The poor woman must be cursing the day she ever met them. While she waits for Anna in the Ladies, Maria's mind hops, skips and jumps back in time a few hours, back to when she forced herself to walk calmly up the rest of Mrs Halpin's path.

Anna had jumped up from the table to greet her, her smile framed by the milk moustache curling above it. The tableau in the kitchen was as homely as an advert. Porridge with a stir of strawberry jam in it steamed in a bowl. Toast soldiers stood to attention in the rack. A boiled egg waited its turn on Mrs Halpin's placemat. The spout of her brown teapot protruded from its pink cosy. The radio spitter-sputtered. Maria recognised the newsreader's voice: Martin O'Donnell is often in the canteen, chatting and laughing, moving from table to table while drinking cup after cup of tea.

'You're squashing me.' Anna disentangled herself from Maria's embrace. Her jam-sticky hands patted her mother's face. 'You're freezing, Mummy! Touch the teapot – it'll warm you up.'

'You look perished, that's for sure.' Mrs Halpin shut the kitchen door behind them. 'Sit down by the fire and I'll put a fresh pot on.'

Anna recounted the excitement of waking up. One minute she was dreaming and then the next, well! None other than Chuzzlewit was asleep on the bed beside her and her in her vest and pants still!

The letterbox rattled and Maria jumped for the door. Mrs Halpin was ahead of her and out in the hallway before Maria could stop her.

He said he wouldn't. He promised.

'Post's early for once.' Mrs Halpin pottered back into the kitchen. 'Now, Maria, what were you saying? How's your friend?'

'Fine, thanks.' The tale she had rehearsed the whole way home had vanished. She searched frantically inside her own mind for it, but it was gone. The life had been strangled out of it with that single word from John's mouth. 'Her arm. It took a while to get it checked out, but she's fine. Strapped up.' She gestures at her own shoulder. 'A sling.'

'And finally, in Dublin last night,' Martin O'Donnell said from the window sill, 'four women were arrested in the city centre, in Mullerys public house.'

'I thought you said it was her leg?'

'What?' Maria said, distracted by the radio yet noticing the sharper turn in Mrs Halpin's words.

'Her *leg*. On the phone last night you said it was her leg.'

'The publican, Mr Laurence O'Toole, alleges that the woman demanded to be served against his wishes and that her companions stole alcohol when she was refused.'

'The paving stones by the new flower pots on O'Connell Street, wasn't it?'

'Um . . . Yes.'

'The women, who it is understood are part of a city-wide gang, have been charged.'

'Yes arm or yes leg?' Mrs Halpin's lips were pursed.

'And now, with the time just approaching half past eight, Radio Éireann brings you this morning's weather forecast.'

'Well?'

Maria stared at Mrs Halpin as though she had never seen her before. She tried to rerun the previous minute in her head, to split herself in two.

'Leg,' she said finally. 'I meant leg.'

'I see,' Mrs Halpin said, her tone suggesting that she saw something completely different. 'Anna, I'd say you'd better get your satchel. My Norma would have been long gone out of the house by this time.' Maria was puzzled at Mrs Halpin's frown, at the arms folded and pulled up high under her chest, then suddenly understood what it meant: Mrs Halpin thought Maria had abused her hospitality – worse than that, her good faith – so that she could spend the night with a man.

Well, Mrs Halpin's suspicions would just have to wait. Maria swallowed hard and decided it would be safest if she pretended to leave for school and instead took Anna straight to work with her. Martin O'Donnell hadn't said their names, and she clutched this thought tight as she stood up. She caught sight of herself in the mirror over the telephone table in the hallway. Her pale cheeks were hollow and her eyes framed by dark smudges. Snow and coal together. She walked to the front door and opened it a crack. He had promised he'd be gone.

Dear God, she thought, let him not have been lying.

CHAPTER TWENTY-THREE

Eve turns away from the window and lights a cigarette. The cherry blossom tree outside has shrugged off its winter gloom and its branches are now furred with pinkish, soft-as-snow petals. Smoke curls around her red hair. 'What are you going to do?'

Maria bites the nail of her forefinger. Dots of red have sprung up from the white. The sweat on her hands stings the fine rips she has torn round her nails. It's Friday evening and she still hasn't slept. She has been awake since the previous morning or maybe a year before, she can't tell.

'I don't know. I'd have said anything to get him away from the street. I was so scared Anna would be waiting at Mrs Halpin's window and I didn't want him to know which house I was going into.'

'And you don't know how he found you?'

She keeps her voice low. 'He said a friend on our old street in London had our address.' Maria shakes her head, forlorn. 'I don't understand how, though – I've been so careful.' But it was only a matter of time. She knows that now. John would find snow in the desert. He's that type.

'Why didn't you tell me before, what he was really like?'

'I tried to, once,' Maria recalls the Pandora's box of her heart that night in the Chopstick, 'but I couldn't make the words come out.'

'I mean, Maria, I just wouldn't have thought that *you* . . .' She lifts her hands in such a way that Maria can't tell whether Eve wants to shrug or applaud her.

'That I what?' Maria snaps. Eve has some nerve, always thinking she understands more. That she lives a bigger life than anyone else.

'. . . would ever do something like that.'

'Something brave, I suppose you mean?'

'No, that's not it at all! I just didn't think you were the sort to do something quite so . . . so . . . final, as to kill him off like that! Don't get me wrong,' she adds quickly, seeing Maria's face. 'I'm on your side and always will be. I'm surprised, that's all.'

'When it was just about me, I think you're right. I was the sort who'd never have done something so, I don't know, big. But when it wasn't just about me . . .' Maria's anger is gone. The side of her thumb is between her teeth again and her eyes are wet. 'When it became about Anna, too . . . that had to change everything.'

'And does he know?' Eve taps her cigarette in the general direction of the unlit fireplace and grey ash flutters down onto the carpet.

'That he's dead?'

'Yes.' Eve tries to swallow a giggle but fails.

'No.' Despite herself, Maria can't help but smile. 'No, he

doesn't. And I thought I was in trouble enough when all I had to worry about was getting fired!'

'You've not been fired.'

'Not yet.'

A song meanders down the corridor from the bathroom on the return in the stairs and floats towards the open door to the flat. Eve and Maria stand in silence and listen.

> *Fling them out from the darkness,*
> *My lost love, Macushla,*
> *Let them find me and bind me*
> *Again. Ifff. Theey. Wiiiiiill.*

The door opens and Anna twirls in, waving her toothbrush like a baton. At the sight of her unexpected audience she drops into a curtsy and Eve laughs. 'Encore, Miss Mills, encore.'

'What does that mean?'

'It's French for "again".'

'"Macushla" is Irish, Mrs Helping told me. It means "darling".'

'The exact translation,' Eve says, 'is "pulse".' She tabs her cigarette and puts the stump back in the box. 'Waste not, want not. Anna, have you your bag ready?'

'Yes, sirree, Bob.' Anna puts the toothbrush in on top of her slippers and snaps the clasp on her cardboard vanity case.

'Have you got Jocky and Pocahontas?'

'Wrapped in my nightie.' Anna nods.

Maria kneels down to close the wooden toggles on her duffel coat. 'Mittens?'

Anna checks her patch pockets. 'Yes. Goodbye, Mummy.' She throws her arms around Maria's neck. Anna is no longer her little girl made of sugar and spice and everything nice.

She is made of stronger, hard-won smells: Pears soap and crayons; last year's coat aired, never washed; hair dried by a spitting coal fire.

'Mummy?' Their arms are entwined around each other and Maria hears the whisper through the thick muffle of her own hair. 'My toggle's digging into me.' Soft breath tickles her ear. 'You're too squeezy.'

Eve blows Maria a kiss, and as they clatter down the stairs hand in hand, Maria hears Anna say, 'I saw a few pieces of confetti on the path outside from the tree. Would you like some? It looks pink on the tree but when you pick it up it's white.' Her presence in the room fades as her voice recedes. Maria feels the want of her as a beat in her body; as she would her own trembling pulse. *Macushla*.

She looks around the room. Sits. Smokes. Stands by the window and watches. When she bites her nails they taste of cigarettes. It's not a long time, but it's a long wait. She hasn't switched the lights on so shadows pile up, dense black drifts in the corners. For once, she is glad of the gloomy room and its slubby brown wallpaper.

The front door downstairs is on the snib. He appears soundlessly.

'So this is where you've been hiding yourself, Maria.' His voice sounds astray in her flat. Its walls are used to quiet, female sounds. To giggles, songs and tales of dolls, cats and school. His is a deep, exaggerated version of Anna's own fading accent. It's all wrong. 'Where's Anna? Why isn't she here?'

'She's away at a friend's. She's been looking forward to it for ages – she'd have been so upset if I let her down.' And because you're a ghost, she thinks. You don't exist. Because you're a dead man.

He nods, lights a cigarette. Maria doesn't offer to show him a recent photograph and he doesn't ask for one. He doesn't ask anything else about his daughter, doesn't seem particularly interested in her; she will be the easy part, once he gets Maria back. It is Maria he has come for. He needs to talk seriously to her, he tells her. Wants them to put everything behind them. He's willing to forgive and forget. He couldn't be sadder, or more apologetic, or more full of new, box-fresh promises.

'I know I've done wrong by you – both of you – and I'm sorry, I am. You come back and it'll get put right. I miss you both. It's God's honest truth. I'd have come to get you sooner if I'd have known where you were.'

'*It*, John? What's *it*? How can you put anything right? I don't even believe you want to.' She looks carefully at him. He's too contrite. Suddenly she understands the difference between this time and all the previous ones: he's talking like he's the one who needs her. 'Are you in some sort of trouble?'

At first he protests. No, no, it's not like that at all. And then he concedes that, maybe, there's been a bit of bother in the last few weeks. It's nothing. Some petty business with the police back in London. He was in the wrong place at the wrong time and none of it was his fault. (Of course it wasn't, she thinks. It never is. But she stays silent.)

'That said . . .' John raises his hands wide, the gesture of a man willing to forgive all his enemies, no matter how grievously done by he is. He is staring straight into her eyes as he sits down across from her. '. . . we'll give London a skip from now on, maybe head up north. Manchester. Liverpool, maybe. Fresh start.'

'John, I—'

'I'm sorry, Maria,' he says, soft as a caress. He is leaning forward now, only the oxtail-brown of her narrow table between them. 'I know he still haunts you,' he says, and reaches for her hands. She watches as fingers, like snakes, move towards her.

Francis. It slips from his mouth and sits between them, an invisible tide flowing between their two bodies. She has always pictured the name Francis as a grin; it was impossible not to smile at the wide *an* in the middle. She looks up, startled. John never spoke about him, would never even say his name.

Francis. He has said it again, and it sounds different, narrower than the way she says it. 'I'm sorry,' John repeats. She's confused. Sorry? But he blames her, she knows he does. He must do or else he'd have talked about him, cried over him, wouldn't he? But his *sorry* is a crack in her flesh and his *Francis* the tiny trickle of water that permeates the crack and seeps inside, deep into her parched heart.

'It's not your fault, Maria, and I'm sorry that I ever made you think it was. It did for me, too, his dying like that, only I didn't know how to say it.' His fingertips are touching hers now, but she doesn't move her hands. Isn't it possible – just maybe – that this could be for the best? She's failed here, that much is obvious. Who is she to judge another's pain? Isn't she in trouble with the police herself and about to lose a job that she's already proved she can't do? Anna's best friend is a pensioner. Their flat is a dump. She's a failure. And perhaps what he's saying is true, that he has changed. People do, don't they? They can try again.

As though he can read her mind, he says, 'Give me a chance and you'll see the truth of what I'm saying. You'll feel the truth of it, Maria.'

The crack opens a little wider and into the gap rushes one thought: Please, save me. His fingers are warm. Soft hands are a sign of a man who'll never do a tap. She can't remember where she heard that, or if she ever believed it. But what she does remember is how good, how safe, it once felt to have her own hands enclosed between his. The backs of his are smooth and even, whereas hers are seamed with raised, blue-tinged veins. His fingers move down and stroke her palms. She stares at the topography of her skin until she is aware of nothing. Below the papery, pale surface stamps an army. Life tramping through her body, working as her master and servant, ceaselessly campaigning to keep her alive. She is only a body: an automaton for eating, crying, dreaming.

Her breathing slows. His fingers edge closer, moving higher over the backs of her hands, up her wrists and onto her arms. The very smell of him caresses her. Without looking at him, she is aware that he is leaning across the table, that his mouth is moving to meet hers. Little boys are made of slugs and snails and puppy-dog tails. Men are beer and sweat and the loamy tang of damp earth.

It's not your fault.

She exhales. People can change, can't they? Machines can be taken apart and put back together again. Machines can be oiled and cared for. Hasn't the way she's lived her life here just proved how much she needs him? Failure is relentless and exhausting. *Save me,* she thinks, as she leans forward, barely breathing. It has been such a long time since she smelt him. Such a long time since she tasted him.

CHAPTER TWENTY-FOUR

'Come to see if I'm dead yet?' The door opens a little further. Tess is pale, slighter than ever. Brown hair with white and grey roots streels down to her shoulders. It must have been wavy once, Maria thinks, picturing a mass of curls like Eve's bouncing around that narrow face, and those sharp eyes blazing with youth and spirit. Tess coughs, a hacking sound that seems far too loud to come out of such a small body. She lays a hand over her chest as it subsides into a wheeze. 'Holy Mother,' she walks down the passage to the kitchen, 'the hounds of Hell are let loose in there.'

The fire is lit and the room is stifling hot. Condensation blurs the window and falls in thin rivulets onto the empty jam jars, matchboxes, broken crockery and other junk dumped on the windowsill. A tarnished bud vase stands empty, its silk nosegay lying beside it on the damp paintwork. The kitchen and pantry jut out into a high-walled, narrow yard. Despite the fire and the March daylight outside, the room is shadowy, with inky corners.

'I brought you a bottle of cough syrup and a few messages,' Maria says. 'I thought you might like a scrambled egg.' The bread, milk and eggs look as uncomfortable in Tess's hands as if Maria had handed her a baby to tend. She turns about in search of a landing place, finally stacking them next to the sink. The egg box teeters on the dull grey edge of a pile of pots and pans.

'It's like a game of shove ha'penny in here.' Maria is reminded of Patrick's desk.

'I always was good at that.' Tess pushes the bottle onto the windowsill. 'Did you get any cigs?'

'Here.' Maria reaches into her basket. 'And this, too.' She hands her a naggin.

Tess grins. 'If that quack over on Beechwood Avenue prescribed this I'd be better already.' Maria extracts two dirty teacups from the clutter in the sink and gives them a swift swish under the tap. 'I didn't think you'd be the lick-and-a-promise sort,' Tess mocks.

'There's plenty I'd say you hadn't thought about me.' Maria puts the damp cups down. Hers has a pattern of intertwined violets and green leaves; Tess has faded rosebuds in pink and chipped gold. Maria remembers the woollen tea cosy that was posted in as a relic, made to keep a man's seat at his table warm. She pours two fat fingers of whiskey into each cup. 'I've come to apologise and to say goodbye,' she says.

'That's two different things,' Tess replies. 'And as I've no interest in hearing out the first, you'd do better to get started on the second.'

Once upon a time there was a woman whose baby died and whose husband grew to hate her for it. Once upon a time there was a woman who thought she could unwind the skein of her life and spin it afresh. Once upon a time there was a woman who didn't understand how the story should be told. Or how to get to the end. Or the middle. Or even back to the beginning.

Maria hears herself going through a sequence of cause and effect, push and pull, unsure as she speaks if life could ever be as straightforwardly consequential. What is it, she wonders, to tell another person a tale? Whatever essence she is trying to capture is immediately freed again in Tess's imagination. Maria's own memories are put into words only to be translated back into a second set of different pictures.

Tess says nothing, but smokes and sips and taps her cigarette against the ashtray in a neat triangle of movements.

Maria takes up the stitches of her story at the moment she'd left Tess asleep in her bed – can that really be only two evenings before? It feels like a hundred years – and talks until she has caught up with herself, until she has knitted herself back to this untidy table.

The whiskey slips down easily this time. The warm sensation that follows the initial burn in her throat and chest is almost pleasant. It is a relief to feel its slow numbness take over her limbs. In John's hands the night before she was aware of every inch of her body awakening from its long enforced sleep. But it awoke only to betray her and now she desires only nothingness again.

What she doesn't tell Tess is what happened afterwards. After John had taken her hands, after he'd leant over. After her body had recognised the smell of him, the touch of him. She thinks of what happened next – *andthenandthenandthen* – but she does not speak of it in this room, or that this morning, when they'd woken up, he'd said, 'We'll get you packed up, head straight for Manchester.'

He unwrapped himself from around her. Got out of bed and fumbled on the floor for his clothes. 'I've already sent my things to a mate's up there. Didn't want anything left lying around in London.' Maria sat up in bed and tugged the straps of her slip onto her shoulders. He smiled as he watched the peep show of her breasts disappearing only to be immediately visible again, round and firm, through the transparent beige nylon. In his gaze she recognised a familiar expression: the hard-won pride of a man surveying his property. He ran the flat of his palms across his hair and said, 'Start getting your stuff together. Shouldn't take long.'

She watched the curl of his mouth intently for a moment. Despite where his lips had just been, she could not see love on them. No care, or need, or want. His expression was that of a victor over an enemy. Her heart quickened. She felt desperate suddenly to cover herself. She shivered and pulled a cardigan on over her slip.

His coat lay puddled on the floor and he picked it up, his voice light. 'And just in case it might occur to you to change your mind today or anything, just so's you know, Anna will be coming with me, even if you don't.'

'Anna goes where I go.' Her voice cracked. Her lips felt swollen and bruised, her throat dry.

'Not if I say so, she don't. Not now.' He pulled Friday's *Evening Press* from his coat pocket and threw it on the bedspread. 'Ain't you been the busy little wifey, out on the town with your pals?'

He laughed as he pulled up his braces. When she leant forward to pick up the paper, she could feel the last trace of him leaking out into her slip.

Young Women Arrested in Public House Affray

Four young women were taken into custody in Pearse Street Station last night following an affray in Mullerys public house, Eden Quay, Dublin.

It was alleged that they demanded to be served pints of porter and when refused by the barman, stole a number of other drinks, totalling 10s 5d.

Reports suggest that they are part of a gang that has plagued the city centre for some time. The barman on duty in Mullerys had received information from a local publican that they were in the area and had alerted the gardaí.

The women were named as Aoife Ní Amhalghaidh (28), Alicia Cassidy (30), Mary-Anne King (26) and Maria Mills (29). They claimed that they were protesting against the regulation forbidding the sale in on-licence premises of pints of beer to women.

Local parish priest Fr Leo Horan, who was near the premises at the time and witnessed the incident, told this reporter: 'They were drunkards. This was unbecoming behaviour from ridiculous women, unfit to be children of our nation and its future mothers.'

The four women are expected to appear in Court in the forthcoming weeks.

'And before you tell me there's more than you going by that name, I know there ain't,' he said. 'I went in that pub yesterday before I came here. Checked. It's you.' He leant over her, his breath on her lips, his hands on her cheeks. His fingers were warm – she could smell herself on him.

There it was. The flash in his eyes. She recognised it finally, recognised all of it, and hated herself for her stupidity. Those fingers were the ones that had been wrapped around her throat one lonely summer night the year before. Those same palms had pushed her back on the day she'd thought Anna was going to tip boiling water over herself. Maria's heart and head once more remembered who he was. The machine of her body had chosen to forget. And as if he had been in the room with them, the chubby body of baby Francis slipped once more out of her grasp and under the waves, until he was no more than a dark twist of seaweed curling away across the top of the water.

Pains and fears and the spill of tears. That is what John is made of. And what he says is true: she has to go with him. With no job, and a court case looming, what choice has she got? A woman who told the world her husband was dead, then got herself arrested for theft? What judge wouldn't hand Anna to him and be grateful to John for taking her on? Because of her stupidity he owns her now and they both know it.

But she tells none of this to Tess.

What she does instead is to put down her cup, swallow and say, 'So, I think it's best if we leave. Give it another go, as a family.'

Tess stays quiet, a silence that bloats, filling the room. Maria raises the naggin and refills their cups, wishing she'd bought a bigger bottle. What else is she meant to do? Mop an ocean with a single rag?

The clock on the mantelpiece strikes twelve. Tess says, 'If I had the wireless on, we'd be hearing the Angelus now. All over the country, everyone hearing the one sound, muttering the one faith.' She sounds scornful, almost angry. She switches on a lamp at the far end of the table. A warm yellow light illuminates their cups and the whiskey glows like spun gold deep inside. She turns to face Maria. 'Does the child know?'

'No. She stayed with Eve last night. He hasn't seen her yet.'

'And what will you tell her?'

'It's going to sound strange whatever it is . . . that the accident turned out to be a mistake and it was some other man died, and it all only got straightened out a few weeks ago, when there was that explosion on the oil rig.'

Tess sighs. 'Could happen, I suppose. There were some called dead in the war only to appear bold as brass back on their own doorsteps months later. More usual the other way round, mind. When do you leave?'

'He's calling for us late tonight so's we can get the morning ferry.'

August to March. It's not even seven months, yet she was becoming a different person. One who might in time do more than just want a better life for her daughter, but provide it. That is the feeling that was growing in her on Thursday night. Maybe Eve was right about that, too, and being arrested should be nothing more than another link in the chain. That the chain is what matters, not any individual link.

The pattern of violets on the cup is pretty, though roughly painted. Some petals are larger, thicker, than others. Maria traces the leaves with her fingertip. A stranger painted them, many years before. Another fired them on the tea set. Another sold it. The world is bewilderingly full of strangers. How is she ever to find her place in it when she can't even find her path in the company of the people she knows?

'You don't want to go, I can see it. So why are you sitting there jawing on to me about it?' Tess says. She holds her gaze.

'Tell me, Maria Mills, how long before you have to put yourself between your husband and your child?'

'He won't touch her. He said so. He promised.'

'He's a liar.' Tess pushes her cigarette hard into the ashtray. Her words thump onto the table. 'You know it and I know it. You're afraid of him, I can see it. And where there's fear there's cause for fear. You mark my words.'

Maria swallows too much too quickly and splutters. Her eyes fill and burn, her sinuses flush with pain as she coughs up the whiskey. Tess fishes around in the scummy waters of the sink and produces a milk jug. She fills it from the tap. Maria turns it around to tip water from the spout into her mouth. It tastes sour.

'Yes,' she says, when the coughing ends. 'I am.'

Tears fall down her face and onto the table and Tess reaches across to touch her arm. Her bony fingers are all wintering twigs, their touch so different from that of the confident, knowing hands that had held her hours before. Yet she is gentle, with an unexpected warmth. Tess says nothing, then stands and leaves the room. Maria sits there, grateful for the stale, overheated peace, for the hiss and splutter of the fire. From next door she hears schoolboys' faint shouts, the repetitive clang of their ball hitting a dustbin.

Maria wants to sit there for ever. She glances around the cluttered surfaces and the floor but, once again, there is no sign of the Cumann na mBan medal. Hardly a surprise in this room. Tess's belongings have the freedom of stray cats. They roam at will, and there is something admirable about their disregard for order.

Tess reappears with a book in her hand. Maria recognises it and the shock of this familiarity embarrasses her. The old-

fashioned cover and closely written, carefully inked pages
are not the strangers to her that they should be. 'It's all right.
I know you've been in it.'

'I'm sorry, I really am,' Maria says. 'I didn't go hunting, I
just saw it there on the floor and picked it up. Forgive me,
Tess, please. It was wrong of me.'

'I'm slovenly and I knows it, but I'm not stupid, Maria
Mills.' Tess holds the book closer to the light and flicks past
page after page. 'Nobody finds nothing that I don't let them
find.'

Tess turns the book towards Maria, then sits back in her
chair. 'I used to think it was what a person *did* that could spell
their ruination, or the slide towards it. But it's not, Maria. It's
the things you don't do.' She lights a cigarette and smokes,
her head back and her eyes half shut, as Maria takes the book
in her hands. The page Tess has opened begins on the day she
was arrested and taken to Holloway. Maria reads the story as
quickly as the spidery, faded writing will let her. She stops at
a large ink stain, and holds the book closer to the light.

> Damn & blast me but I dropped my pen & ink's blobbed
> all over my page. Doesn't matter, Dr M. always says,
> Minnie's allowed give me new pages whenever I want
> them. But I don't. Then I'd just have to write the page
> out again & I might want to change the words if I do
> that, & I don't want to change it. The story is the story,
> going back over it won't make it the story any more, it'll
> turn it into makey-up. The spilling has to stay part of
> the story.
>
> I wasn't sure if I'd be able to put words on it. If I
> even knew the right words for what happened. Words for

the doctor with the towel around his neck, & the traitor women at his side holding the pint of Benger's like it was a cup of tea, & the suffocating in my throat & the tearing pain in my chest & him saying to the nurses, we've an easy one for the tube here, with these gums, & him squeezing my arm between his thumb and forefinger like he was a witch getting me ready for the oven & going, Three would fit through together here. Words for the rips in my gums. Words for how as I had the Monthlies but they wouldn't give me anything for it but instead left me lying there in my own blood & vomit.

Dr M is a prison visiting doctor at Pentonville as it turns out, & he knows a prison doctor at Holloway & lo and behold he got a copy of the report on me. He keeps his desk locked but Minnie can put her hand to anything. He's out on rounds now so I've an hour. Minnie is keeping sketch.

Doctors are meant to make you better, is what I was brought up believing. The man I met, the man who wrote the letter that is about to be forthcoming, he has no right to call himself Doctor to all the world. He's no better than that Jack the Ripper. He must know it too. The man's a murderer. His victims just ain't died yet.

8 December 1909
The Prison Commissioners,

Gentlemen

I have the honour to report that today I saw and examined Tess Mary Keating at H. M. Prison Holloway, in consultation with Dr Raglan. I also took part in the artificial feeding by the oesophageal tube. Tess Mary Keating is about 18 years of age, a spare, pale-complexioned woman but severely neurotic.

She was sentenced on 1 December to four weeks' imprisonment. From the records I find that on committal she weighed 112 lbs, & today she weighs 108 lbs. Her height is 5 ft 4 in. Her lungs and heart are quite healthy; respiration quiet; pulse 72 regular, fair volume, medium tension, capillary circulation active. Tongue clean; teeth in great disorder with eight missing & five in various states of disrepair; no distension of stomach or abdomen; bowels regular; menses regular; knee jerks excessive. Her throat is rather small and slightly granular but not inflamed.

On passing the oesophageal tube there was a slight spasm at the upper end of the oesophagus 5 to 6 inches from the teeth; this no doubt increases the discomfort of the passage of the tube, but it can be easily got over by using a fine, moderately stiff tube with only one side opening near the end of the tube and in the stiff part, as is common practice.

Personally I would be inclined to leave her without food for two or three days and by that time the spasm will have passed off. Any ordinary individual can survive with only water for a couple of weeks, and there is no damage to life in a healthy individual from any loss of body weight up to 25 per cent, or say 20 per cent, including the weight of the clothing. This woman therefore can afford to lose 21 lbs without any risk.

I have the honour to be, Gentlemen,
Your most obedient servant,
Edward N. Trench

I've tried now. I have.

Dr M can't say otherwise. But putting the words down didn't make the gristle dislodge from my chest. But worse, even worse, is knowing that it will happen again.

Last night I had a dream where I floated over the Thames, it flowing dark & treacly below me like Metropolitan Mixture. I soared out over London like a bird & dropped down to land in the Square. On three sides were huge houses decorated in frills and ruffles, for all the world like fancy iced cakes. The Dublin Mountains filled the fourth side but didn't touch the houses. Snow sat on the peaks & flowed down the sides. Miss Billington was there, too, & the both of us dressed in tea gowns of shot silk from China, all the colours of the rainbow spilling & splashing together & the beautiful stuff of the fabric glistening in the sun.

And when I woke up I understood that the summer day I first saw her in Cavendish Square was the true Beginning. I've tried so hard to make my brain go back to that day. To all the days since, when hundreds of us had our feet beating in time, & I felt strong as the wildest wind because we were together. But I can't. They're gone. Because in prison I saw what happened to that lady with the green cape & it pains me I don't know her name. Because in prison I was a body with half her teeth missing, held down by three women while a man shoved tubes into her. If I stay it will happen again & I won't be able to bear up against it.

If that day was the Beginning then this must be the End.

I'm no suffragette. I'm Tess Keating, coward.

Once again, Maria wills herself forward nearly sixty years. The kitchen rings with the heavy clang of steel doors, the echoes of boots on grated landings. A voice trying desperately to scream in pain, to beg help from the women holding her down. Pleading with them to be her sisters. A broken life sits between them on the table.

'Tess, you're not a coward. This proves it.'

'No, it doesn't. Because I couldn't go through it more than that one time. I was too scared. And that's the truth of it. Going on hunger strike once isn't a brave thing to do. It's foolhardy, acting how you think a hero acts. Or it was for me, anyways. It was like something out of a penny dreadful, the way me and Minnie used talk when we didn't know better. But doing it twice, knowing what it means and the slow agony of it, and the fear that your own body will kill you itself . . . That's what brave is. And I didn't have that in me. I ran away sooner than get put back into prison. 'Twas years before I dared go back to London.'

'What about the others? Minnie, what happened to her?'

'I never saw her again. I did hear years later from a woman I chanced upon in the street that she kept going with it and the forcible feeding broke her health. She went to live in Hove for the sea air, but it didn't do her any good.'

'Why are you being so cruel to yourself, Tess?'

'I let my own fear rule me. And that's what Minnie warned me from the start not to do. She told me I was putting myself in the way of something that was bigger than any single one of us and I didn't understand her. I thought I knew it all. But I didn't.'

Maria nods in dizzy recognition. 'Eve said something like that once. About acting for the future, not your own past.' Can it really be possible to live, to act, so entirely outside yourself?

'That's what the suffragettes were about,' Tess says. 'They – we – saw how it should change. And that's where I failed them. Failed myself. But being a coward will snarl at your heels like a cur. And you don't know what manner of kick you'll give it some day out of anger, just to prove to yourself you're its master.'

Tess taps her finger on the table. 'That's why you're doing wrong if you go back with that man. There'll be no salvation for you if you go into it knowing what these tears tell me you know.'

What these tears tell me you know.

Maria's tears are a river flowing from the bottom of her soul, carried along by Tess's long-hidden words, the whiskey and her own exhausted confusion. Yet now they suddenly stop, dried up by rage. How can this woman lecture her on what's right and wrong? To detail another woman's private duty to her own life? Tess is hiding things still. Maria's not forgotten the flash in her eyes when she broached the subject of Cumann na mBan, or her fury at the mention of Lily Byrne. Maria isn't the only one in this room with a life of secrets and lies inside her, she's sure of that. You bloody liar, she thinks, feeling unsteady and furious and betrayed. She pushes away her cup and rises from the table.

'Do you know what, Tess? We must both be cowards in that case!' She is leaning too close to the older woman's face, her words still thick from crying, but she doesn't care. 'I'm a liar and a coward and I know it and there's no one to care about me if I pack my suitcase and live out that lie in England. But what about you? Your fight didn't end with the suffragettes, did it? You've no business to be lecturing me about squaring up to my life, to' – she nearly spits it – 'my daughter's life, when you're hiding away in this tip, refusing to look your own past in the eye.'

She is gripping the edge of the table, her nails digging into the wood. Whiskey-soaked anger is her fuel. 'Don't you dare make a liar out of me, just because you've made one of yourself.'

Tess says nothing, but takes up her diary in both hands. One finger traces along the marbled veins in the cloth of the cover as gently as if it were a map and she were planning a trip to the country. When she speaks her voice is calm – she could be talking to herself.

'Since you first called here, I've gone and read all my diaries again. My "Written Notations, or What Tess Keating Saw", I used call 'em. I was a fanciful young one. Dusting the master's books in the library was one of my jobs, though all I'd ever do was the long bits that faced out and a quick flick across the top, and I got the idea of keeping my own book from the names of some of his. *London City*: *Written Notations of a Capital* was one – I thought it sounded very grand. *The Secret Diary of a Maid-Servant, or What Petal Saw* was another.' She shrugs. 'That was a different class of book altogether, as it turned out.'

She plucks a crochet hook out of the mess on the table and skewers her hair into a bun. 'Time,' she says quietly, 'is a cloth. It polishes memories smooth.' So much so that she had let herself forget it wasn't always like that for her. That she was once on the other, the *before* side, of those days, then unmade and remade by them.

'Stories in books always go the same way. This happened at the beginning, then this happened, then this and this, and it goes on and on until the last page tells you "The End", and even if the story doesn't finish the way you want it to, it's still over and everything's left sorted, tidied away.'

This reminds Maria of the way she had blurted out her tale to Dolores but she says nothing, and Tess continues, 'But life's not like that. Life is about doing the same thing day after day and being meant to be grateful for the chance to do it at all. And I'd forgotten for a long time how much I hated my life when I understood it didn't have to be like that. And when you appeared on the door, carrying on with your stupid questions, it all got stirred up in my mind again.'

'All what?' Maria snaps.

Tess is doing nothing to appease her. She's not far off ignoring Maria as she goes on in the same soft tone: 'And now I'm left asking: how did I let myself away with it?'

'With *what*?'

'With the curs I kicked out at and those I didn't.' Her fingertips beat out a rhythm on the diary. 'A man told me once that when you wind up the clock you should stay to hear it strike.' Maria and Tess both glance involuntarily at the travelling clock in the centre of the mantelpiece. Daniel looks at them from his home next to it, his dark eyes smiling solemnly out at his mother. 'But it's more than that. You should stay until it's unwound itself back down to nothing.' Tess stares up at her young son. His sturdy legs in their flannel shorts look solid, unbreakable. 'You should be there for the end, even though you don't know when that will be.'

'Be there for the end,' Maria repeats softly. 'Yes.' She nods. 'The end.'

Tess lifts her teacup to meet Maria's, and her pink roses tap against the tiny violets.

CHAPTER TWENTY-FIVE

He wants to know why she ain't ready yet.

Because she isn't. Won't ever be. Not today, not any day. His face darkens.

'No.' It is both the quietest and the loudest word she has ever spoken. She is unable to move from her seat, she's clenching her buttocks so tight. Afraid she'll soil herself even, she's that frightened. But this minute is everything. Everything she wants for herself, for Anna. Everything she now knows she wants them to be is here, in this minute. 'Go on.' She forces her eyes to meet his and says quietly, 'Just try it.'

He's taken aback. 'What are you playing at? We're leaving.' She knows he's not used to this. According to John's script, next should come the tears, then the soft voice calming, reasoning, begging him to see sense. He's not used to playing against this version of Maria, and he's lost. 'You've not got any choices left, Maria, remember?'

'Were you talking to me?'

He jumps back. 'Who the fuck are you?'

'Eve Cawley.' She appears from Maria's scrap of a kitchen. 'Have we met? No? You're quite right, we've not. I've heard all about you, though. Didn't like any of it.'

'Fuck off, whoever you are,' he says.

'What a coincidence, Eve. Neither did I.' Alicia. Tall and broad-shouldered, standing in the doorway to the bedroom. She moves closer to him. He looks up into her face. Her expression doesn't change as she says, 'Isn't *this* a fine way to treat your wife?' Typical of sharp-tongued Alicia, Maria thinks, to use his own words back on him.

'Very fine,' Eve says brightly. She walks to the window and glances out into the street below.

'The finest.' Alicia nods, takes a drag from her cigarette. 'And yet . . . when he said, "Fuck off," just there, I did wonder, could he be talking to me?' She looks down at him, her eyes never leaving his face. He must feel her breath on his forehead. He mutters.

'What was that? Oh, right, got you. It's the accent, you see. Ladies, John here wants to know what the fuck is going on,' Alicia says. 'Can either of you help him out with that?'

'Nothing, John. Nothing's going on,' Eve says. 'That's right, isn't it, Maria?'

'Yes.' She has to fight her own fear to match the strength in their voices. 'Yes.' Her hands are clenched under her, where no one can see them shake. 'And you're not staying and nobody's going. Not me, not Anna.'

'Not true, Maria,' Alicia says, her snake-charmer voice unchanged. 'He's going.' She is just as she was that evening in the Percy French. That calm tone. Disconcertingly playful yet all the more threatening for it. Maria could know Alicia for a hundred years yet never know her at all. 'Aren't you?' Alicia's bluish smoke curls around his black hair and, in the mess of the smoke and the shadows, John seems to shrink. But Maria knows him, knows he fights in rounds.

'Get them out of here. I'll be back in half an hour,' he says, but he's looking confused. The room is darkening, the shadows in its corners coming to take him away.

There is a sudden clatter outside, and the door to the flat opens. Two burly guards spill over onto the mat. Behind them Maria catches a glimpse of tight grey curls and two currant-bright eyes. 'Are we on cue?' Mrs Halpin asks, her cheeks pink as she slips past the guards and to Maria's side. 'Ada's looking after you-know-who,' she whispers, just as the larger guard begins, 'Are you John Mi—'

'Oh, I'm so sorry, Garda!' Mrs Halpin says, mortified.

'Are you John Mills?' he repeats, with a frown at the source of the interruption. 'Our opposite numbers in the Metropolitan Police in London suggested you might be visiting us in Dublin. They've been looking to have a nice chat with you. Stolen property, I believe they mentioned, wasn't it?' He turns to the younger guard next to him. Maria, relieved to recognise neither of them, blushes at his 'stolen'.

'And fenced,' the shorter guard adds.

'You can't prove anything,' John says, but he's faltering. She can see it.

'You're right. But we can tell the lads over in London you're here, and we can make your life a misery while we're waiting for them to come over and collect you.'

'I'd say,' the guard says, 'you'd be better off leaving now, don't you? In case we decide we'd sooner take you with us.'

'That'd be best,' the first says, 'for sure.'

Maria knows he has cursed them to Hell, has shoved past

them, has slammed the front door. She knows he is gone and that, incredibly, the final bell of the fight has been sounded by none other than Anna's own Mrs Helping. And yet she is left with the strangest sense that he has shrivelled away into nothing. That she has filled every last corner of the flat with herself and he has been sucked into the dark walls of Redoubt Terrace, gone for good.

CHAPTER TWENTY-SIX

Granite, with a black limestone heart, Nelson has stared out over the city for one hundred and fifty-seven years. If those sightless Portland stone eyes could have seen, what would Horatio have made of the city that unfurled around him? Trains, trams and cars have, over the decades, drowned the sharp clip of hoofs. Hats are no longer doffed. Hems have risen until ankles, calves, knees and now thighs saunter past him every day. He has stoically ignored the panting dead-of-night frolics against his very own railings and been woken daily by the plaintive cock-crow of early-morning deliveries. He has stood immobile as wars were fought with and against his own countrymen (even those wars fought simultaneously).

Stuck atop the Pillar to stand sentry over thousands of lives in all weathers, he has commanded views over Dublin Bay, across to the Wicklow Mountains and on a clear summer's day, it was claimed by some, even as far as the Mourne Mountains. Nelson has outlived King William's statue in College Green, which was blown up in 1929; the equestrian George II in St

Stephen's Green, detonated in 1937, and all 168 tonnes of Queen Victoria, which were ousted from Leinster House in 1948 lest the very sight of her bulky sovereign skirts offend the sensibilities of the Free State government any further.

A memorial to Nelson was originally mooted within a month of his death, and since the first morning his giant body stonily witnessed the sun rise high above Sackville Street, there were campaigns to remove him. The *Irish Magazine* of September 1809 wrote: *The statue of Nelson records the glory of a mistress and the transformation of our Senate into a discount office.*

'"... until at one thirty-one in the morning of today, Tuesday, the eighth of March 1966,"' Hilda reaches her crescendo, '"down he went!"'

She looks over the top of the newspaper. From her seat at the head of their favourite table (best view of the swing doors), Hilda has been reading aloud from the *The Irish Times*.

Central Dublin Rocked by Explosion. Nelson Pillar Blown Up: Gardaí Search Rubble for Possible Victims blares the front page. As Michael commented earlier, the timing of the explosion was ideal. Nelson made all the morning editions.

The canteen is chock-a-block. The tea ladies' elbows rise and fall like pistons. There is nothing like a newsworthy event to bring out a thirst and the urns are doing some mighty trade. Nobody is talking of anything other than Nelson and his sudden, shocking end. Between sips of tea and the business of lighting, smoking and tapping cigarettes, Michael, Deirdre and Mags are listening intently to Hilda's history lesson. Deirdre is teary, her nose red and glistening.

'Rudolph's taken it a bit personal, hasn't she?' Michael whispers to Maria. 'No wonder.' He nudges her side, his breath stale and smoky. 'She was stood up under it often enough!'

Maria isn't listening. She has no idea what he's going on about. Her hands under the table are unsteady. Her cup sits untouched. She doesn't want tea anyway.

'"A young taxi driver, Mr Steve Maughan of Beaumont –"'

Deirdre blows her nose, and the trumpeting interrupts Hilda's flow. She briefly breaks off her recitation to glare across the table before clearing her throat pointedly and continuing, '"– was cruising slowly past the pillar just as the explosion went off.

'If the lights had been red I would surely have been killed,' he said."'

She turns the page. '"The demolition of the Pillar was obviously the work of some explosives expert. The column was cut through clearly just below the plinth, and the debris fell closely around the base of the monument, with some stones being hurled just as far as the entrances of Henry Street and North Earl Street.

'"CIE bus driver Michael Ennis, driving the ghost bus – a bus used to take CIE crews home at the end of work – passed the Pillar on his way back to the Ringsend garage seconds before the explosion took place. 'I noticed the time as about one thirty-one,' he said. 'It just went wham! It reminded me of the bomb that dropped on the South Circular Road during the War. I felt the bus lift with the force of the explosion.'"'

'Our house had its windows blown out in that one,' Mags says, glad of an opportunity to stake her claim close to the action. 'A German pilot got lost and thought the Grand Canal was the Thames or something.'

'Ahem?' Hilda rattles her paper.

'"Dublin Corporation workmen were called to the scene

and cleared the rubble from the street but gardaí were expecting huge crowds of people this morning to seek pieces of the Pillar as souvenirs. The Pillar held the names of four of Nelson's great battles – the remains still are blazoned with them – Trafalgar, Copenhagen, the Nile and Cape Saint Vincent. Nelson's famous blind eye was turned at the second – Copenhagen. Early this morning, the only recognisable part of his statue in Dublin, the head, was lying amid the rubble beneath the foot of the Pillar looking down North Earl Street. Behind it, unseen, the word 'Copenhagen' remained engraved in the stone of the still-standing base."'

'He's lost more than an arm this time,' says a voice from behind Hilda's shoulder. Michael sniggers.

Hilda throws him the disappointed, exasperated look of an owner whose puppy has done its business on the floor. 'There's no need for disrespect,' she snaps.

Dolores ignores Hilda and leans over the table. 'Can I have a word, Maria?'

Dolores had told her to stay home on the Monday so any fuss could die down. She was to tell anyone who asked that Maria had phoned in sick. And in the Nelson-inspired excitement and confusion filling the corridors and the canteen on Tuesday, nobody has even thought to ask if she's feeling better.

Hilda stares straight ahead, desperately ignoring Dolores' seamlessly upholstered left breast, now suspended just inches from her cheek. A waitress swoops to take away their trays and Hilda reasserts her control. 'Break's over.' She folds the newspaper with a definitive snap. That, clearly, is enough of that. 'Take hold of yourself.' Hilda turns on the still-snuffling Deirdre. 'What's it to you to be so upset?'

'It's a miracle nobody was hurt.' Deirdre wipes her pink-rimmed eyes. 'It says that Burton's and Best's windows were destroyed and the glass flew everywhere, and that big neon sign fell from three floors up! Ten foot long it is. Was, I mean.'

'Ooh! Do you think there was any looting?' Mags asks.

'From Burton's and Best's?' Michael is disdainful. 'If there was, the looters will have brought the stuff back by now.' Dolores laughs, an unexpectedly open-mouthed guffaw, and Michael beams.

Once again, Maria walks down the stone steps in her mind. The turn, turn, turn of them makes her dizzy, even in memory. She remembers the warm, clear air on the viewing platform and the shock of the damp, marrowless core of the Pillar on the way down. She imagines the Pillar as she first saw it, aged ten, with her father.

Poor Dad, she thinks, and realises she hasn't thought of him in this way for a long time. After he'd left the bank in disgrace he'd got a job as a salesman and Maria had been shipped off to boarding school in Sligo. She remembered Aunt Josephine had called him an *embezzler*, which had confused Maria at the time because it sounded like an exotic acrobatic act. Typical of Aunt Josephine to get so annoyed about a circus! He travelled around the country for years, selling weighbridges to cattle marts. The last time she'd seen him she was eighteen. Passing through, he announced, when he showed up one day at the secretarial college to take her for lunch in Sligo. Glued to the hotel bar as always, everyone's friend and no one's. He had died in an accident a month later, when his car hit a bridge. There was no other car involved. All he owned was the suitcase on the back seat.

'Do you remember our outing to the Pillar?' he had said to her more than once, as she ate her hotel lunch that day. He hadn't changed, was still drinking his red lemonade and barely eating. 'You'd been at me for ever to bring you to the Pillar, and for a day out in town to get a new doll, and so I did. It was the best day. Wasn't it?' She had nodded. 'This old sales lark is temporary,' he said. 'It's great, and I'm doing great, but it's temporary. When I'm fixed up permanently, we can get a house again. If you want to, that is.' He had looked bewildered, as though the passage of time had taken him by surprise. 'Now that you're grown up.'

After lunch they had shaken hands and she'd left him in the bar at the Grand Hotel. She couldn't face two hours of typing practice so went straight back to her digs. With her coat on, she'd lain on the bed and felt herself float away into nothing. Her eyes were dry, yet ached as though she had been crying for a week. Family ties, she thought. This is what it is to have none. Nothing to tether me at all. This is no life. She would go away to London as soon as she was able. She'd find a new life there. And she'd not be alone either, she'd make sure of it.

She had found herself thinking about her father a lot in the days after she'd visited Nelson's Pillar with Anna. Of the mess he had made of his life. How he didn't seem to know who was true and who was false. She was glad she'd got to climb the Pillar again, as an adult. To hear that babel of unknowable foreign voices and accents mixed in among the Irish. The hazes of sky and sea, and the black line of a plane bisecting the blue. The mounds of the hills in the distance, holding the city in like a high pastry crust. Strange, to think of it being gone just like that. *Boom*. The platform turned into wire and stone and lumps of rock, and bits of Nelson scattered all over O'Connell Street.

'The Pillar's just the start!' Deirdre's eyes are huge and her lower lip droops. 'What'll be next? The Wellington Monument? My boyfriend works in the Phoenix Park. Is he to be blown to smithereens for the sake of some stupid statue?'

'Oh, stop fly-catching, Deirdre!' Hilda wears her reading glasses attached to a chain around her neck and now lets them drop onto her cardigan where they sit on the broad shelf of her bosom. 'Nelson had it coming to him. There's been talk of replacing him for donkey's years. Now get back to work. You go on, too, Maria,' she says, as though the timing of Maria's tea breaks is still in her gift. With a sniff, she adds, 'You look miles away anyway, you might as well. I'm sure there must be something Robert Ryan needs taking care of.'

Michael ignores Hilda's signals to get back onto the leash. 'Who do you think should be up there instead of the one-eyed adulterer?' he asks. Nelson's destruction has disrupted the daily grind of the day and he's not going to let its power dissipate easily. Deirdre cheers up enough to suggest that maybe Robert Emmet is due a turn, but with no seconders she quickly moves on and claims, in the heel of the hunt, she'd be all for the men of 1916, what with it being the jubilee year and all. Narrow it down, Michael tells her, but she can't decide between Collins and Pearse.

'Roger Casement, then?' Mags says. 'You don't hear much about him any more, and him hung for his troubles.'

'How about him and Pearse up there together?' Michael retorts.

'A traffic garda.' Dolores turns to Michael. 'Hat and raincoat and all.'

'Stop the lights!' Michael says. Dolores laughs again, and Michael rolls at her feet, his paws waving in the air, begging to be tickled.

Hilda snorts in derision. Honestly.

'Come on, Maria,' Dolores says. 'I need to talk to you in the office.' She turns and saunters off, calling back over her shoulder, 'Don't do anything I wouldn't do, Hilda.'

Not so easily vanquished, Hilda says to Dolores' retreating back, 'Maybe Robert Ryan should get the Pillar. Seeing as how he's so incredibly *popular*.'

Maria pauses before she follows Dolores and looks around the table. 'I've just realised: if you're all here, who's in the office?'

'It'll be fine by itself for a while,' Hilda says. 'On a day like this, we can't be expected to adhere to the usual routines. We've all had a shock.'

The route to Robert Ryan's office takes them past the copy room. The sound of its ringing phones chases them all the way to the stairs to the second floor. Robert is out. Dolores props a *Woman's Own* against the plastic cover of her typewriter. Today's jumper is that bit tighter, her hair that bit higher than last week. She glances into a compact and pouts before rubbing non-existent smears of coral shimmer lipstick from her teeth.

'Am I to be fired?' Maria asks finally. 'Is there a letter here for me? Oh, Dolores, I don't have to type it myself, do I?'

'It's all taken care of.' Dolores laughs. Her disinterested shrug suggests she could be reading a story that she may put down without finishing.

'What do you mean?'

'You won't be fired. A note is meant to go on your file, but I'll be able to sort that with Personnel. Hardly anyone knows what happened because I called a friend in the newsroom and asked him to make sure the story didn't go out again. I went through all the newspapers I could find on Friday afternoon and yesterday and threw the city news pages into the bin. Good old Nelson's taken care of the rest.'

'But what about when it's in court? It'll be back in the papers then, from the court reports.'

'The charges are being dropped. I expect you'll get a letter from the gardaí any day.' She flicks open the problem page. 'Listen to this one. "Dear Cathy, My husband insists on turning the light out before we can have intimate relations. Is it possible he doesn't want to look at me? I would like to see what's going on for once. Will he think me forward if I ask him to leave it on? Yours sincerely, Christine M."' Dolores sighs. 'You and the rest of the country, Christine M.'

Maria flaps her hands to reclaim Dolores' attention. 'Dropped?'

'I called the owner of Mullerys, whatever his name is . . . Liam Rowe? Told him how none other than Mr Robert Ryan himself was interested in making a radio programme about the best public houses in Ireland and was curious to find out more about Mullerys, what with it having such a good reputation.'

And who could resist the prospect of being interviewed by none other than Double R himself? Certainly not Liam Rowe, a man who, Dolores recounts, chewed the ears off her about how none other than James Joyce himself used drink in Mullerys.

'I thought he'd never shut up his blethering about it. He said, and this is his expression I'll have you know, not mine – the bar is "immortalisised" in *Ulysses*.' The way Dolores tells it, Joyce used trot from St Stephen's Green to seek out a perfect pint of plain in Mullerys as often as his legs would agree to take him there. 'And that Simon Dedalus – these are Rowe's words again, not mine – gets "banjoed in Mullerys in manys a chapter".'

Dolores flicks expertly through the magazine. Hairstyles and make-up, easy-knit matinée jackets and family fayre recipes zip past their eyes. The world in fast motion, in miniature. She bends her head low over the *Hollywood Lights* page, ablaze with the gossip that a sequel to *Charade* is to be filmed, with Cary Grant and Audrey Hepburn's characters now married and living in Paris. Her eyes locked with Cary Grant's, Dolores says, 'So then I said that a rumour of some bother in the bar had reached Robert's ears and was giving him cause for concern. And what a desperate shame it would be, I told him, if Mullerys wasn't the right sort of establishment to feature in *Robert Ryan's Rovings* after all? And that was that. Sure wasn't it all a storm in a teacup, wasn't he just after deciding that minute that he wouldn't be taking it further. "Great!" said I. "You look after that bit of nonsense and we'll be in touch in due course about the programme."'

'Dolores . . . I just don't know how to thank you.' The relief is enormous. Her grip on the parapet had been slowly slipping. She had been hanging on by a single finger.

'You don't have to.'

'I do, I really do. You've no idea how much this means.'

'You don't have to thank me because it wasn't my idea.'

Maria's stomach flips again. Please, God, let Dolores not

have involved Robert Ryan. That will just defer her firing to another time, when he's annoyed with her about some stupid trifling thing and remembers how he was persuaded to lend his name to a lie.

'I'm not talking about Robert.' Dolores laughs at the bewildered look on Maria's face. 'He hasn't a clue. It was all Patrick Keady's idea.' She tosses the magazine into the wastepaper basket under her desk. 'Though I wasn't meant to tell you that.'

'There is such a condition as stenographer's elbow, you know.' Hilda straightens up and flexes her arm. Her call has lasted forty-five minutes. 'Honestly, you'd think he'd been standing underneath waiting to catch Nelson's head.'

Maria has her own receiver tucked under her chin while she turns the pages of her notebook. She was drafted back into the copy office after lunch to help manage the flood of excitable reports that started as a trickle early that morning but soon became a free-flowing deluge. Back in her former seat, she is answering, transcribing, typing, filing.

What a long day this has been (for everyone except Nelson). The pay phones in town are heavy with RTÉ-funded coins this afternoon. A reporter tells Maria rumour has it that none other than President de Valera himself took up the phone to the *Irish Press* to suggest the headline *British Admiral Leaves Dublin by Air*. Maria watches the hands of the clock approach ten minutes to five. She counts down in her head, wondering to what extent the ripples from O'Connell Street will be permitted to disturb the closing routines of the copy office. When, at ten minutes to five, Hilda begins her departure, Maria finds herself smiling. All is right in this world. It is unshakeable. Nothing that happens outside can breach its ramparts. Routine is the president and Hilda its taoiseach. It is a world of such predictability and ease, at so many removes from the life of the city around them, that it surely cannot last.

Maria looks at the flushed faces around her. The air in the room has been overused and made everyone headachy. Ears are pink from the pressure of the phones, while necks and shoulders cramp. Even Michael, a man who once described his attitude to his job as 'easy listening', looks hot and bothered.

'Dring, dring.' He picks up his silent phone. 'The Club? Calling for me? On my way!' He shakes out his shoulders and heads for the door. 'Is Maria coming? No? She doesn't know the half of what she's missing.'

'I do, Michael,' she says, 'but thank you.' And she smiles to herself as she scrabbles under the desk for his typewriter cover and carefully drapes it over his machine.

Anna is in the garden, where spring is beginning to make its presence felt. A few snowdrops and crocuses have appeared. Their small heads bob about, curious about life above ground. Mrs Halpin is sanguine about Nelson. Like Hilda, she, too, thinks he had it coming.

'And it's not as though it was during working hours when the street would have been full of people,' she says, as though the issue was primarily one of timing. 'I'd say Mr Halpin is looking down and laughing. He never did think much of that Pillar. Mr Onions, now,' she purses her lips, 'he'd have been more of a Nelson man, I dare say.'

Maria pauses and they both listen to Anna, singing to herself in the garden, her tune just audible through the open window. Mrs Halpin potters around the spotless kitchen. She only ever sits to jump up again. Watching her is like seeing light to Tess's dark. Maria leans her back against the draining board. A *plink-plink* from the cold tap into the sink behind her harmonises with Mrs Halpin's *tut-tuts*. Does she hear that desperate noise? Mrs Rogers knows a little man: she'll have to get him in to do the washer. Butter dish goes back in the fridge. Wipe, tidy, clean. Maria watches her move around her kitchen.

'I knew something was up, though we got the whys-and-wherefores wrong,' Mrs Halpin says. 'You don't bury two husbands without learning how to spot another widow. You never really had the look of one, we thought.'

'We?'

'Myself and Ada,' she says, adding proudly, 'There's not much gets by a woman on the Committee of the Irish Housewives Association. We decided you never had a husband at all.'

'I did, unfortunately. Do. Did.'

'What have you told Anna?'

'Nothing yet, but I will soon. I'll tell her he's not dead but had to go away and we don't expect to see him again.'

On the Saturday afternoon Maria stood up from Tess's table feeling that, with a single word, the suffocating weight of her life had lifted from her. Her rage at Tess fell away. The tap of Tess's fingers on the diary was a drum, a call to arms. The idea of volunteering to put herself back into a life where her very breath would depend on the mercurial anger of another was completely, entirely, wrong. And choosing to put her daughter there would be to deny her a future. Maria was no longer afraid of what could happen. Instead, she was afraid of what might occur if she did not act. She would have to leave Dublin at once: that much was clear. But now, with Anna, just the two of them . . . We've done it once, she reasoned to herself, we can do it again.

Next stop: Mrs Halpin's.

'There's something – a lot of things, really – I need to explain.'

'The leg and the flowerpots, is it?' Mrs Halpin said.

'No. Actually, yes, that, too. But that's only a tiny bit.'

Mrs Halpin listened open-mouthed. *Husband, baby, pain, fear, run.* She had a handkerchief tucked under the wristband of her watch and her fingers twitched towards it over and over. *Pint, arrest, cell* earned a 'Jesus, Mary and Joseph!' Her expression turned thunderous at the mention of departures, of midnight berths and ferries, of Manchester and Liverpool.

'But we're not going back with him. He thinks we are, but we're not. I don't know yet where, but I'm going to take Anna away today. He's only come for us because he's in some trouble with the police over there. I'm sorry I lied about what happened the other night. And about John . . . I should have told you about John months ago. I just . . . I thought it would be better this way.' She realised she was gabbling in her haste to explain and apologise and say goodbye and leave.

'Better? Better for yourself, you mean.' Mrs Halpin ran her hankie under her eyes.

'For everyone.'

'Your Anna has given me more joy these last months than

I've had in years.' Mrs Halpin looked past Maria and towards the window. 'Years,' she said again. 'Families aren't always safe places, Maria. That's the tragedy of it. But your decisions aren't hers, and neither are your lies.'

Hankie back under her watchstrap, she picked up a knife and a cob of soda bread and cut slice after slice, though there was nobody there to eat them. 'There's some who emigrate with one eye over their shoulder their entire lives and others who throw their past into the fire along with the ticket stub. I know which my son is. He won't ever be bringing those grandchildren home to me. I don't know why,' she sighed, 'but at least I've learnt not to have expectations.'

Maria looked at the floor. Everything was her fault. The unhappiness she was about to inflict on Mrs Halpin! She had been so half-hearted about this arrangement, resolving to find someone else only to weaken at the prospect of upsetting Anna. She had used Mrs Halpin's goodwill and generosity because it suited her. And now her own deceit and selfishness had forced the end upon all of them. Anna was going to be heartbroken to leave the woman's care and it was all Maria's doing. How wrong she had been about Mrs Halpin. She wasn't looking after Anna out of boredom, or the chance to earn a bit on top of her pension. She was caring for her out of love.

'There was no leaving husbands when I was your age. Put up and shut up. That was what we were told to do.'

'I tried, I really did.'

'Then you've done enough. Mr Onions was that type. Maggoty with drink on a Saturday night and in the front pew of a Sunday morning. Cowards push and push as long as you let them, but one good hard shove back and they won't push no more. That's the trick of it, though, to make that one push your best, if you take my meaning.' She rubbed at a stain on the red and white gingham oilcloth that covered the table. There was a faded, pinkish patch where her teapot usually sat. She put her cloth down and turned to face Maria.

'Come with me,' she said, 'and we'll put a call through to my Norma's George.'

CHAPTER TWENTY-SEVEN

The seating in the reception area is low, uncomfortable and fashionable, all chrome curves and padded leather. Tess is like a wriggling child, shifting from side to side against the back of the chair. She's refused to remove her overcoat and the dark tweed is wrapped around her, like a blanket. Maria notices the bulge of her tongue making its quick-fire progress around her cheek. Eventually she stops fidgeting with her bag and headscarf. She slows and settles, tucking herself to one side of the seat.

'This yoke had better not tip me out,' she whispers to Maria.

'It's quite safe – it just doesn't look it. Honestly, Tess, there's no need to be nervous.' Maria doesn't believe this is going to happen. There's time yet for Tess to walk away, to change her mind. To decide that she has forgotten everything, or made it all up, a story to amuse herself.

'There bloody well is,' she replies.

In the constant flow of people through the reception area Maria recognises one of the two men who wrote the note on

Michael's copy sheet. She hasn't seen him since that evening in the Club, and stares stonily at him until she catches his eye. His lips twitch nervously before he hurries off.

'What're you grinning at?' Tess says.

'Nothing.' Maria smiles. 'Nothing at all.'

Tess glances up. The ceiling is constructed of unvarnished concrete in a pattern of large indented squares. 'You lot like working inside an egg box, do you?'

'And this must be the one and only Tess McDermott!' Robert Ryan has materialised in the doorway. He bestows on the entire reception area a smile designed to melt even the most frozen housewife's heart. His arms are flung wide, he would embrace the entire postal district if he could. Maria struggles to her feet to introduce them but Tess has already hoisted herself up and has a hand extended.

'It is none other than she,' she says, with a haughty dignity.

'Now, Tess,' he holds her small hand in both of his, 'what I want you to do is to think of the interview as no more than a chat, the sort I'm sure you're used to having over the garden wall.'

'I will not do any such thing!' She pulls her hand away. 'And if you think I'm here to talk about my life as if it's no more than a gas over a fence, then I don't give a fiddler's for you or your programme, Mr Robert Ryan!'

Robert's Saturday-night smile disappears. Bloody hell, thinks Maria. Here it comes. He'll have a go at both of them for squandering his precious time. Tess didn't even get as far as the control booth. She'd better offer her the bus fare home at least. Maria looks from one to the other. Tess is holding his gaze. Her tongue lies quietly in her mouth; her cheeks are still. She is pale, solid as if cut from marble. Robert opens the door and stands to one side. He shakes his head, and says, 'You're absolutely right, Mrs McDermott. Please accept my apologies.' Maria follows Tess through the door, and as she passes him, Robert murmurs, 'Relax, Maria, you look more worried than she does.'

By rights the recordings for *The Women of 1916* should be taking place in the Radio Éireann studios in the GPO. But when one of the first interviewees refused, saying she'd 'never set foot in that God-forsaken building again, not even to buy a blasted stamp', the producers had decided it would be wiser to move to neutral territory. Probably just as well, Maria thinks. How disconcerting it would be for a woman who had fought in that building – or, worse, who had lost a loved one between its walls – to sit on its third floor and broadcast her story.

Tess had refused to do a preliminary interview with one of the researchers on *The Women of 1916*, so Robert has no notes on what to expect. She would only tell her story once, she said. That would be it, then. The book will close. *The End*. Robert prefers his path of his interviews to be scripted, right down to his off-the-cuff remarks. Because of this, he was reluctant to meet her. It was Dolores who suggested that the very fact Tess *wouldn't* talk to anyone other than him meant the interview would have a real freshness to it. A power, a spontaneity. And wasn't that exactly what plays to Robert's considerable strengths? He had nodded seriously. How very true. And didn't Dolores finish up by saying (while Maria stood silently nearby, inwardly applauding her technique), if the interview works out, use it. If not, then what harm has been done? Cut it short after ten minutes and send the old dear home with an autograph and her year made.

The studio is a large room with a smaller booth tucked inside it. In the main room, an engineer sits at a vast recorder, silently spooling tape. The door next to his desk leads to the recording booth, which has space for a table and chairs. Two microphones wait expectantly on the table.

The wall between the rooms has a glass panel. Maria isn't allowed into the recording booth but the engineer tells her to sit near his control desk so she and Tess will be able to see each other. He settles Tess in front of her microphone, distracting her as one would soothe a fractious child. She won't take her coat off and props her handbag up against the microphone.

'I'm Tommy,' he says, with a wink. 'Don't you mind that Robert Ryan. I'm in charge here – he just doesn't realise it. If you pay attention to what I say you'll be grand.' He gently moves her bag to the floor by her feet.

Maria goes to the canteen to fetch Tess a glass of water and on her way back happens upon an impromptu 1916 Programmes Committee meeting that has sprung up in the corridor, occasioned by Hugh's bumping into Keith Kirwin.

'Have you made space on the mantelpiece?' Hugh is cooing. '*Easter Rebellion* is one for the Jacob's Award, I'm sure of it.'

A St Brigid's cross as distinctive as that in the Telifís Éireann logo itself, but mounted on a base of Connemara bog oak and marble, it is rumoured that this year there'll be a new Golden Trophy award to reward exceptional programming talent. Keith's smile is self-deprecating yet he raises his hands as though he can already feel the cool heft of the marble, the ancient wood. The Jacob's Awards! What a great night that will be.

'From the first minute I put an eye to the script I knew

it was a winner.' It sounds as though Hugh has decided on his rightful place in what will become the history of *Easter Rebellion*. 'But, then, I have a very keen eye, as you know.' Keith, Hugh exclaims, has taken the idols of 1916 down from their pedestals and turned them back into men. Heroes, yes, but human ones, virile creatures of flesh and blood. The script is a mastery of its craft, it's true. The editing a triumph of excising non-period detail. But the direction!

Keith's bashful demurs suggest to Maria that he has already spent time imagining the Taoiseach presenting him with his award, and is fretting that Hugh's exuberant praise might somehow jinx it. 'Just between ourselves, Hugh,' Keith has said variations on this many times in the last few days; Maria herself has overheard him at least twice, 'I did receive a green sheet I was very happy with.' The director-general issues his memos on distinctive green paper. Congratulatory missives are rare as hen's teeth and both men know this single sheet is worth more to Keith's career than any number of Jacob's Awards.

From out of sight, a set of footsteps gets closer. The owner of the feet is singing to himself:

> *Dublin is sound asleep when what do you know?*
> *Nelson gets blown to bits and down the Pillar does*
>   *go!*
> *He was on the ground when we rose from our beds,*
> *Scattered all round and what d'you think we said?'*

It is now three weeks since Nelson was toppled and two weeks since the Irish Army nipped into town to finish off the job and remove the dangerous stump that had been left behind. And the army blast, as people the country over said to each other with much satisfaction and no little surprise, did more damage than the first. Written by the Nappertandy Three within days of the explosion, 'Night Night Nelson' is at number one in the hit parade. Michael launches into the chorus just as he rounds the bend in the corridor.

> *Night night Nelson, so say all of us,*
> *Here's your few bob now, go get your bus,*
> *Night night Nelson, your Pillar's done,*
> *Off you go now, time for you to run—*

'Oh, hello, Maria.' He breaks off his song but not his stride. He shifts a pile of folders from under one arm to the other and continues down the corridor.

Keith and Hugh frown their disapproval at Michael's retreating back. How frivolous. The Pillar features prominently in many of *Easter Rebellion*'s exterior scenes at the GPO. 'Whoever it was that took it upon themselves to topple him,' Keith says, 'I'm bloody grateful they waited till March.'

Maria smiles. She is grateful that she got to climb the Pillar again as an adult. Bombing seems such a gritty, ignominious fate for it. Already Nelson has become nothing more than a problem spared for Keith Kirwin and a silly ditty that the pop charts will soon discard. Do such things only resonate when they're personal? What starts out so vast, stronger than any single individual, becomes filtered through the small histories of our lives until it is laid to rest as an anecdote. Relics and keepsakes. Maybe that is the true heart of storytelling: it is the sum of memory plus time. Maria is about to re-enter the studio when the next door down opens.

'Ah, Eamon!' Hugh calls out. 'I'm just congratulating Keith here on a truly excellent production. Magnificent. I'm sure you'll remember I said so all along. History has been made, wouldn't you say?'

'History has been remade,' Eamon O'Mara retorts. He is clearly still bristling at losing a skirmish during the last committee meeting. He had (at some length, as Patrick commented) presented a case for banning advertisements from all the jubilee programmes. The purity of the programme content would be impinged upon, he insisted. And hadn't enough liberties been taken already? Hugh for-heaven's-saked him. With the ratings *Easter Rebellion* is sure to get? Ireland, he sniffed, is no place for that sort of Reithian nonsense. Eamon's final, unsuccessful salvo at the meeting was 'All things considered, you should hope you're not up against *Peyton Place* on Ulster.' Keith scowled in response. He had campaigned to be given the coveted *Hitchcock Presents . . .* slot at eight forty-five but it seems that even rebellions are not permitted to overthrow the master of suspense.

And that, Maria recalls, as she shuts the studio door behind her, had been the concluding piece of business at the last official meeting of the 1916 Programmes Committee. She gives Tess her drink, then returns to her seat on the other side of the window. Maria will be able to hear the conversation between Robert and Tess but they will hear only each other.

'And ready to record in five,' Tommy says, as the *Recording On* sign glows red behind Robert's head.

Five. It is Monday, 4 April 1966. Easter Sunday will fall on the tenth, less than a week away.

Four. In some parts of the country uniformed members of the armed forces have been banned from taking part in commemoration parades. But in Dublin *Easter Rebellion*, featuring the Irish Army dressed as their long-dead British counterparts, is in the can and ready for broadcast.

Three. The commemorative *RTV Guide* is at print. A two-page spread is devoted to photographs of the 'Relics and Keepsakes' submitted. The Frongoch tea cosy is one of them, much to Maria's delight.

Two. The Women of 1916 is waiting only for Tess's interview and for Robert to record his closing words.

One. In a week, it will be fifty years since the Easter Rising of 1916.

And we're recording. In Donnybrook, they are ready for battle.

CHAPTER TWENTY-EIGHT

It is impossible to look at anyone other than Tess. Once she begins to speak, her words seem to come from another place. Somewhere deep inside her, a hidden well of hope and strength. Maria has seen glimpses of this before, but now it is as if a cover has been pushed back and light spills up from the depths below. Maria had been worried Tess would be nervous, would skip about in time in the way Eliza O'Mahony's memories tugged at the frayed edges of her story until they unravelled into an incoherent mess.

But Tess is perfect.

Robert begins by asking her the same questions he asked the other women he has interviewed for the programme. He had used the questions as reins, tugging sharply at them when he felt the interviewee was veering off course. However, it is soon obvious that Tess knows the road ahead, and he stops interrupting her. He allows her words to flow like a river out into the studio, through the streets of Dublin and across the Irish Sea until she drifts ashore in London. She explains briefly about the suffragettes and that final, fateful march.

'And that was the incident that led you to Holloway Prison, isn't that correct? What happened to you there?'

'Where do you want me to begin?'

Where else is there but the beginning, Robert gently chides her.

'So you believe in beginnings, do you, Mr Ryan? I did too, in those days. For me, gaol began in the van. Me, a pal of mine called Violet Burrow, two posh sorts I'd not seen before that day, and a woman called Nellie Potter were shoved into cages in the back of a van to be taken from Bow Street to Holloway.

'The cages had small iron gratings to look through. They were filthy and I couldn't help but think how disgusted our housekeeper Mrs Judge would have been. Couldn't help but think either as how I'd have given anything to put time back to a day before and be in Cavendish Square feeling the wrong side of her temper. We had to hold the bars going around the corners, only I didn't want to because they were so dirty. But I was so sore from the kicking I'd got at the march that I had to grab them in the end or else I'd have fallen over.

'We'd been given a bowl of stirabout at Bow Street but I couldn't touch it and I was dizzy with hunger and thirst. I could feel my breath getting short and there was a feeling in my head like a door was slamming over and over. Panic, I suppose. I made myself count the freckles on the backs of my hands to keep my mind busy. Every time the van lurched my ribs shot through with pain, which made me lose count so I'd have to start again.

'We stopped five times and each time the door opened, another wretch got flung in the back with us. God forgive me, but the state of some of them. Nellie Potter spat on the floor, over and over. I remember noticing her arms were thick and brown as rolling pins. This wasn't a new journey to Nellie. She used to follow Flora Drummond everywhere. Flora was known to everyone as the General, and Nellie the General's Gundog, though you'd get a swipe of her claws if you dared say it to her face.

'In the prison yard they pulled us from the cages to shake ourselves straight. There hadn't been a mutter out of me the entire time. The whole day was too big for my mind to fit it in. When I climbed out of that van I thought I'd been swallowed up by Holloway Prison. Earlier that morning before we started out on the march, just as my pal Minnie and me were checking our pockets for the hard-boiled eggs, she asked me if I remembered the first time we went to the ABC at Oxford Circus and if I still had the cutting from the paper. "Do you remember where it says it's a life and death struggle?" she asked me. And I remember, clear as if she was in this room now, what she said then: "Tess," she goes, "this part now is the truth of that."

'We were in the yard of Holloway Gaol and one of the posh ladies from the van asked her pal did she think her hair would be cut off. Nellie Potter turned on her. "Yer 'air?" she said, and spat on the ground. "This ain't the carneys." I gulped so loud I thought she'd poke me in the eye for my troubles.

'A guard grabbed Nellie's arm and pulled her forward. "Look who's come back to me," he shouted. "It must be love. Or mebbe you just like how we serve the food, these days."

'The posh lady stayed silent after that. When we were brought in she was just ahead of me. Her green cape had a big rent in the gathers at the back, as though handfuls of the fabric had been ripped out. Her shoulders were shaking so bad it made the silk ripple like leaves in the Square. I was only ever to see her one more time after that, may the Lord rest her.

'My cell was about the size of the butler's pantry in the house, and when I was pushed into it I had no notion of what was waiting for me there. How could I? Hearing about it was nothing, just nothing, compared to the real life of it. There was a Holy Bible in the cell and, no word of a lie, a book called *The Home Beautiful*. A whisper went through the gratings that Nellie chewed hers up for want of tobacco.'

Through all this, Tess remains completely calm, her voice almost flat, which somehow makes it sound even worse. Robert gently guides her through her description of being force-fed and even Maria, who has already read Tess's diary, winces in sympathy. The engineer looks horrified and brings a hand to his mouth as though he might vomit. 'Tommy!' Maria hisses. 'Don't. You'll distract her.'

'I had to leave London then,' Tess says. 'Gaol had broken me. The month I was there would never leave me. It was under my skin. No, more than that: it felt like a new skin, and dirty with it, no matter how much carbolic I scrubbed myself with.'

Maria leans forward in her seat. From here on, the story is new. Robert's researcher wasn't the only person she'd refused to tell it to before today.

'My friend Minnie's employer took me in for a while. He was very kind, but he couldn't have me in his household for long, and me not doing a tap of work. It would have caused talk. There was a queue of girls anyhows, needing his help. I didn't know it when Minnie first brought me there, but I wasn't the first to benefit from his kindness, nor was I to be the last.

'I never did get what I was owed in wages. When Minnie went to collect my box Mrs Judge told her there wasn't anything she could do. Mrs Judge had tried to cover up for me, God bless her, but it was no good. The master said his vote would be for me to be kicked in the backside from one end of the Square to the other. Minnie bumped into Betty, the maid I used to share a bedroom with. I'd munged up my life, according to her, which wasn't much by way of a goodbye after three and a half years in our attic together.

'The doctor gave me my fare, and in January 1910 I arrived back in Dublin. It felt a different sort of cold, grizzling place from the city I'd left five years before, but that's as may be. He had written me out a reference as though I'd been his own servant and it got me a live-in general job easy enough with a lady called Mrs Somers in Rugby Road. I had a good year there. Mrs Somers ran the post office in Rathmines, with her daughter Elizabeth as the junior clerk. She was lovely, Elizabeth. She wasn't much older than me but she had a very grown up way about her. They moved to Dalkey to run the post office there but I didn't want to go with them. I wouldn't know what to do with myself outside of a city.

'It was Elizabeth first got me introduced to Cumann na mBan. I've often wondered did she regret being involved herself, because her mother was dismissed from the post office when customers complained that Elizabeth was using the premises to give out leaflets and take in the subs.' Tess pauses and sips her water. Maria smiles through the window but Tess is staring into the convex glass of memory and doesn't appear to see her.

'Before Mrs Somers moved to Dalkey she helped find me a new position with a woman in Harold's Cross. Mrs Johnson knew about my past. Elizabeth must have told her. One day I opened Mrs Johnson's front door and who was there? Only Mrs Despard, who was well known to me by name from when she'd been in the WSPU in London, though by now she was long gone from it and was in the Women's Freedom League. Mrs Desperate, as she used to be called by some behind her back, had been in Holloway twice, and by virtue of us having been in the same prison, she treated me as though we were baptised into the same church.'

Robert Ryan chuckles and Tess looks at him as if she'd forgotten he was there. 'So you joined the Irish suffrage movement then, Tess?'

'I swore I'd leave it all alone, after London. But I couldn't, as it turned out. A key had been wound up in me and I could no more stop than I'd have run around the street in the altogether.

'Like I said, it was Elizabeth got me involved first. I went to an Irish Women's Suffrage Federation meeting with her – it must have been about a year after I started in service with her mam. I thought it all a desperate waste of time at first, all politeness and *can-we-have-the-vote-please-sir*. It made me think that men band together because they want to fight something, and the women start because they want to organise it. *The Irish Citizen* was the paper they took in the house, and I used be given it to read and then for the fires when they were finished. It used carry a daft advertisement for a clerical and ladies' tailor. "Suffragettes always before the public eye need to dress well," it went. That was what it was like at the first meetings I went to.'

'Did other women there feel the same?'

'Some were there only because of what had gone before.

They were angry, called it a noose around all our necks. Others cared only for the future. They wanted to own it, to take it before it had even happened.' She pauses. 'It only began to get rough here after that business in 1912 when Asquith had the hatchet thrown at him. That brought about the forcible feeding. Artificial feeding, it was called here. I decided I'd burn in Hell before suffering that again. I hated myself for it but I put my head down and kept quiet again awhile.

'Then the war started and everything was for changing. I got in with Cumann na mBan in 1914, not long after it began. I've often thought of this in the years since, but I knew well its constitution said that we'd bear arms and that we'd use them. But we had no notion then – well, I for one didn't at any rate – that we'd get so caught up in such a rebellion. I wonder does it sound to people now that we were like an army, mobilised and ready to fight? The history books make it all sound more joined-together than it was to us who were living it day by day.

'There was a lot of rattling tins at first. Flag days and céilís and concerts. Quite a few of them were mad into the traditional dress. There was a Volunteer Tweed uniform we were asked to make or buy. Some looked like they were put together with a blunt knife and no fork, they were that badly made. I wasn't bothered with it. I'd been so long earning my maid's uniform as to have no interest in saving up for any other.

'I joined the first-aid squad to get away from the tins. Bandages coming out my ears, I had. A few times we were brought to the Dublin Mountains in our full first-aid packs and carrying stretchers. We were taught about guns, too, how to clean and load them. And yet I still never had the thought that I might have to pick one up in the name of battle. It was nothing more real to me than polishing the silver in Mrs Johnson's house: I knew where she kept the Pextons polish, and how to use it, but I never expected to be offered a drink from some fancy goblet.'

Her flow falters for the first time and there is a pause before she says, hesitantly, 'But . . . but not expecting to do something is no excuse. So there's no pretending that I didn't know what I was doing when I lifted that soldier's gun off the street that Easter.'

'And so, Tess,' Robert's eyes light up and his nose twitches as though he can smell the feast about to be set out in front of him, 'what was *your* Easter Rising? Where were you and what happened?'

'The morning of Easter Monday, we got the order in our branch to mobilise at Weavers Hall and off we marched to Emerald Square in The Liberties. I loved that name, but there's no glitter to the place. We were told to bring rations to last us twenty-four hours and not to wear any uniform or our brooches or anything. We obeyed, too, everyone that I saw or heard of, apart from a woman from Glasgow called Margaret Skinnider and, of course, Countess Markievicz herself. She liked her uniforms, did the countess. Margaret's was more of a ragbag get-up. Whenever us girls saw her we'd snigger, because on the Monday all Margaret did was pedal around the city from garrison to garrison, changing in and out of her rig-out as she went and calling out, "It's on," to everyone she met. Margaret got wounded for her troubles, mind. "She'd no outfit picked out for that," a man said to me, and we all wondered what had happened to the detonators for bombs she had hidden under her hat. She wrote her account of it all the following year. "A successful revolt becomes known as a rebellion, and an unsuccessful one is an insurrection." That's what she wrote, and she was damn right. It's the winners' reward to write the story of victory. But maybe Madame Markievicz wouldn't agree with that.'

'Did you know Countess Markievicz?'

'Not to speak to. From all I ever saw of her she seemed a strange one. She'd an odd, gloating way about her, going about that week with her revolver swinging from one hand and a cigarette in the other. That's not the way to do business, I thought.'

'And that's how you thought of it?' Robert prompts. 'Business?'

'That's what became of it, no matter what it was you'd signed up for to begin with. I was no countrywoman in a kilt fighting for freedom. For me it was about the vote, about getting women recognised as equals. Didn't the very tricolour the men decided to march under belong to us first? No one remembers that now, for all the nonsense that's in the papers about showing the Irish flag this Easter. They were Mrs Despard's colours long before they were draped over any man's coffin.

'It was the women were out on the streets during that week. All the telegraph and telephone wires had been cut so we were like those pigeons you see with notes tied around their necks. One woman had the job to carry another's typewriter. We did everything the men did that week but the only difference was we didn't get executed afterwards.

'On the Monday evening I got sent to St Stephen's Green with a message. The Green itself was locked since that morning and men were digging trenches inside the railings.

Dug for seven, eight hours straight they did. There was a man shot who fell down dead into his very own trench. I had to run from St Stephen's Green across to the College of Surgeons and I was hurrying for all I was worth and I heard some old pair – out for a stroll by the look of them, which was madness in itself but there was plenty doing it – saying, "The cut of her with no hat on!" like I was a scruff out on my half-day.

'Mrs Johnson had a blackthorn cane and I had cut a hole in my skirt and dropped it inside, like a third leg. Old suffragette trick, a lot of us did it. Some nurses wearing the Red Cross bibs even had knives hidden inside.

'There was great supplies in most places for the first day or two. But when they ran thin there was a few whose job it was to get fresh and distribute them. A pal of mine held up a bread cart, another stole cans of milk. There was a lot of looting too. I was in the Marrowbone Lane garrison then, and a woman appeared with three calves on the Thursday. They were butchered, and it fell to me to bring a sack of cutlets to a group who were minding an arms dump over in York Street. I was skirting along by myself, alone for the first time in two days. It was near dark and quiet and I was slipping down the laneways, careful to keep an eye out but moving quick. And then I saw them: the soldier and a woman I knew a bit by the name of Lily Byrne. She'd a Red Cross bib on, too. He had a gun in one hand and her hat in the other. His back was to me. She spotted me but had the sense not to let on. All round them on the ground was ammunition – it had come pouring out of her skirts like hailstones. He was shouting abuse at her, waving his gun back and forth, like you'd draw a carving knife across a whetstone. Then he grabbed her by the hair. And still he didn't see me so I got my blackthorn out of my pocket. He was very tall and I couldn't reach up to his head so I clipped him across the back a solid whack.'

Tess stops abruptly and a darkening look comes over her face. Maria recognises the rumbles of thunder in the storm clouds that flit across her eyes.

'Yes, Tess?' Robert says. 'What happened next?' His voice is neutral, light, as though he is merely asking her to describe the plot of a play she once enjoyed.

'Are you sure you want to hear it?' she says. 'Because when I tell you it's yours too. All of yours. There's no un-owning of it. You're calling up the dead.'

Robert glances through the glass at the engineer. Tommy nods slowly and rotates his arm, as if rolling a large spool of invisible thread. Keep going, his arm is saying. Maria is sweating.

The studio falls silent as Robert waits for Tess to draw a breath and continue. The silence lasts for longer than a breath, than two. Robert says nothing but nods and leans forward just enough to touch his fingertips to the back of her hand. She closes her eyes. 'And I picked his gun off the pavement and shot him in the back of his head.'

'Christ!' Maria says, her eyes locked on Tess's face.

'Bloody hell!' gasps the engineer.

'And then?' Robert's tone is low, even, yet the brightness in his eyes shows how pleased he is.

'A bit of his skull flew off to one side and I looked at it like it was nothing and I was somebody else. It was very white and clean. If I hadn't seen where it had come from I wouldn't have known what it was. Lily was gathering up her ammunition and stuffing it back into the bags sewn inside her skirt pockets.

'I went over and looked at his face. He was young, which

surprised me. I don't know why, I hadn't thought him young, from the back. A young man with a black moustache and his blood spilling down the pavement. And it was only later, when I washed the spots of blood off my hands, did I wonder what his name was and his age and where his sweetheart was.'

'Where exactly did it take place?'

Maria thinks this an odd question. What does it matter? She has admitted killing a man! But Tess is looking across the table at Robert with something rather like respect.

'On Peter Street, by the steps of an insurance firm called Shipman & Cox. Drops of blood had splashed up as far as the brass nameplate, and even as I stood there I thought, That'll be a bugger to polish if it's let dry in. Isn't that terrible? And now the building's gone. Some other new-fangled thing got put up instead and it made me sick to my belly, the day I realised that even the site of his death was gone. There should be a mark made on every spot in every street where blood is spilt. Because what's left? All of this?' Her gesture takes in the studio, RTÉ, Dublin, Ireland. 'All of this shenanigans? None of this is about people like him. It's all leaders and museums and colour supplements in the newspapers. None of it remembers the ordinary ones.

'Lily Byrne had a rosary around her neck. Lots of women wore 'em. Hers was brown beads with a shamrock emblem joining them together, and she took it off and I thought she was going to say a prayer over him but she didn't. She waved it over him, like it was a curse.'

'You're admitting that you killed a British soldier?' Robert wants a succinct admission. He interviews with an ear to the edit and the ten-second clip that will be used to advertise the programme (and played at the Jacob's).

'Yes.'

'Were you caught?'

'No,' she says, quiet again. The word is an exhalation that seems to take many long seconds to leave her mouth. 'No.'

'What happened next?'

'We ran. Got out of there as soon as we could. Across to Aungier Street and up Camden Street, going in and out of the doorways if we heard a patrol. And me with the gun in one hand and the bag of cutlets in the other without even thinking what I was doing.

'I hid out for a few days, and once I heard the surrender was done, I got out of Dublin as quick as I could. It was nearly ten years before I came back.'

'Do you feel any remorse?'

'At the time, none. And it's a terrible thing to say. It was a war, was what we kept saying to each other, and war's rules are not man's rules. That was what so many men believed when women were dying in the name of the vote. And I had believed myself a coward in London, and after that day, after protecting Lily, I wasn't a coward no more.'

'Is that what you think now?'

'Twenty-five odd years later my own son went to fight on the side of the British and he died. And that's how I learnt the truth of what I did, of what war is. A child is a parent's heart lifted out of their own body and put into another. What I stole that day on the street was some other mother's heart.'

'I know our listeners will think it brave of you to tell us your story fifty years later.'

'I'm not brave, Mr Ryan,' she says, with a glance through the window at Maria. 'That's where this all started.'

Robert wraps up the interview with his prepared script

about all the women who took part in the rebellion and how little history has recorded their involvement. How stories such as this remarkable true one, told for the first time to Robert Ryan on *The Women of 1916*, need to be heard. Isn't this the time, fifty years after those tumultuous days, that Ireland needs to listen? To listen to these voices – all of them, men and women – before they fade for ever and become lost to our nation's history and from its future generations? To listen and to learn, he says. That would be the true legacy of the Easter Rising.

The engineer switches off the *Recording On* sign. Robert leans over to shake Tess's hand, but Maria can no longer hear what they are saying. Tess looks old, exhausted and suddenly frail, her strength dissipated.

The locked box has been opened. So this is what it was. Tess, too, had a death kept secret, a death worn as punishment. Francis floats into Maria's mind and she lets him breathe there for a minute before softly tucking him away again. The two women look at each other through the thick glass. Maria stands up and, as if worried she is about to abandon her, Tess rises quickly, too. Maria shakes her head. *Wait*, she gestures. *Sit down.* The engineer takes the broadcast permission forms into the booth for Tess to sign.

The door to the corridor opens. Eve, with a message for the engineer.

'He'll be out in a second.'

'I'll wait,' Eve says. 'So, how did the interview go?'

'Just wait until you hear it, Eve. It was . . .' Maria struggles for words. 'It was . . . something to be proud of.'

'Good.' Eve grins. 'That was what we wanted, wasn't it? Oh, before I forget, I bumped into Patrick Keady on my way here.

He asked if you'd stop by his office later on.'

'What for?'

'No idea, though I'd have sworn he was muttering something to himself about ice-cream.'

Neither Maria nor Patrick has ever mentioned her arrest or his part in its resolution. Neither has he mentioned that she is due back at her old desk in the copy office in two weeks' time. She is curious as to how their paths will cross now that the work of the 1916 Programmes Committee is complete. Soon the committee will exist only as minutes on paper. The arguments and reconciliations will be over, the spats and misunderstandings tidied away, stored equitably alongside the good ideas and the bad. All those spent words locked in a filing cabinet. What else is there to be done with them?

And where will life take them from here? What will Anna's future be? Maria thinks of the two of them on Nelson's Pillar, staring out at the brittle elegance of a tarnished city. And now the Pillar is gone, destroyed in the name of something and nothing.

Let that be an end to it.

How she had desired a small life! One like the cardboard doll's house she had made with Anna. A world made perfect only by scale: complete, entire and hers to own. How foolish, she thinks.

She looks through the glass into the booth. Tess is rising again from the table. There is a heavy lift and fall to her chest and her hollowed cheeks are flushed. The stuffy air in there must have got her wheezing. But she looks calm, a clock unwound all the way back to nothing.

We are all running away from something, Maria realises, and she feels the thought as a quickening inside her. And running to something. Yes, that's the truth of it, that's the part she had forgotten all those months before. Every escape can be – no, more than that – *has* to be another beginning.

Maria pictures her daughter's smile, that moment of sunlight captured in a jam jar. Let this time, she thinks, this Easter Sunday, be the start of new, hopeful things.

ACKNOWLEDGEMENTS

With many thanks to Éilís Ní Dhuibhne and James Ryan; to Catherine O'Mahony; and to Tony, Clare, Feargal, Cal and Rosa.

History changes. Research continues to show that more women were involved in the 1916 Rising than previously thought. (Mrs Halpin would be shocked.) The period covered by this book is well served by non-fiction, and I found *Window and Mirror – RTÉ Television 1961–2011* by John Bowman, *Renegades* by Ann Matthews and various newspaper archives particularly helpful sources of information. Needless to say, Maria, Tess, Mrs Halpin & co. are fictional, and any errors they make are mine.